The Big Waste

By C.W. Ashley

For Katerina

Contents

Your first day in The Big Waste can often be your last.

-Citadel Warning

Chapter 1: The Pit Maneuver

They were gaining on him, the delicious buzz of the wheels in the wasteland tearing through the orange sand and patchwork tarmac was the music of the hunt. Cook's bandits had found a courier in a Class A vehicle. After blasting an entire day's worth of ammo during the chase, they started to ram it.

The driver of the vehicle, a freelance cargo transporter, was still defiant as hell in the face of the assault despite the fact it was his first day running a delivery. After repeatedly wiping sweat and dirt from his driving goggles he tore them away from his eyes so they snapped uncomfortably on his bushy hairline. Bleeding from a hole in his leg and without any weapons of his own, all he could do was grip desperately to his consciousness and steering wheel every time the cheap metal of the pursuers' off-road mini-beast slammed into his car door.

The Big Waste smelled blood.

I refuse to fucking die today.

He was determined to convince himself.

I've got a full tank of gas. These fucking powder-heads can't drive like I can. I have to survive this. Then I'm heading back home and staying there. I never should have come out here.

The driver known as 'Ignition' liked to talk to himself in times of desperation – it always made him feel less lonely when he needed friends around him the most. Now he was in the middle of nowhere, trying to survive a failed delivery run while being chased by two of Cook's bandits in a Scar-Buggy. The gash in his thigh just added to those things reminding him he needed friends now more than ever.

Eyes open Iggy! You can still drive...

The gurgle and scream of the dueling engines were loud enough to wake sandworms from hibernation. They sang in chorus with the howling jeers of the powder-addled bandits desperately smashing Iggy's beloved car, the **Blockgain Chaser.** The scrap they'd be stripping from it was almost as exciting to them as the cargo they hoped to steal. The buggy they were in had been modded to hell and back, with enough power under the hood to keep up with a high-end Chaser. If Iggy wasn't on the brink of death at a ridiculous speed, he might have been impressed.

"You **ain't shit** without that ammo! Last chance to run back the outpost, waste-rats!" Iggy yelled from his broken window as the bandits pulled closer for their next attack.

Iggy wanted to be intimidating, but he was used to demolition derby rivals in controlled citadel tournaments. Not murderous bandits so high on powder they couldn't even respond coherently. His threat only seemed to excite them even more as they pulled a hard-left side shunt into the Chaser for the 4th time with exuberant screams.

The impact wasn't enough to cause Iggy to spinout, but more than enough to splash the pumping blood from his bullet wounded leg all over his dashboard. The metallic stench of his quickly-drying sticky blood was so putrid it kept him conscious; like some sort of crude smelling salt. His blurring vision made out that the area around him was an endless looking sea of flat wasteland. No roads, or shortcuts, no alleyways or mountains, just a wide-open space for him to die.

I need something to ram them into, like a rock or a steel post. Hell, even a guard rail to grind them against would do it...why is the waste so empty?!

Iggy clenched his teeth and grunted weakly as the pain began to overwhelm him. The shallow pool of blood in his lap made him feel like he pissed himself. The rushing cold air felt like a blizzard as his life energy was literally draining out of him. The Scar Buggy was gearing up for another sideswipe, looking to put him to sleep. Iggy knew as well as they did, he would never wake.

Keep it together! Stay alert! It's the last round of the seasonal qualifiers, take them out, Iggy!

Feeling the blisters on his palms split open as he squeezed the wheel with a desperate surge of survival strength, he pulled his Chaser into a minor right turn – just enough to lose a little speed. The Scar buggy's over modded engine made ugly sounds as it tried to slow down, but with all the upgrades in the world, it was still just a poorly made bandit buggy. It couldn't re-adjust like a derby vehicle and that split second in the screaming inertia was all Iggy needed.

Hello **PIT Maneuver***, I've missed you!*

Iggy cranked his vehicle into a hard left while diverting fuel to his custom petrol boost, a standard function in all derby machines. The front end of the Blockgain Chaser plowed into the side of the Scar Buggy's back wheel with the impact of a scrap cannon.

The Blockgain Chaser's ramming power turned the bandits into protein spread. The meeting of flesh and bone against the metal of their own vehicle cut their whooping screams of bloodlust viciously short by the much louder crunch of them being churned into their mangled vehicle as it split in two. Iggy's car spun out like a tornado after the crash, and the dizzying effect along with the impact robbed him of his last bit of consciousness as his car skidded to a halt. The last thing he saw before passing out was the pale severed hand of one of the bandits landing on the roof of his car, before sliding off with a trail of gore on his windshield.

The Blockgain Chaser had wrecked its 173rd vehicle, and Iggy had killed for the first time in his life.

Chapter 2: Animal

"Ignition to Citadel depot...do you copy?" There was nothing but static. Iggy had the communicator close to his bloody face as he held down the button. "Ignition to Citadel depot, I am still carrying package 320, I'm...in an unknown patch of the Waste, please respond."

Iggy had awoken with a tongue like sandpaper, and with all the adrenaline of the high-speed chase now gone, his body was deathly weak from his injuries. Although his leg had stopped bleeding, he wasn't confident he could walk if he needed to. The radio device was slightly damaged but it was still working, Iggy knew someone was listening.

*Pick up you bastards, you **can** hear me.*

Suddenly the fuzz and crackle came to life, and a heavily muffled voice responded. "Copy Ignition, this is Rayko, Depot office. You're over an hour late."

"Y-yes Depot, bandit raid. Cook's men, I think. I barely escaped with my life and my vehicle is-"

"What of the cargo, is it intact?"

Iggy sighed, noting the emotionless tone of the officer. His head was still spinning. It was hard to focus. Yet he had no reason to believe the grey strongbox in the back of his car would have been damaged; the material of the cargo's casing was stronger than the armor of the Blockgain. But he thought he'd take a look anyway.

"Just confirming, there was a collision and-"

"And what? What is the status of the cargo?"

It wasn't there.

Everything in the atmosphere suddenly became much more unpleasant. The wind became salty and dry; the screech of the crows became that much shriller and the glare of the pale orange sun felt excessively harsh. This was the effect of panic setting in.

It was definitely here...how long was I out for?

"I repeat, what is the status of the cargo? Please repor-"

Iggy ended the call immediately.

He knew what was coming next, no matter how rational or fantastical his excuse; the depot would hold him responsible for the missing cargo. The price of the cargo was seven thousand standards, the delivery error fee was another two thousand, and every day he failed to clear that debt he would be charged another thousand up to a month.

The Citadel was a day away, assuming he could get back right away. That was ten thousand standards. Even selling all of his assets and stripping his accounts wouldn't be enough. They'd send him to one of the debtor's prison camps, a death sentence for sure.

Returning to the Citadel was no longer an option.

Iggy slammed his fist into the dashboard. He shoved open the car door and attempted to climb out. He realized the pain in his leg was gone, due more to the fact it was numb rather than that the wound was healing. The bleeding had stopped but only due to a gruesome-looking scab over his heavy-duty cargo jeans. He briefly picked at it. The scab was the only thing keeping the grit out, protecting him from infection. He left it alone.

Swinging both legs outside the car; he grimaced as the hot sun beat down on his back. The waste stretched on endlessly in all directions and the only scenery apart from the discolored sand was the remains of the Scar Buggy that he totaled.

Scavenging wasn't something Iggy ever considered himself doing. As a minor celebrity in the Demolition Circuit, he had the luxury to look down on those who were forced to dive in junkyards as a means to live – and those were the folks **inside** the Citadel; the wasters outside of it were basically living like animals. Regardless, it was survival time and supplies were top priority before the dreaded sundown.

Walking was very uncomfortable. His injured leg dragging along behind him, he desperately crossed the 30 or so feet between his car and the smashed buggy. His sleeveless duster felt heavier than ever and his armpits itched ferociously as large droplets of sweat trickled down the inside of his wiry arms. He tried to lubricate his throat many times by swallowing. It only exacerbated the issues caused by his tongue, which was rough as granite due to the onset of dehydration.

Do powder-heads carry water?

A couple of steps away from the front half of the buggy, Iggy was met with the repulsive sight of one of the passengers. The bandit's upper body had been torn from the abdomen with a trail of intestines painting a bright red trail back to the front half of the vehicle. The heavily tattooed, bare-chested corpse laid face down in the sand with its two broken arms stretched out in separate directions.

In the left hand was a large dark grey revolver with an engraved cream wood handle. Iggy leaned over and grabbed it. The barrel was still warm from the recent fire. He checked for ammo. There were two bullets remaining. He sighed with disappointment but shoved it in his pocket; a gun was a gun, and there could be more ammo over on the buggy.

Breathing as shallowly as possible, Iggy limped to the front half of the rival vehicle and did his best to rummage through the debris. Apart from a few bags of powder, there was very little of value. There was a canteen with a small amount of liquid but Iggy decided against drinking it until he could be sure it was water.

Searching the back half of the buggy was a little more fruitful. He found a spare half canister of fuel which miraculously didn't explode upon impact when Iggy smashed into them, plus a nasty looking nail-bat that had a few strings of razor-wire around the end of it. Iggy liked the weight of it as he gave it a few light swings. A chill went down his spine. They'd have used this to turn him into Bull-chow once they took out his car. He shuddered and took a few deep breaths.

Not this time fellas...not this time.

That minor pleasant turn was instantly soured by the sight of the 2nd corpse. Although still in one piece, all of the limbs were heavily distorted and deformed from the crash. The face had the horrifying final expression of life plastered across it, with gory holes for eye sockets were the waste crows had plucked them out for an afternoon meal. Iggy wretched, but the dryness of his throat kept him from bringing anything up.

He wasn't built for this kind of violence. There had been fatal accidents in some of the derbies he was in, but he very rarely had to see the state of the victims in the aftermath and *never* up this close.

I sure don't want to do this again; it can't be like this all the time in the waste, can it?

The introspection was cut short by a sharp, stabbing pain in his leg. The feeling hadn't returned fully but it was enough of a contrast to draw immediate attention to his crusted wound. It almost felt like a *bite*.

Still holding his new nail-bat, he used his free hand to immediately grab his leg where the pain was shooting from. The scab was coarse and sticky and he was met with a slight sting when his blistered hand felt it. But the throb of the pain was coming from somewhere *deeper inside* his leg, underneath the scab he felt something *moving*.

Panic hit him like his old driving instructor smacking him across the face with a heavy glove. Iggy dropped to the ground as he abandoned all fear of pain. He tore at his scab, searching for the source of the movement. Bleeding to death was preferable to dying from some sort of parasite devouring him from the inside out.

The thick layer of stiff encrusted flesh came off. Iggy was met with a horrific sight. Something bulbous and slimy was lying there, **pulsating** and feeding on his leg. Iggy had no interest in trying to waste precious seconds wondering what it was. He wanted it off of him immediately.

He could barely get a decent grip on it before he began to pull. It was a pale yellow color with blotches of a wine-red shade across it like the pattern of a spotted super bloom mushroom. As Iggy squeezed it to tug, the color morphed with the pressure of his hand, turning a passionate blood red like a fist-sized pimple ready to burst. Iggy's panic and anger were the only things keeping him from passing out due to shock.

Get off, fuck, come on....

With a desperate yank, Iggy removed the fleshy bulb from his skin and it flew from his hands as fast as he pulled it. His scream of fear and pain was matched by a terrifying high-pitched wail that came from the thing itself as it flew across the sand.

Wh-what the hell was it?

Iggy didn't have to wonder long. Through the blur of his teary eyes, the source of his panic took shape. The bulb opened to show a gaping wide mouth and two protruding black eyes. It was a **Bloodtoad**.

Of course…I mean what else?

Fairly common across the more remote areas of the wastes, the very small Bloodtoad would burrow its way into the body of a much larger host, usually through an open wound, before secreting a blood-clot toxin which would cause the opening to rapidly close up and scab over. The blood-toad would then begin to dig deeper inside and drink blood from the host gradually enough to go unnoticed while growing with every gulp. Some reports described the toad inside a human for days or even *weeks* before being noticed depending on how slowly it would drink. After reaching a certain size and strength it would deliver a knockout toxin and fully devour the host from the inside as they slept.

Dinnertime is over, you fucking animal!

Iggy rose to his feet, unbalanced from the fresh surge of pain and staggering as his body registered the blood loss. The toad was too fat and bloated to scramble to its feet in time to make its escape. Iggy closed in and cocked his new bat back to swing for the fences.

The sound was repulsive but to Iggy, it was like the finest music. The bat found its target perfectly. The blood-sucking monster exploded upon impact. Sweet-smelling blood splashed in every direction, a purple-red slime covering Iggy, the corpses, and the remnants of the buggy.

…Nice….

Iggy reveled in the small high he got from ridding the world of the beast. He wasn't certain he had saved his own life, but destroying that slimy pus balloon felt just as good.

Then came the growls.

I must smell pretty tasty right now...

The sweet scent of the toad's blood was already being carried on the wind. It had already caught the attention of something hungry. That wasn't hard though, everything was hungry in The Big Waste. He was a little too dizzy to hear exactly what direction it was coming from but it was getting closer.

Raidlion...Gamma-Grizz...Plentipede, what are you?

His brain gave his damaged body several orders to dash back to his car and escape. Drained from his blood-toad home run, he was barely able to take two steps before stumbling to the ground; his legs wouldn't carry his weight. He was now using every ounce of willpower just to stay conscious. Being devoured wasn't going to be pleasant at all; he could only hope that dying quickly would spare him the agony of being digested.

Maybe I can hold my breath...it eases the pain...I just want to sleep now.

It was widely understood that citizens like Iggy were never meant for The Waste. It was no more apparent to him than now as he lay there, blood pouring from his leg, listening to the growls of the beasts around him. The growling was now ravenous and shaking the air around him. Curiosity caused the doomed driver to stare right at the source of the guttural sounds.

Ugh...another frog...of course it'd be.

It wasn't actually a frog but a Gecko of the waste variation. About 6 feet long and covered with rough yellow scales and huge black eyes with a red tint. Its lengthy tongue lashing back and forth, tasting the air for a source of food, which was now right in front of it.

Iggy wasn't scared anymore, there was nothing he could do but show defiance, he wanted to look straight at this beast and sneer, cursing it for not being the high powered muscle car he always assumed would kill him in a derby.

As the salivating reptile closed in, Iggy relaxed his eyes and let his breathing crawl to a sedate pace. It was going to come soon. Nature was going to take him back to wherever he came. He closed his eyes and he heard the sickening crunch of powerful jaws gnashing into flesh and bone. There was no feeling, only sound.

Fucking Animals.

Chapter 3: Bright Eyes

The Big Waste was home to all manner of living things. Humanity's grip on the hierarchy of the wild was very loose since the end of the skirmishes. The disfigured mutants known as **Blights** controlled most of the geographical space, making use of well-organized underground tunnels and fortified outposts that had an unparalleled network of communication. As these blights were primarily soldiers and excavators during the skirmishes, their training put them ahead of desperate human scavengers too poor or unskilled to live in an advanced 'Citadel' or even a more modest 'Shell'. They would be killed, hunted and enslaved by the Blights. Humanity had turned their backs on them and they had no intention of showing compassion in return as a society.

Some humans were in bandit gangs or worked as well-armed mercenaries that made them less vulnerable to the Blights, but apart from rival gangs, the biggest threat to life was the wildlife itself.

There is little information on what kinds of weapons were used in the skirmishes; reports range from wicked science to arcane magic but the effect they left on the world is undeniable. They changed the very make-up of the creatures that survived it. Large cat-like creatures with gills dart through the waters like trout. Oversized bloated Rhinos spew toxic waste during mating season. Squirrels combust into flame as a self-defense mechanism and a fly-trap plant species that will snatch a person walking by and drain the volume out of them, leaving them as powdery husks so light they are carried by the harsh winds or buried by the pale sand. Almost everything was a carnivore; food crops were hard to come by and were more valuable than any drug. The creatures of the waste adapted to live off flesh, the food chain was circular. Everything was eating everything.

A large wolf-creature with white eyes dashing across the plains was about to become one of them.

She wasn't completely certain why she was running but she was finding a lot of peace in her aimless high speed. Her silver-white paws seemed to barely touch the sand as she sprinted gracefully towards her unknown destination. Her powerful shoulders fit sleekly atop her toned forelegs covered with a fine coat of shimmering white-grey fur that matched her pale grey-blue mane. Her eyes were focused, yet free, her breath was strong but measured. Her appearance did not match the toxic, fragmented background of the waste, but she moved through it as if she were its ruler.

Her midday run began to find direction as her powerful stomach began to churn and gargle with the oldest urge of any living thing. *Hunger.* Letting her nose become her targeting system, her instincts cycled through the proximate scents for the best source of food. A few carcasses in one direction, probably too rotten. A nearby source of water to be kept in mind to visit later. A burning smell, maybe an explosion or two...but it was masking another scent, one of another animal. No, **two** animals covered in the stench of panic and desperation. The two sources were becoming close, directing her to the meeting point. A live hunt maybe? A perfect source of food for the wolf.
Her speed increased to a breakneck pace as she closed in on the curious pair of whiffs. Her eyesight was good but it was far behind her sense of smell, her crystal white eyes left the job of locating to her much more adept nose, and it was doing a fine job.

Finally, even in the harsh uncomfortable sunlight and the dusty air, her vision began to perceive a shape in the distance; the source of the smell, a tasty body of living meat. She came in at such a speed that the target didn't even have time to react. The sheer impact of this powerful wolf beast's tackle snapped the target's neck and most of its spine. It was lifeless before it flopped to the ground, turned over. She wasted no time in taking her first bite. There was an audible crunch of gnashing jaws crushing bone. She had caught a tasty lizard.

She was so busy feeding she barely noticed the badly wounded, barely conscious human right next to her, quivering with his eyes closed. None of this mattered to her, as she was hungry.

Chapter 4: Wheelhouse

The sky was a pale orange now, the nuclear weather worked in mysterious ways but every now and again it would find a way to be beautiful, whistling with a gentle breeze as it maintained a comfortable temperature. This was the fortunate face of the waste that Iggy awoke to. He felt he must be in the afterlife, though he expected it to be a little more *cloud*-like.

She was feeding like one would expect from a beast, her mouth barely closing before another bite was taken. She gave herself no real-time to savor the taste or pick the leanest parts of meat, just letting her maw act as a chaotic factory of consumption. She was eating as a monster would. But a monster was not the creature before Iggy, it was a person – a wild looking female with pointed ears, large canines and grey eyes so bright they almost looked white. She was a fascinating being of ambiguous humanity.

Iggy's clouded mind attempted to process his current situation, taking in the familiar bleak sight around him with a very heavy heart. As his tongue became reacquainted with the torrid air of the waste, he concluded that he was probably still alive due to the stranger in front of him. His 'rescue' seemed dubiously swift but his curiosity was halted by what he saw. Gratitude for his life saved dissipated as she continued feasting, tearing through the very ribcage of his would-be devourer. The carcass was gone; beyond the desert scales, the lizard was unrecognizable. Its skull had been mostly chewed off; its limbs were gone. Its chest was open like a volcano.

How did someone her size, tear through that motorbike-sized lizard so quickly? And how hungry will she be after she's finished with it? Do I need to stay to find out?

Just as Iggy sat up and began to pat himself down to see if he had lost anything, the female's head snapped up from the food in response to Iggy's nervous motions. She stared at him with an animalistic intensity that could be read as either caution or curiosity. Iggy's defeated expression was all he could offer back. He wasn't even completely sure if he was alive, and if he was how long it would actually last.

The silence was broken a guttural grunting sound from the woman. It was so deep and strong it reverberated the air between them. It had the short sharp bang of a dog's bark but sounded like a word.

"Mine."

Her eyes narrowed, now with something that looked a lot more like anger. Iggy gasped weakly in confusion.

"I...ahh..."

"MINE!"

This time she sounded like a gunshot. The sudden sound made Iggy jump, almost dropping the blood-soaked bat he had been gripping without realizing. It was now clear what she meant. She was claiming the kill.

"It's yours...you earned it...I'm gonna go to my car now...OK?" Iggy pleaded, trying to not make sudden movements.

As he attempted to crawl to his feet, he made waving motions toward his car behind him while keeping his palms open to show complete pacifism. Even if he wasn't half-dead from his ordeal, she had just made a meal out of waste reptile that could have easily swallowed him.

Not someone I want to fuck with.

Her head tilted with a mild bemusement as she looked at the car behind him. Her gruff voice was less of bark now and more of a growl.

"Wheels...Wheels house, yours!?"

"Yes...wheels, but not house. It's a car, my car."

"Cah...house...cah?

"Just car."

"Cahr... where...sleep? House...Cahr."

Well I guess I'll be sleeping in the car for a while, won't be back to the Citadel anytime soon

"Yes...it's a wheelhouse...car," Iggy said coyly trying to hold a neutral expression. "I'm going inside now"

Still utterly perplexed by the situation, Iggy rose to his feet trying to find his balance on his near useless leg. The woman also stood up, seemingly more interested in the vehicle debate than the half-eaten prey.

"House...strong...sleep...nice."

At full standing height, she was about 5'8, a couple of inches shorter than Iggy himself. Her hair was long and silver, bushy but less tangled and dirty than one would expect it to be. Her face was angular with sharp features. Soft but pursed lips covered a pair of inhumanly sharp canines as she spoke. Her nose was small, delicate and slightly pointed.

Her shimmering eyes were set a little deeply into a youthful pair of cheeks which didn't match perfectly with her mature jaw. It was clear she wasn't fully human but she looked more attractive than any mutant or blight that Iggy had ever seen. Her body was roped with toned muscles covered by a light grey skin that showed full definition. She was completely naked aside from a loose piece of cloth on her shoulder that was being worn like a baggy poncho reaching down far enough to cover the top half of her thighs.

As far as Iggy was aware no person in the Waste dressed like that. She looked like a fantasy creature from a pre-skirmish novel. It was interesting to observe her, despite the pain he was in.

Relaxing to a level of mild panic from existential terror was significant. He was pretty sure if this woman wanted to kill him, she would have already done it, and any predator that came in their direction she would decimate, so he felt he wasn't in any immediate trouble. Picking up his bat and confirming he was still carrying the scavenged revolver; Iggy attempted a weak smile, nodded at her, and limped back to his car. He may have not been in imminent danger, but every hour meant a higher price on his head from the Citadel depot. Iggy didn't get 6 steps from his car when he heard the light patter of quick footsteps behind him. In a silvery flash, the woman was already in front of him with her clawed hands searching all over his car. Despite being very protective of his beloved Blockgain Chaser he was equally careful with his tone.

"H-hey…careful, that's all I have you know!"

Weird mutant girl with her mitts all over my windows…

"House…Nice House…Nice…Home,"

Her voice was no longer a harsh bark. It was still gruff, but even though it retained its primality, the tone began to resemble that of a human female. Iggy even picked up a hint of happiness.

"It's a nice car, yeah. That's my Blockgain Chaser, my 3rd car. I built her up from a high-profile wreckage in the 230th Athens regional. The supercharger is brand new but I had to source the roll bars from the…"

Realizing his chirpy rambling was probably all but intelligible to her he stopped to observe her further. Not only was she fixated by his car she seemed to be *affectionate* towards it.

Both her arms were spread across the hood of the vehicle as if she was giving it a hug. Iggy felt like he may have inhaled some of the blue powder from the wreckage because he wasn't sure what he was seeing was real.

"Best home…my home…will stay inside."

A feeling of cold shock washed over him as he realized what she was getting at.

"Listen, lady. I'm glad you like my car, but I'm leaving in it now," Iggy said as he turned to the great empty pseudo-desert of the Waste. "I got people coming after me, more dangerous than that lizard too. So just keep all the food and I'll take my, uh-house."

She stopped hugging the vehicle to face him with her sharp pale eyes fixed into a very serious stare, clearly understanding but not pleased to be hearing it.

"House mine now. Open it."

The bark was back and it was now more authoritative than wild. It appeared her mind was made up. Iggy's throat felt like a slimy cave of terror and sickness. He gripped his bat and attempted to take a defensive stance for his car only to hop into a painful limp once he put any serious weight on his leg. The woman broke her stare to observe his clear injury, tilting her head in analysis.

"Cut, rotten...leg needs Clear-wet, or leg will come off," she grunted as she sniffed the air between them. "Open home...we find Clear-wet."

Clear-what? Is that a brand?

Iggy was taken aback by her interest in his leg, and also very impressed with her improved diction with every sentence. It seemed as if she was now offering something for letting her inside his car. Hearing her say 'we' reassured Iggy she didn't want to car-jack him, but maybe hitch a ride.

I don't think I have a choice...and she's right, my leg is probably infected at this point, and I won't be near a clinic anytime soon. Not soon enough at least. Whatever this Clear-wet is...well it might be the only chance I got.

"Well I doubt I could stop you, but if we are going to be riding together, I need to know what to call you," Iggy said. He put a hand on his chest as he introduced himself. "I am Ignition...or Iggy."

He turned his hand to point at the woman. She seemed a little taken aback and paused for a moment before responding. "You...Ignishin...Nishin...I am...Sil."

Sil? Okay. My passenger is a mutant girl called Sil. This is my life now.

Nodding in acknowledgment he slowly opened the door to his vehicle, tossing his new bat in the backseat and swatting away the severed bandit hand on his bonnet. Sil picked up the hand took a bite out of it, holding it like a takeaway burger. Iggy barely kept himself from vomiting at the sight. She finished the hand with a second bite, the crunching of bone in the mouth very audible, chewing through it like it was a piece of toast.

So, she does eat human flesh then...good to know.

After she was finished, they both stepped into the car. She wasn't sitting firmly in her seat but instead stretched out all over the place like a lazy dog. She was at an angle where she was between facing

Iggy and the front window. One of her legs was propped up on the side of his seat, while her other was crossed over her own. Iggy did his best to not leave his eyes wandering near her now fully exposed lower region, but she didn't seem to care. Her eyes were darting around the car and she had a look of genuine wonder on her face.

Despite all of his confusion, discomfort, and sense of dread, Iggy couldn't help but notice her fascination and smile.

Chapter 5: Free Trade

The **Blockgain Chaser** is a heavily modified muscle car tuned and specialized for high-level demolition derbies. However, it was so expertly engineered it can basically be used for anything in the hands of a driver like **Ignition.** He was raised poor by an alcoholic Grandpappy in the slums of the grand Citadel of Athens. Despite most young boys in his area becoming money-dips and pit-fighters, Ignition made the most of Athens' motor craze and learned everything he could about cars from his Grandpappy's garage.

He started out fixing local cars and salvaging wrecked vehicles in the garage when his Grandpappy was passed out on the couch or bleeding his standards dry at the slot arcade. Iggy would also take joyrides in the Junkers he fixed, developing an early skill for driving a wide range of vehicles in the tight streets of his neighborhood. By the time he was 12, Iggy was self-sufficient; making money for car repairs and betting on Citi-Races. His knowledge as a repairman allowed him to accurately assess the aptitude of the racers and get a near-perfect win rate. Driving came so naturally to him that he turned professional at the age of 17, which made Ignition the youngest driver in the Athens Premier League. Over a derby career of nearly 10 years, he rose up in the ranks to peak at #4. It was very safe to say that Ignition was a very good driver. But it wasn't enough. The challenge wasn't gripping him anymore. He had to do something else.

But why…why did I enter the waste? What did I expect out here? Would the invitational tournament really have been that bad? I could've jumped to #2…

"There! Turn house there!"

Iggy's somewhat peaceful introspection was interrupted by the now-constant barking of Sil's passenger-side directions. There was no left, right or general estimate of distance; just a very frantic series of jumping in her seat while pointing and barking. This made Iggy feel like he was taking his driving test all over again. They must have been driving for 20 minutes and Iggy had no idea if they were anywhere close to this source of 'Clear-wet' that Sil spoke of. He could only guess she was following her nose as she seemed to inhale sharply before every barked order.

Iggy's leg was feeling waves of heat, itchiness and brief numbness. It was clearly infected but he was somewhat impressed that his leg had lasted this long. Being shot, having a toad drink the blood from his leg, and passing out twice made him think his leg had extra lives or something. He could only hope the ointment that Sil was so determined to locate was going to be the real thing. Iggy was barely surviving the Waste with two legs; he didn't even want to think about trying with one.

The land around him was beginning to look different, the orange sand was now more of pale beige and there were patches of golden-brown sand along with tiny ponds of shallow water. It still looked like a hellscape but one that could much more reliably sustain plant life. The sky was now a light purple, still bright enough to see but the glimmer of the night stars are showing very faintly.

"Here, found here!"

Iggy winced at the volume.

"Where, near the ponds? What am I looking for?"

"There!! Leave house there!!"

As Iggy pressed on the brakes with his weak foot, he circled around the area deciding where to park but noticed Sil was growling fiercely at the window.

Is she seeing something I ain't?

Iggy brought the Blockgain to a halt and scanned the area from the car window before stepping out. After finding the most comfortable weight distribution between his legs to stand, he limped out of the car. He was barely able to keep up with an impatient Sil. He noticed there were small amounts of plant life around him. Not just the moldy grass but a few weeds and even something that looked vaguely like a flower.

Even inside the Citadel, plants were extremely rare, and there were almost never seen by folk like Iggy. They were reserved for the central districts were the 'Zens' lived, mostly to make their high-rise apartments and marble halls more attractive on promo vids. Sil rushed past Iggy like a blur and started to shout in her barking tone when she got close to a small turquoise cactus.

"Mine! MINE! Don't take!!"

Please don't be another fucking dead lizard....

Iggy hopped out of his limp to painfully jog towards Sil to see what the commotion was about; only to see three figures of human shape standing about 12 feet away from them. Sil was now steadily moving to the front of the cactus as if she was ready to guard. The three figures all had brown cloaks on, which were typical for scavenging nomads. The figure in the middle raised their hood which revealed a human face.

Under the hood was a man of about 40 years old with a thick medium brown beard and rectangular black goggles. After taking a step out in front of the trio, he held his hands out as a passive gesture, desperately signaling that he didn't want any trouble. One of the hooded figures behind him seemed to be rummaging through their cloak and it was making Iggy nervous. He decided to speak up before this escalated any further.

"Hey, what's going on? Who are you?" Iggy said in an even but direct tone.

As Iggy called out, Sil's barking stopped and morphed into a low growl, as if to give backup to his words. The bearded male stepped forward and removed his goggles to reveal a set of warm friendly eyes. He spoke with a slight rancher's accent.

"My name is Novak sir; behind me is my wife, Trass and our prospector, Clive. We don't know what's got your girl so upset, we ain't bandits, and ain't tryin' to take nothing from her."

The hooded figure who was rummaging removed their hood to reveal a female face that had a few scars around the cheeks, blue eyes and short red hair. She was roughly the same age as Novak, and she spoke with a much thicker rancher dialect.

"Ain't got none ta steal from her even if we was, lady's nearly as naked as the day she was born. Ya need to keep your girl in line waster, well mutant-girl…"

Sil's beaming eyes narrowed and her voice shot up.

"Sil not Mutant! Need clear-wet, go back!"

So, she isn't a mutant?

Iggy tried to de-escalate by meeting Novak's tone.

"Listen, she is trying to find a medicine or something for my leg," Iggy explained as he winced on a step. "I don't know what we are looking for but she can get protective of things that seem minor. Tell me what you're after so we can keep out of each other's way."

Sil's back arched and her huge fangs were on full display. She was allowed the conversation to continue, watching everyone carefully.

Novak and his wife, Trass looked at each other before looking back at Iggy cautiously.

"Uh okay that's fine, we aren't after that, we just want some water," Novak said as he nodded at his wary wife. "The pond behind you looks pretty clear so it won't take too long to filter, some of the puddles 'round here can take up to an hour to clean even with Clive's help and we got a lot of families back at the convoy," Novak detailed.

Novak's words were sincere enough for Iggy to relax. He nodded slightly at the trio and turned to Sil who was still intensely focused on them. He attempted to speak to her in a firm but diplomatic manner.

"Sil, they just want to go to the pond for water. We will move out of their way and find the Clear-wet...okay?"

Sil turned slowly back towards Iggy letting her arched frame return to a more standard wild woman's posture before speaking firmly herself.

"Clear-wet **here!** No one take, **only leg!**"

Iggy noticed that she was motioning to the small cactus as she said Clear-wet, which explained why it looked like she was guarding it.

"Alright Sil, we will take the cactus, they just want the water, no problem."

Iggy's mostly rational voice warbled as a new wave of sore pain washed over his leg, which he masked poorly with a false cough. Novak, Trass and their hooded friend 'Clive' began to walk towards the pond. Sil watched them closely in her defensive stance, looking like she was ready to pounce.

"Nishin…" Sil said in a hush.

Sil's eyes began to dart between the trio and Iggy frantically as if she was trying to tell him something. Iggy was an instinctive person, but he didn't pick up on anything out of the ordinary about the nomads, apart from 'Clive' remaining both silent and hidden under his hood.

They walked past Iggy and Sil carefully making no sudden movements and passed them in a wide arc as if they were being repelled by Sil's low growls. It was only when they got to the lip of the pond Sil seemed to relax a little, which in turn caused Iggy to exhale deeply.

"Nishin...clear-wet is here. Hold still, only one chance to save leg."

With the fate of his leg in Sil's hands, Iggy nodded before moving closer to a highly focused Sil and the apparently important cactus.

Sil took a deep breath as she ran her clawed grey hands over the cactus gently as if she was searching for something. The sharp-looking bristles on the cactus seemed to have no effect on Sil's clearly non-human skin. After a few seconds, she leaned forward, smelled the plant and took a large bite out of the top. The sound was loud wet crunch which caused Iggy's eyebrows to jump, but his voice to hold. He had followed her thus far and wasn't about to question her now.

Sil didn't chew or swallow the chunk of cactus in her mouth; but instead crawled over to Iggy on all fours with her face now level with his beltline, humming smoothly before looking up at him.

Looking down at Sil on her knees made Iggy's neck hot and his breathing quickened. Her skin seemed to glow in the afternoon light and her pronounced cleavage was made even more visible through the window of her low hanging body poncho from his line of sight. Her shimmering eyes seemed less primal and more empathetic to Iggy; leaving him to wonder how much of an impact his car had on her perception of him. Despite his pain, Iggy didn't want to think about anything else but what he could see in front of him.

And then she bit him.

Her head moved so fast it looked like an illusion; her fangs sinking deep into his nasty wound, and the pain was so sudden and so unfamiliar that Iggy didn't even make a sound. He was in shock.

She's gonna kill me right here, eat me alive and steal my car...

Trying to keep his mind focused, his hand slowly moved to his jacket, feeling around for his holstered revolver. Without moving her mouth from his leg, she restrained his wrist with her powerful hands. With the feeling of being held by iron shackles, he felt like she could crush his bones like a plastic cup if she really wanted, but she only held. As her eyes fixed on his; the pain of the bite began to lessen accompanied by an odd tingling feeling through his lower body, starting to feel bizarrely pleasant.

"S-Sil...what's happening?... ugh"

The sensation was both invigorating and slightly arousing, waves of subtle electricity through his legs were finding their way to his groin and his manhood began to react accordingly. Sil somehow looked even more desirable to him now than before she was biting him. Acutely aware that the trio was still close enough to hear any moan he let slip, he tried his best to hold his voice. Just as it began to overpower his senses, she removed her teeth from his thigh.

"No fucking way...I don't believe it!" Iggy exclaimed.

The wound was gone, the feeling of his leg had returned completely and apart from a small itch there was zero pain. His festering, heavily scabbed bullet wound was now a slightly bloody scratch, no bigger than what a mildly annoyed kitten could deliver. He was instantly healed. Sil and the Clear-wet were the real deal. The wild lady rose to her feet and faced Iggy, and her soft lips expanded into a toothy smile.

"Leg is saved. Clear-wet works." Sil said softly, her striking face mere inches away from his.

Every fiber in Iggy's surprised mind was telling him to lean in and kiss her but he was unsure if she would even understand what that meant. He took a gulp and closed his eyes but the 'moment' didn't last long enough for him to make a move.

"RANDALL GAINSBOROUGH, AGE TWENTY-SEVEN. BOUNTY ACTIVE."

The voice sounded like a car alarm mixed with a steel factory. Iggy's eyes sprang open like he was rudely awoken from a good dream and spun his head to face the sound so quickly he felt his neck sprain. The obnoxious clamor had just blared out Iggy's full name; something he hadn't heard out loud since adolescence.

The nomad trio had made their way back over from the pond, carrying the water they came for, facing Iggy with the third traveler fully revealed.

'Clive' was a Tin Man.

Early model synthetic humanoids, known as 'Tin Men' in the wastes, were very rare but instantly recognizable. Pre-skirmish they were primarily used in simple support roles; assembly workers, tour guides, groundskeepers, and office admin, but never combat roles. Humanity was paranoid enough to not make A.I. soldiers, lest they are used against them one day. But now in the wastes, the remnants of the synthetics had been rebuilt and reprogrammed for a whole range of survival-based tasks. Personal bodyguard was one of them.

A Tin Man?! How did these nomads get their hands on one?

Clive's face was a cheap mockery of humanity, a ghoulish plastic-looking light blue mask for a face with two flickering orange lights as eyes. Behind the mask-face was a crude network of wires and spark plugs with a rusty tripod that seemed to form a 'neck' for the Tin Man. He stood just over a head taller than Iggy and his limbs were long and gangly.

Clive was a very early model; the amount of work done to repurpose him seemed to be rushed and amateurish. After blaring Iggy's information, it raised its hand to extend a rusty claw-like finger that pointed at him with an emotionless prejudice. Slowly Novak and Trass came over from the pond, with backpack flasks full of water and long poles fashioned into spear-like weapons. Sil was now in a crouched position between Iggy and the Tin Man Clive, her growl so deep that it was felt in the pit of Iggy's stomach. Her head was darting between the three in a rapid pattern.

The bearded male Novak spoke in his usual soft tone.

"You gotta understand we've been a struggling convoy since the shell evicted us, we have been living from scavenge to scavenge. We can't really hunt food out here and only a couple of us know how to use weapons. But anything worth eating out here is dangerous and we don't want to risk our dwindlin' numbers, fella."

His red-head wife Trass stepped forward, speaking with a scratchier and slightly more aggressive voice.

"Ya spoke well too good to be a Waster, Mista Randall. I had Clive runna background on ya. Figured you for a Citi, but never reckoned you'd have a bounty that fat on ya neck. Ten thou would take tha whole convoy a long way, we got our own twelve-year-old boy plus six other kids who ain't been eating good for weeks now, ya'll know we gotta do right by em."

The bounty has been launched already? Guess they don't like being hung-up on. I thought I'd have at least another half-day before the registry update. I don't want to fight these people...much less kill them...but....

Iggy's hand once again found itself reaching for his revolver. He obviously had an advantage with a firearm, but he only had two bullets against three opponents not even sure he could hit two of them. Guns being as rare as they are, most people don't get the opportunity to use them, much less practice.

Would a bullet do anything to a Tin Man?

Having non-existent experience with synthetics, he wasn't feeling super-confident standing in front of Clive, even with his freshly healed leg. He attempted to negotiate with a voice he couldn't keep from quivering.

"L-listen, you don't need to do this, there are plenty bounties out there".

Trass smirked and Novak sighed in response, now walking closer to Iggy with his spear outstretched and pointed at his throat.

"If you come along peaceful, we can collect this bounty without any violence, I know the debt camps are kinda rough, but you're still young, do the smart thing, mister."

Trass turned to her husband after glancing behind Iggy.

"Ya know Novi, his veehickle would probably go for nearly as much as the bounty, or we could add it to tha convoy…"

Iggy had heard enough.

"Fuck that, you ain't taking me or my car, *back off*."

Sil had also heard everything she needed to.

"HOME is mine! NO-ONE takes!"

Sil leaped into action before Iggy could even draw his gun. She was so fast that Novak and Trass could only respond as a splutter.

"Clive! Get her! You gotta…"

"Fuckin save us, robot!"

Clive's arm, shrouded under a heavy sleeve until this point, rose up to reveal a rusty forearm-weapon. Crackling with blue sparks at the wrist, revealing it to be a stunning prod. Clive's body squealed painfully as his rusty joints moved into action, but despite his age and model, he was still incredibly agile, leaping out of the way of Sil's charge but also barely missing with his own shock-prod counter move.

They were now in a fight.

Trass had already begun flanking Iggy as soon as Clive jumped into action against Sil. The wild woman and the Tin Man were now circling each other, with an automatic acknowledgment for each other's speed. Iggy stood horrified at how fast a gangly humanoid-like Clive could move. His body looked like an overgrown metal spider, with his arms and legs bent wide and moving laterally in a jerky motion. Iggy then spotted the red-head nomad make her way to his left and he drew his pistol, not confident he could hit her with a shot.

"Dang it Trass, stay back, let Clive handle it!" Novak shouted to his wife while cautiously staying put in his original position. But Trass' eyes were now wild with the fire of conflict. She couldn't hear anything rational right now.

As her battle-grimace turned into a small grin, Iggy wasted no time in pulling his revolver and aiming it at her center mass. The trigger felt stiff and uncomfortable with the weight of the gun seeming unfit for one hand. Iggy had no idea how to tense for the recoil, he let off a shot that had a sounded like a monster truck backfiring. But apart from a slight crouch by Trass and a flinch from her husband it was clear that the bullet didn't hit anything living. Iggy cursed his bad aim and now reduced ammo. Trass saw all she needed to close the gap on the young driver with impunity and Iggy doubted she was going to miss with her spear thrust like he did with his gun.

Sil's ears pricked up as if she 'saw' every aspect of the fight despite only watching Clive and made her move. Without even waiting for an attack to counter, Sil achieved speeds *even faster* than before. She darted right toward Clive and grabbed the wrist of his non-stun-baton arm and yanked hard in a half pivot motion, tearing the synthetic arm right out of its socket.

"GAAAARRRR"

A metallic whine from Clive's chest followed the sickening ripping sound of wires and joints as Sil snarled with moderate effort pulling the appendage from the rest of the frame. Iggy, Novak, and Trass all stood looking slack-jawed at the violent action and Sil didn't waste a single second of their shock to capitalize.

In the same turning motion she used to tear off the arm, the wild female swung the metal limb as a makeshift club with blistering force at Trass' head with such power the impact took most of the head off. Sil's fluid and precise motion contrasted with her primal nature. Iggy cringed in disgust as he heard the smack.

Wet chunks of Trass' skull flew across the sand, covering almost everybody except her husband Novak who was a few paces behind. The recently widowed man dropped to his knees immediately and began wailing in immediate grief as her half-headed body slumped to the floor ungracefully.

"Holy Shit!" Iggy exclaimed.

Before Iggy could even comment on her violent technique, Clive; now coated in the mechanical fluid that pissing from his shoulder stump, was regaining balance and preparing to zap Sil with his still functional electro-prod arm.

But the Tin Man never stood a chance.

Sil spun back around in reverse, now using the severed limb like a sword. In a motion as fluid as the last, she impaled Clive's chest with his own arm. Iggy had to shield himself from the bits of bolts and scrap metal that exploded from the chest in all directions. The Tin Man was standing but silent, with his voice function no doubt being obliterated by that move. With a slow and glitchy looking behavior, it finally staggered back from the fight, its circuits going a mile a minute trying to react to the major damage. Iggy wasn't about to wait to see what happened next. In one swift motion, he pointed his revolver and got up right close to Clive before putting the gun to the Tin Man's temple.

The oversized revolver cracked the air with another boom.

The kickback of the shot almost sprained his wrist, but this time the bullet hit its target and the true power of the gun was realized. Clive's unnerving plastic mask of a face was almost disintegrated by the sheer impact of the shot and the Tin Man went completely stiff before hitting the floor like a wrecked steel pillar.

The after-shock of the gunshot finally dissipated. All that could be heard was the blubbering of the last surviving man in the trio, Novak.

"P...p...p... please folks...I know we d-did you wrong trying to claim t-that bounty, but I gotta little boy back at the c-convoy. Let me just get my wife's body and I'll be outta ya way...please...?"

Iggy breathed the hot air out of his lungs and began to feel more civilized again, giving the adrenaline time to settle. He holstered his gun and spoke with an angry but clear tone. "We never wanted this! I never wanted this! Take your wife and go. Bounty hunting is a nasty business, if you really care about that community you have then you'll stay the hell away from these kinda risks, got it?"

Novak dropped even further down in a pathetic bowing motion as the spit, snot, and tears from his face began to heavily soak the ground beneath him. "T-thank you kind sir, I wish Trass hadn't talked me into thiss...oh god...my Trass...I'll do right by the convoy sir...you're a good man, I'll spread your good name, we can sort you with some supplies and we----**ackkkkk!**"

The Nomad's sorrowful apology was cut deathly short when his torso was severed violently from his shoulder at a crude diagonal angle. The amount of blood was unbelievable, spraying in all directions not too different from the Bloodtoad that Iggy himself had killed. As the mutilated corpse gargled its death rattle, the blood-soaked killer Sil rose to her feet picking up a chunk of Novak's flesh to chew on as she walked over to a shocked Iggy.

"Sil, he was surrendered, he wasn't going to fight us...why?" he asked solemnly.

Sil looked at Iggy confused. Her beastly battle expression replaced with her innocent wonder. She was now the curious drifter who was fascinated by the car.

"All threaten life…all lose life…even metal human…and must eat too yes?"

Sil held the chunk of Novak's half-eaten flesh to Iggy's face with a charitable expression expecting him to take a bite.

"Hey! What the fuck you doing Sil! That's a person! I'm not eating that; you shouldn't have fucking killed him any way you **animal!**"

Iggy wretched and jerked back, instinctively backhanding the meat from her grasp. Sil raised an eyebrow before slapping him with a dismissive snarl sending him flying a full 5 feet backward effortlessly.

Every fiber in Iggy's body told him to immediately regret calling Sil that word and he was half expecting it to be the last thing he ever said. But sure enough, Sil stayed fairly calm and retrieved the chunk of bloody meat from the floor before popping it into her mouth with a neutral expression.

"Clear-wet save leg, but won't save hunger. Should eat, Nishin."

Sil's voice was back to being a low growl of mild indifference. She turned towards the pond immediately and jumped in. No doubt to drink and wash after a very dirty fight. As Iggy watched his new companion splash around in the water like a proud but happy tiger, he began to contemplate the state of his life.

So, she's really a killer, I don't know how much further I can travel with her. She isn't going to fit in with any Shell society, definitely not a Citadel. Not that I could go anywhere with this fucking bounty on me. Why the hell didn't I pick something a little safer? Why did it have to be Waste Cargo-runs, Ignition? I still can't believe that Clive called me Randall, even paps stopped calling me that…

After a few more minutes of introspection Iggy finally pulled himself back to his feet and began the nasty chore of scavenging the torn-up trio for any supplies and items.

My leg does feel better though...

Chapter 6: Finding Your Way

Holding his breath to block the smell of drying blood, Iggy's shoulders hung weakly as he walked between the pile of bodies and his car. After dropping the last bit of scavenged loot in his trunk he took stock of the items he collected. The nomads had some basic tools along with a decent amount of food for their trip. The recently collected purified water and the two makeshift spear weapons with a folding function made them easy to store in the trunk. Mainly out of curiosity, he also salvaged a few parts from the decimated Tin Man too. He took the shock prod arm attachment and a fairly intact component inside the burst chest that looked a little like a palm-sized version of a car engine, which had Iggy's interest immediately.

After packing everything up, he opened his car door just in time to see Sil emerge from the pond. Her dusty silver hair was now a much cleaner shimmer of brightness, and her previously blood and sand stained poncho was now closer to its original beige color. Her skin was still moist from the water; clear and smooth looking, with some noticeable bristles of fine light-colored hair on all of her limbs. Once again Iggy was in absolute awe of her appearance.

Any sensible thoughts of getting as far away as possible from this murderous creature left Iggy's mind as swiftly as the fresh sand being carried by the wind. As she walked past him to climb into the car, she glanced at him with the same indifference as before but now with a hint of added curiosity. He cleared his throat and tried to sound focused.

"We better get moving, it's nearly dark and even I know how deadly the waste is when the sunsets. Luckily, all outposts and settlements will turn their signal lights on, so as soon as one becomes visible, we will drive towards it."

Sil made herself comfortable in the passenger seat of the Blockgain before responding, her voice was so relaxed she sounded more human than ever, if not a little gruff.

"Move home to light...yes okay...take it there Nishin."

Her eyes met his with new softness and sincerity. They hadn't discussed the practicalities of her traveling together after finding the clear-wet, but she made the entire situation seem so casual that Iggy had nothing to protest. He nodded, jumped in his seat and gunned the engine.

I guess I gotta get used to this, but for how much longer?

She had her back reclined all the way into the pit of the seat with her well-toned legs high and across the dashboard. She was a little fidgety and couldn't seem to find how she wanted to cross or tuck her legs in for the car journey. Leaving Iggy to force himself not to stare at her exposed lower region that was being pathetically covered by her loose and constantly shifting poncho. They had been driving for only 15 minutes or so and he was already hard as a rock. He said extremely little to her on the journey so far, mainly asking quickly if she could see any lights in the distance with her superior eyesight. But nothing came up yet.

If Iggy had been on a street with other cars, he would have crashed multiple times by this point. He couldn't focus on the road. Sil refused to sit in her seat like a regular human.

Iggy shifted in his seat a few times to try and manage the uncomfortable nature of his fierce erection, but it failed to do more than make him look like a flustered, grunting mess. Sil suddenly stopped stirring and trained her bright eyes on Iggy in serious consideration. Iggy snapped his head to his side to glance at her before wiping his brow and re-focusing on the endless path of shadowed land in front of him.

"What is it Sil? Another cactus?"

Iggy pushed through a forced chuckle in an attempt to take the tension off, it didn't work.

"Nishin…is wanting to-"

Sil leaned over to Iggy, brushing her skin firmly against his before pressing her face near the upper part of his leg. Iggy recoiled in shock and the Blockgain took a jerky turn, in response.

"Sil…what the fuck?"

Sil began to inhale softy, pulling her head up a little to now actively sniff around Iggy's tented groin area.

"Nishin…wants to…push?"

What the…

Iggy began to shake his head in a mix of disbelief, annoyance and slight fear. "Push? I don't know what that is, something to do with the car…err home?"

Sil stared at him for a moment with mild confusion and quickly rose to a seated position to remove her poncho. Exposing her previously obscured torso to reveal her medium-sized, shapely round breasts and dark grey nipples, which matched her ashen skin. Her stomach was a tight six-pack of solid muscle and her lower entrance was covered in a fair amount of black hair, but less than would be expected for a woman of the wild. Without any warning she climbed on to Iggy's lap to face him, blocking his view of the front window.

"Sil! I can't see it! Wha…?"

Iggy hit the brakes pretty hard but the sudden stop barely moved her, as if she was anchored to her new seat. She then pressed her chest against his face softly as her sharp fingers began to comb through Iggy's coarse dark hair. Her voice was now a low, suggestive purr.

"Nishin...push...push with Sil," she said as she knotted her fingers in his hair.

Her terminology became crystal clear as she timed her statement with a grinding stroke of her naked behind against Iggy's pulsing member, almost teasing it with the hope of freedom from his cargo jeans. Her breath was like a furnace with the stench of blood still thick on her exhalation. Iggy ignored it, his body was telling him to make peace with his hang-ups about her actions and to give in to his instincts.

I can't think of a good reason not to anymore.

The sky seemed to get darker, and Sil's gleaming eyes blazed in the low light around them. Her tongue glanced past her white fangs and flickered around Iggy's face as she pressed into his lap a little harder. Iggy's hands went on auto-pilot, one finding itself on her back, the other frantically trying to loosen his belt with limited success. Sil purred aggressively as she took notice of his attempt and began to move up further close to him; pressing her breasts right against his face, and moving into a half squat over him. Iggy gave up trying to pull off his loosened pants with his now trapped arm and just focused on kissing her firm breasts, attempting to be sensual at first but quickly falling into a lusty lapping motion around her nipples with an occasional nip every few seconds excitedly.

This is...amazing.

It had its desired effect. Sil's purrs were now mixed with resonant, jumping whimpers and she put her half crouching position to use. Using one of her feet she hooked her toes on the inside the waistline of Iggy's pants and dragged them off by pushing her foot downwards.

There was a slight scratching from her sharp toenails but the motion was so erotic the pain was unnoticeable. With his pants around his ankles and his underwear just below his knees, Iggy's manhood pointed skywards. Itchingly hot and slick with sweat and early fluids of anticipation. Sil's parts were just as wet but even hotter, roasting the inside of the car like a high-powered radiator. Her eyes were wide with hunger and unmoving primal confidence her tongue was lashing around his face like a whip. It was strange to Iggy, but it felt good. Gripping the driver's seat firmly she began to find her way on top of Iggy's pulsating tip. It was so erect she didn't even need a hand to guide it.

"Sil...Nishin...push...*ahhhhh*"

She found the touch, then the prod and in one fairly quick motion she sank down around him, letting him slide almost to the hilt before exhaling with the first shock of pleasure that was in chorus with Iggy's own with more volume. The soft heated caverns of Sil's insides were an astonishing contrast with the strong surface of her body. Iggy's jaw stretched open with a gasp, filling his mouth with even more of Sil's firm breast. Her wild hips began plowing into Iggy's lap powerfully, her wetness engulfing him completely and finding a smooth but exciting motion that had him bucking his pelvis in near-perfect rhythm with her.

Iggy's heart nearly jumped out of his neck; his body had not had this sensation in a long time. Drunken one-night stands with pit groupies after the demolition matches were barely as satisfying as masturbation, sometimes less so. This natural, dangerous, beautiful creature who basically saved his life twice was now locked in coitus with him; inside a vehicle that she seemed to love as much as he did. He did not understand her, he understood the situation even less, but at this moment he felt genuinely happy.

"Sil, ahhh, slow down...damn," Iggy heaved in slight discomfort.

Sil's impressively built body steadily increased in force and speed and didn't seem to have an upper limit. Her inner walls were closing in on him ferociously and her grunts were becoming more animalistic. Iggy's fear of coming to soon quickly morphed into fear of his physical safety. Her superhuman strength was being reined in by very little control.

"**Oww Sil…**slow down…it **hurts,**" he pleaded.

Sil said nothing, simply giving him a slightly confused half-smile before licking his face again; her hot tongue felt like a small steam-iron pressing his cheek. She placed one of her hands on his shoulders, and her mighty vice grip was apparent as Iggy felt the ligaments near his collarbone begin to give.

Iggy's was panicking; he could hear the suspension of his beloved Blockgain being tested by the impact of the powerful humping. Despite his mortal fear, he was still in too much carnal ecstasy to think straight, and could only beg for mercy with his wide-open eyes.

"**Push,** push **more**, Nishin!" Sil demanded gutturally.

His penis was a pillar of pure pleasure pumping sexual streams of energy to all corners of his body, but his bones felt like they could snap like toothpicks in the next minute. As his bruised pelvis throbbed like a punching bag, he realized that a regular non-upgraded man might not be durable enough to survive a round of passion with whatever Sil's species was. Iggy wondered if she was even concerned for his safety anymore, or was she going to devour him after sex like a black widow arachnid? The unknown becoming less exciting and more terrifying by the second.

Iggy, knowing he had to do something, took a gamble once again.

"You want me to *push*, Sil? Okay!"

Sil's eyes flickered with wild anticipation and half-smile was now a full, almost villainous grin, clearly liking what she heard.

Placing one hand on her back and another on her chest right above her breasts, he took a gulping breath and gave her the hardest shove he could muster. He knew he couldn't push her off with her naturally perfect balance, but with any luck…

"Ah…**Nishin**…*mmmm.*"

Sil noticed the effort, and all of Iggy's strength managed to budge her maybe an inch before she willingly gave into his momentum and let him push her back against the dashboard; where he was now the one leading the hip motions in top position. Her eyes widened with glee, she liked it. Switching to missionary saved his life.

Increasing his grip on her helped him fully appreciate how solid her muscles were, it was like squeezing a palm tree. The only difference was her relatively soft skin that was covered in light amounts of hair instead of bark. He took care to moderate his hold as to not break his fingers.

He was now thrusting at an angle that not only gave him plenty of pleasure but driving Sil to unmatched thrills since they started. Her voice was no longer a growl, purr, grunt or anything else remotely animalistic. Her full-throated cries of pleasure were very human and very female. Iggy had a brief illusion of power and dominance as he smashed his hips into his wild partner with full force, his body pulsing with the natural high of being alive.

Sil's cries of escalating pleasure put her deadly set of fangs on display, large jagged yellow-white molars with curved bladed canines almost like a saber-tooth. Iggy once again acknowledged the pure danger he was in being around this creature, let alone inside of her. She gave him an approving glance as to signal an approaching climax and wrapped her legs around his waist. The strength of her thighs clasping his midsection almost stole his breath but her simple sign of physical affection was all it took to push Iggy over the edge, he held on as long as he could.

"**Ahhhhhhrrrr!!**"

Iggy shouted powerfully from his chest as his orgasm exploded through him and his primed member blasted several rounds of his seed far inside of his undomesticated companion. Sil inhaled with a mix of pleasure and fascination with Iggy's orgasm as she arrived at a milder peak herself, careening out a low hiss to go with it. Luckily for Iggy, she was content with the experience, and eventually released him after purring with the after-glow. He slumped back into his driver's seat, feeling like an empty tube of toothpaste as if there was nothing left inside him to keep him together. Sil crawled across him, sitting in his lap with her arms over his shoulder and began licking his face once more.

"How was it for you Sil?" Iggy asked with a weak chuckle.

She paused her licking and looked at Iggy like a small pet, responding through a smile while stroking his sweat-soaked head.

"Nishin so soft, Nishin push gentle…"

Gentle!?

Iggy rolled his eyes before kissing Sil, catching her lapping tongue with his own to try to guide her into a human kiss. She responded awkwardly by attempted to emulate before pulling away. Leaving his lap, she grabbed her poncho to pull it back on, glancing out of the window with a face of mild concern.

"Nishin…sky gets dark".

Iggy pathetically raised his arms to the steering wheel as she made her way back to her passenger seat and began to drive. Still breathing heavy, he stepped on the gas and began to drive through the waste feeling a little confused.

Well, Ignition, what did you expect? A cuddle?

After two near-death experiences and the hook-up of a lifetime Iggy had so many unanswered questions and this was the first moment since meeting that they had some peace. But she was no longer the naturally curious traveler with constant energy and comments. She was now still and silent, sitting almost like a human would in her seat looking out into the black night sky as if she was mesmerized. Her face was covered by her messy post-coitus hair that blocked Iggy's line of sight but was certain she didn't have her usual perky expression. He could take the silence no longer but didn't feel bold enough to discuss the sex just yet.

"Sil, where are you from? I don't think you mentioned."

She didn't move to respond and paused a moment before she did as if her mind was in a far more important place. "Sil was away from home...now I home, for now."

Although it was the most complete sentence she spoke since they met, it still made no sense. But Iggy knew that further questioning probably wouldn't get him anywhere. "I'm from Athens, you know the Citadel?" She said nothing, but Iggy kept on talking to keep the silence at bay. "Athens is the only Citadel in zone 11, apart from my away derby tournaments I never really left it until today. Something about driving for a living but never leaving one area after an amount of time..."

Iggy found himself slightly caught by self-reflection before finishing his thought.
"It just felt like a trap, like driving in circles over and over again. Different names on the betting odds, different demolition maps, and different cars to smash. I went up in rank, but I never felt like I was going anywhere..."

Iggy wiped a stream of sweat from his forehead as he refocused on the endless path in front of him and checked his half-empty fuel gage. He wondered if anything he said was making sense to Sil.

I mean, I'm not even sure it makes sense to me. But I had to get out. I had to.

"Nishin...is still home?"

Whatever the reason she calls it home, it makes sense for me. In the Blockgain, I feel safe all the time, even after today. Maybe it is my home...maybe it's our home....

"Yeah I guess I am Sil, I never really left."

The dry corners of his mouth cracked a little as a small smile crept across his face. It was his first smile since accepting that cursed cargo run. On some level, he felt understood by Sil, which added to his already complex feelings towards her.

"Nishin...did like the push?"

Well, I'm glad she brought it up, holy shit.

"Yeah it was...nice," Iggy said in much understatement. "Look not that I'm complaining, but why? I mean why me. Why here and now?"

Although he was talking to a wild creature of the wastes, he still didn't want to sound needy and whiny. Sil still remained motionless but let out a small sigh before speaking.

"Nishin wanted push...from when Nishin first saw Sil, could smell. Sil wanted home so Sil and Nishin push in home..."

Could smell? Wait, was this a trade? Did she fuck me because I let her in the car?

Sil's voice was now devoid of her guttural beastly tone. Iggy's throat was bitter at the idea of their sex being simply a transaction, as he tried to rationalize an alternative theory.

"Um, did you enjoy uh-pushing with me?"

Sil stayed silent for the longest time, and Iggy took it to be an implication that she didn't enjoy it until she spoke up, now with a voice that sounded almost like a choke and splutter under the breath.

"Sil… can't push again…because Sil must leave home now…before she…**"**

Iggy couldn't make any sense of that and went from feeling bitter and guilty to confuse. Her face was still turned out of view, but now it was intentional as if she was now hiding.

Before she-what? What is she doing?

"**Nishin**, open home **Sil** is leaving."

"Sil you sound strange, let's have a look at you after we get to some sort of settlement, we shouldn't stop out here in the waste while it's dark-"

"OPEN NOW."

Iggy's head spun in the directions of the ear-popping demand to find an unfamiliar face now staring at him. Her eyes were glowing blue-white, her mouth was a beastly snarl with all her fangs on display but they looked even **larger.** Her whole face looked different, her nose and jaw seemed further forward, hard heavy wrinkles gathered on her forehead, and sprouts of bushier hair from her temples and cheeks seemed to have appeared. Covering more of her face than before to form some sort of a mane-like appearance. She looked like she was in the process of rapid mutation, from an exotic humanoid to a monstrous beast.

Iggy clenched his teeth in fear and confusion before slamming on the brakes and sending his car into a fishtailing swerve before the Blockgain Chaser veered into an ungraceful halt. Sil's inhuman growls and were now accompanied by gnashes of her terrifying maw and flares of her larger muscle's limbs lashing around the interior in what looked like a painful rage.

Iggy hit the door unlock switch after narrowly dodging one of her claw swipes and hurriedly opened the driver's door with clammy sweat-slicked hands. He was too wary of her to try letting her move past him so he crawled out of the car first, clumsily making contact with the ground elbow first on to what felt like road tarmac. She shot out of her seat like a catapult nearly trampling him on her way out of the car before standing still for the briefest of moments to glance at the car she called home, and then at the eyes of the man she called Nishin. Not saying a word, she exploded into a deft sprint into the darkness of the waste. In that brief moment, Sil had gone.

The climb back into his car felt like a mountain expedition. His worn-out body and his heavy mood made his movements sluggish and limp and he had a look of numb indifference on his dusty face. His insides ached and churned as if they were suspended in anti-gravity and all he could do was try to make sense of the nonsensical.

*Why did she go? What was happening to her body? Did I do something? Did I **not** do something?*

There was no one to give him these answers; the only sounds were the hair-raising movements of whatever creatures prowled the big waste in the dark. He contemplated Sil's safety by herself, though quickly reminded himself that there was probably very little she hadn't already seen in the waste or killed. With Iggy back behind the wheel, the Blockgain Chaser peeled off in the same general direction he was driving in before her departure.

Once again, he was alone, and with no curious companion to distract his mind from his physical pain he had endured the entire day along with emotional stress of not knowing why she left, Iggy began to cry. His tears-distorted vision created a watercolor effect of the path in front of him that was bittersweet. Shades of black and dark green mixed under the pale blue shine of his headlights creating a dream-like effect that felt like a brief escape from the moment. His mind began to power down, with the murmur of his engine acting as a lullaby to carry his thoughts elsewhere.

Chapter 7: Garage Talk

Despite growing up poor, living in a citadel on any socio-economic level was an extremely privileged position compared to anywhere else in the Big Waste. Local security, clean running water, and basic education were luxuries only Citizens enjoy regularly. Iggy's home of Athens is the 2nd largest Citadel in the known world. Most of its inhabitants go their entire lives without ever stepping outside the Citadel gates, mostly due to never finding a good reason to. But Randall 'Ignition' Gainsborough was not like most inhabitants and Athens was not big enough for him to grow old in.

Below the socio-economic status of the Citadels were the 'Shells'. Mainly towns, cities, and villages that existed before the skirmishes reduced to a *shell* of what they used to be. Derelict burned out buildings, cracked streets, dubious leadership, and dangerous individuals are the reputations of the societies. Shells are large and well-fortified from the waste but never truly safe to live in, even for those with money. Scavengers who earn decent standards from selling materials can usually afford to live in a Shell household, although menacing landlords and deadly debt collectors can make a stay very short for the unfortunate. So, when a very tired Iggy saw the yellow signal lights of a Shell on the horizon after Sil ran out on him, all he could do was gulp and feel the cold sensation of fear fold over his gut.

I can't drive all night; I have to stop somewhere. Shells always have garages and I need to service the Blockgain and refuel. But this damn bounty…can I risk showing my face in there?

Iggy's mind hastily sorted through different scenarios before finally deciding to stop at the Shell. Iggy's bounty was with the Citadel, meaning the money for capturing him could only be redeemed at Citadels. The Shells had their own network of bounties and hunters, and the vast majority of halfway decent Shell bounty hunters had Citadel bounties of their own, meaning they couldn't claim a bounty lest they be captured themselves on arrival. Convoy homesteaders, Nomads and Scavengers like the late Novak and Trass don't have criminal records or bounties with the Citadel. This is usually due to a lack of combat experience and a low chance of being successful in collecting bounties from dangerous high-level criminals or rogues.

The vast majority of all citadel bounties are collected by high-level Citadel '**poachers**'; Experienced freelance mercenaries that are part of an official hunter's guild. Luckily for Iggy the eponymous poachers only get out of bed for 'the big kills' and with Iggy's bounty still only five figures, he would be extremely low on even a rookie poacher's priority list…for now.

The large outer wall of the Shell came into view. It was a network of reinforced steel welded with patches of scrap metal to form a formidable-looking barrier. The outer gate was tall enough to where only the very highest buildings were visible from inside the compound. A few guard towers were scattered outside of the perimeter that Iggy was approaching from, and the odd car screeched by the Blockgain as it was leaving the Shell; the gates snapping quickly behind them with a metallic squeal and clang. Iggy wiped the sweat off his brow before pulling close to the main gate and spotted a large rectangular box that appeared to be an intercom. Pulling up gently beside it, he pushed the button and heard a crackle. As he cleared his throat to respond. A gravelly voice with an outpost accent came through.

"Welcome to Folsom, purpose of visit?"

Iggy was somewhat relieved they didn't ask his name or car's I.D. but he had no frame of reference to know if that was a good thing.

"Need to check into a garage, probably an Inn too," Iggy said, trying to put a little grit in his voice.

The thought of even a semi-comfortable place to sleep made him yawn quietly.

"Entry is 200, stay here longer than a week and you get taxed 1000 every week from then on. There is no Folsom police force but the gangs will kill you if you start too much shit, your car's ID was logged when you pulled up so if we have problems with you the bounty hunters will find you, got it?"

Iggy sighed at the idea of his car being logged but resolved it was probably unavoidable. He handed over a couple of steel cards from his glove box that totaled 200 standards and put them in the slot for money below the intercom speaker.

"Yeah, got it."

The intercom went quiet for a few moments

"Alright, money received. Head in west for Blanch's shop, that's the cheapest garage in Folsom. If you need work then check the Wastelander's notice board at the Iron Knuckle pub just a few blocks further down. Opening the gate, watch your speed."

Huge automated gears on the gate began whirring loudly with steam hissing out of the top of the structure. The scraping sound of the metal retracting made Iggy's skin crawl and he gripped his steering wheel tighter before softly pressing the gas to enter.

His senses were assaulted with an array of neon lights, pollution odors and the chatter and nightlife of thousands. The front entrance was filled with shanty-markets with makeshift lanes for drive-thrus Most of them were takeaway food stalls with the putrid stench of burnt wasteland creatures on display to catch the wind. Iggy ignored the shouts and demands of the store owners for him to try a sample and kept his steady strolling speed until getting to the main crossroad junction. Every structure around him was steel gray, pitch black or rusted orange.

The inhabitants made Iggy feel like a pampered tourist; piercings, tattoos, cheap modifications, and deadly looking mutant pets were as common as a pair of goggles or a wristwatch back in Athens. Trying to remember the directions without stopping, Iggy picked up his speed once he got on a regular street and turned on to a strip which seemed to be mainly bars and clubs. The pulsing neon signs were obnoxious advertisements for places of sex, drugs and violent entertainment. Iggy's breathing calmed as the stench of burnt animal carcasses turned to the odor of bodily fluids and booze, which gave him the nostalgia of his early derby events.

This Shell is a metal version of the waste, just everything is closer.

Iggy rubbed his eyes as they tried to re-tune to the lights, but he managed to catch a glimpse of something important; a large flashing sign that said **Blanch's Box**. Iggy thought it an odd name for a garage but as he drove closer, he saw how accurate the description really was. A pre-skirmish gas station with a makeshift garage door covered in graffiti attached to the side of the main counter. Noticing that the place was free of cars, he pulled in carefully, right outside the garage door.

"Help you, pretty boy?" asked a croaky female voice that he couldn't quite place the location of.

"Uh, I'm looking for Blanch? My car needs a few repairs."

"You're talking to her handsome, aside from a few pubs; your gal is just as pretty as you are. She a custom?"

"Uh, yes. She's a class A built from the ground up, just needs a maintenance check, refill and a window replaced."

"Yes, she does, feel like I seen this whip before. You a death runner?"

Still looking around for the source of the voice he tried to answer as calmly as possible. He didn't want to give away too much but didn't want to be too overly secretive either. Iggy didn't know any death runners who lived through more than 3 years of their careers, so he saw no problem in disconfirming.

"No, never tried one, that purse doesn't mean much to someone who ain't alive to spend it," Iggy paused, thinking of some of the grisly fatalities he had seen on Deathrun vids. "So how much will the work cost?"

There was a pause and then the garage door creaked open before a figure stepped out of the darkness. She was a Blight, as heavily mutated and scarred as any other of the few he saw. Her skin was a pale green and it was peeling. Her face was that of a month-old corpse but with yellow eyes, that seemed to have a soft glow. She had a few strands of pale blonde hair but her scalp was mainly bald and blemished, she was wearing a dark blue mechanic's jumpsuit with a name-tag that said: BLANCH.

"Sugar, ain't no purse gonna be worth the risk for anything out here, you gotta do it 'cause it's fun," Blanch said with a perky rasp.

Leaning out of his car to face the ghoulish lady, he gave her a nod and a smile. He did his best not to look surprised or repulsed by her appearance. Her facial expressions were hard to read because of her disfigurement but it seemed like she was sneering a little.

"Ha, you got a pretty smile considering it's a fake one!" Blanch quipped as her sneer became more apparent. "Listen, I know my kind ain't often seen out of them outposts, but not all of us were front-line before them wars. I was a mechanic in the military and it only made sense that I carried on my work."

Iggy appreciated the candid explanation and relaxed. Blights were the unfortunate casualties of the skirmishes, advanced toxic mutations that give them extremely lengthy life spans, but horrifying appearances that outcast them from most societies. Iggy empathized with the blights like Blanch who chose to live as a minority amongst others.

"I haven't been in the waste long, only a couple of days. I'm just looking for some work I guess, trying not to stay in one place for too long either," Iggy said.

Blanch snorted and her ambiguous expression cracked into an amused smirk. "You and most of Folsom honey, who th' fuck would want to stay here longer than a week other than the gangs? Listen, get your ass down to the Iron Knuckle and do some piss-easy hunting jobs. Most folks can make a living just hunting Plentipedes."

Iggy nodded as he removed his duster jacket and switched off his car's engine. He didn't want to look too much like a cargo runner so he went with just his white t-shirt, which was still heavily stained with dirt and blood. He tucked his empty revolver into his belt but left his barbed bat in the car, not wanting to be wielding it on a busy Shell street.

"Might want to check into a room tonight and get into a shower. The facilities are crap, but at least the Folsom service workers keep the water mostly purified," Blanch suggested.

"Thanks, I will. So how much will I owe you for the service and keep it here overnight?"

Iggy began to check his money looking at the pile of steel cards he had left in his car. He had 600 of his own money left plus just over 190 of what he looted from the Nomads.

Blanch's ghostly eyes scanned him as he counted.

"I take it you haven't had the easiest time getting here, so I'll do the job on your whip for 500, that should leave you enough for a couple of drinks and a room at the Knuckle. You're lucky you're a cute one, I'm getting mighty sick of giving discounts in this hell-shell."

Sweet lady, there are still some good people around, I guess.

Iggy handed over the money and his keys immediately and gave her a genuine smile before closing his Blockgain's door. "Thanks so much, I won't forget this. Is the Iron Knuckle bar on this strip?"

Blanch nodded before waving two garage robots over to push his car into the shop. She grabbed a box of cigarettes from her inside pocket and began patting herself down looking for a light. "Remember hun, tonight's a full moon, Sugar. Every bar and club is always a little more trouble on these nights for some reason."

Full moon? I didn't even notice…

Blanch waved Iggy goodbye and began to stroll towards the Iron Knuckle trying to keep his wits about him but also to stay calm. Also avoiding looking anyone in the eye for more than a split second.

Let's just find this Iron Knuckle, I need a drink and a bed. I can see some work in the morning. Hunting Big Waste bugs should be easy if I just run em over, I guess. But I'm gonna need a plan soon for sure, figure out what to do about this bounty.

Iggy sidestepped a group of men who had matching tattoos throwing dice against the wall, shouting in triumph or disappointment based on their rolls. He also had to walk around a Tin Man that had been modified to blast loud dance music while handing out flyers to a seedy venue called the 'Infection'. While simultaneously holding out a jar for collecting tips.

"Not in a millennium," Iggy said with a strong dismissal.

The thick aroma of stale ale and dried blood wafted towards Iggy and led his nose in the direction of the bar he was looking for. When he crossed the street, the collection of rough-looking locals dotted around the sidewalk began to watch him, silently wondering what kind of profession would lead him into that bar. Iggy kept his eyes forward as he took a deep breath and stepped inside. Hearing the creak of the saloon type doors sway behind him.

The Iron Knuckle was busy tonight. Industrial jazz music pumped out of low-fi speakers in all corners of the dingy establishment. The vision of cheap neon lights on slot machines and snack dispensers were obscured by the heavy blanket of mist produced by the near-uniform level of cigar smoke from the locals. It smelled like **Waste-Weed** mixed with **Gold Powder** but it was hard to be sure. Small tables were completely surrounded and filled by nasty looking bruisers, wearing studded leather and strapped with various nasty looking weapons.

Iggy realized that Folsom must be a fairly tolerant place due to the high mix of Humans, Mutants, and Blights who seemed to be interacting normally amongst each other. Back in the Citadel, Mutants only worked the lowest jobs where they were barely seen or heard by the public, and a Blight would probably be killed on sight with impunity. Iggy was curious about the pressures of the different populations in the waste, but his only real concern was the state of his Blockgain.

Nobody really seemed to notice Iggy enter, apart from a few curious glances from a table of surly-looking blights that seemed to be estimating the value of his clothes. Iggy suddenly became conscious of his 'standard wastelander's outfit. His cargo jeans, hiker boots, and greaser t-shirt made him stand out among the gang uniforms, sanitation jumpsuits and mercenary jackets of everyone else there. Trying not to look intimidated, he walked over to the bar with a measured pace and up-nodded the bartender; a muscular, goblin face mutant that stood around 7 feet tall. He wiped off a sharp kitchen knife with his dirty apron and turned to face Iggy with a grunt before returning the nod.

"Most of this shit I got here will kill a **Soft-neck**, most of em here just stick to the root-water, want a pint?"

Iggy tried not to grimace at the slur and spoke under his breath, "Alright, a pint of that and some of that Hare-Jerky, the spicy kind."

The burly bartender snorted at the order briefly and nodded. After taking 18 standards from Iggy he served up the beverage and food in seconds, before sliding it across the bar to Iggy with perfect accuracy. As he began eating and drinking, he realized how hungry he was since leaving for the cargo run. Iggy's noisy munching and slurping caught the attention of a few humans at the bar that turned to look at him.

The first was a dark-haired man, wearing a studded leather long coat with a large scar across his cheek with attractive grey eyes, he was the closest to Iggy. Behind him was another dark-haired person whose gender wasn't immediately apparent, attempting to light a very large cigar with a tool that looked like a blowtorch. Finally, there was a young-looking male with reddish-brown hair wearing a Wastelander hoodie, along with a plethora of piercings covering his face. Iggy doubled glanced at the trio before pausing his eating, raising an eyebrow slowly.

"Hey don't stop eating on account of us, we ain't creeps or nothin'," The grey-eyed scarred man said fairly calmly. He had a somewhat mature tone to his voice for a man who didn't look much older than 30. The heavily pierced man in the cloak peered from around his companion and looked at Iggy curiously.

"You didn't think you'd get recognized in here? Even Shellers pay attention to the updates, Citi-boy," The pierced man's voice was a full octave higher than the first which could be due to some recent powder use.

Updates? My Bounty...ah shit. No...

Iggy's head snapped around the bar looking for any other exits, but his heart sank when saw how crowded the path to anywhere inside the Iron Knuckle was. He was trapped. Iggy cursed at his own risky decision but also resolved that there was little else he could've done. His heart jumped when he felt a large clammy hand clasp around his forearm. He glanced to his left to see it was the huge mutant bartender who was looking down at him with eyes of mild amusement.

"That's right we know who you are and trying to figure out what the fuck you are doing here," the bartender boomed.

"J-just getting a drink and tryin' to f-find some wor-"

Iggy was cut off by the scarred man.

"When Blanch told Jake here that motherfuckin' **Ignition** was in Folsom, Nails here almost shit the bed," he chuckled, thumbing to the pierced man behind him, who's metal-covered face was now a soft smile.

That's right Iggy you idiot, they show the derbies outside the citadel too....

Iggy exhaled audibly, and his heart and stomach gave him a thousand promises of payback after making them jump so many times in one day. Iggy immediately grinned at all of his new acquaintances and took a confident sip of his drink. The mutant bartender lifted Iggy's gripped arm to shake it with his other, his hand was scarily strong.

"Blanch is always fucking around with me telling me tall tales about soft-necks that walk in and out of here. I had no idea she was being straight with me when she dropped me a message 5 minutes ago, she recognized your Blockgain Chaser right away, it's in good hands with her."

Iggy gulped his root water and returned the shake firmly.

"I didn't think it'd be that noticeable covered in all the blood, sand and bullet-holes!" Iggy quipped brightly. "You guys watch a lot of derbies in the Shell?" Iggy asked, trying to sound casual.

The pierced man who was called Nails leaned forward to answer.

"Kills the time in-between hunts, plus it's actually pretty damn educational. Back when I had a car, I used to use that dirty PIT maneuver on every **bandit** I could find!"

Nails chortled with a grin.

"You gotta use a speed boost for results, Nails." The bartender known as Jake declared, ignoring orders to participate in the conversation. "This means if you get a new whip, you'll have to hunt a LOT of Plentipedes before you can afford a gas charger,"

A cool feeling washed over Iggy's body as he began to relax. Talking about cars over a drink with new fans made him feel more at home than ever. After another 3 root-waters (all complimentary on Jake's insistence) Iggy engaged the 4 of them with his knowledge of car components, recounts of deadly rivals in the derby and slightly exaggerated groupie tales. Along with Jake the bartender and Nails the piercings man, Iggy came to find out the scarred man's name was Malkin and the quiet nondescript person was called Penoli.

They were all hunters who made their living hunting large bug creatures in the wasteland, almost always Plentipedes because of their popularity as a foodstuff. Jake was an ex-enforcer for the Dust-Dragons, a large mutant gang based in the northern zones that occasionally took part in regional races and derbies. Iggy had actually faced and defeated a Dust-Dragon capo in an away match 3 years ago. Going on to become more famous among mutants because of it. It was only an hour of eating, drinking and talking before the four of them and Iggy were laughing together as if they were the best of friends.

"Ah-hah...I tell you what Iggy, if you total a few bandits near Folsom, drag the wreckage back to Blanch's," Jake bellowed while slinging drinks to his numerous bar patrons.

"What? I only need one car, Jake!" Iggy chortled while nudging Malkin and swigging his 4th Root-water.

Jake grinned and lowered his voice a little.

"Me and Blanch got stakes in a chop shop, we make money off wrecked vehicles and we will pay you a nice cut for everyone you bring, Softneck."

"Sounds tasty…but why you keep calling me Soft-Neck? You know it's offensive right?"

Malkin sipped his drink before interjecting.

"Never mind all that Ignition. This ain't a politically correct bar! We all call Jake an Orc; he calls every human who walks in here a Softneck, and all the Blights including Blanch 'Peelers'. Malkin took a second, longer drink with a small smirk. "It's affectionate."

Iggy grumbled under his breath a little but nodded in reassurance to the group to show he was cool with it. Then he yawned a little after finishing his current drink.
"I'm gonna look for some work in the morning, might do a bug-hunt or something,"
Iggy yawned while rubbing his tired eyes.

"Alright, but you're new here, Cook's men like to fuck with some of the freelancers out there if they ain't too known, Iggy," Nails warned with a fairly serious tone.

Iggy's easy smile waned a little as he saw the faces of all of his new drinking buddies go fairly sour in unison with Nails' voice. His mind flashed to the sound of the gunshot that gave him the nasty leg injury, along with the crazed wails of the bandits from Cook's gang. The drinks in his system made his tongue loose, speaking with the vitriol he still felt from the bandit encounter leading to all the events so far.

"I already smashed a Scar Buggy trying to rob me this morning; I ain't scared of those powderhead gangs!" Iggy took a slow bite of his jerky and thought of the mangled flesh of the bandits as he chewed with hot resentment.

"You killed them, where?"

Malkin's voice was lower than ever, without a shred of humor in his tone.

"Ehh, fuck, I think it must have been about 30 miles outside of the Citadel, they were trying to rob and kill me, man, they shot me in the leg!"

Iggy's neck became hot, he didn't like where this was going.

"Your leg looks fine to me, Iggy. Were they trying to steal your car or something?"

Thanks, Clear-wet…do I mention the cargo?

"Yeah they probably were; it's a Class A after all."

The four of them all grumbled a little before getting back to their drinks and the mood began to lift again. It seems as if they found his answer satisfactory, at least for now. The very silent Penoli finally spoke up after taking a long sip of root water.

"Cook's gang-run 30% of Folsom." Penoli paused to look around to see who might be listening. "Some of the affiliates are in this bar. Be lucky you killed them out of zone."

The voice of Penoli was certainly more female sounding than male but he still couldn't be sure. Penoli's face was emotionless and cold. All the words xe spoke were like an automated messaging system. Iggy nodded to her and looked at the rest of the still mostly serious group.

"Listen, Iggy, you did what you had to do to survive, but anyone you grease is gonna have friends, especially in Folsom," Jake stated firmly while cleaning a large pint glass.

The stark reality of the Shell politics hit home to a very sober part of Iggy's mind.

61

"To Survival!"

Malkin raised his glass to concur with Jake and the rest of them nodded with their glasses high in unison.

Out of zone huh? I wonder if any of Cook's gang here knows the two bandits I killed.

Iggy thought of the crash, he thought of his lost cargo, and as much as he was trying not to, he thought of Sil.

Chapter 8: Arrears

She banged on the plastic and metal door with mild but growing annoyance. Her fist was wrapped in a studded black glove and her steel-toe-cap boots were tapping the hollow wooden floor with impatience.

"You needed to get off the premises five hours ago, Jack. Open this door now or I will," she said with a smoky, stern voice.

There was no answer. She banged the door again, now with a more forceful and violent intent. Her single eye had a golden-yellow iris; it was pillowed in a handsome but very mature face that would age her to around 40 by conventional human standards. Her face was partially covered by a blood-red eye patch covering the socket where her right eye used to be. Her bright pink hair was styled into Mohawk that hung loosely as if she grew tired of spiking it every morning and let the hair fall where it may. She stood at a solid 6'2 and was covered in the shredded muscles of someone who knew how to do damage. Although solid with brawn, her body was retained a clearly feminine appearance due to her curvy behind and her large round breasts that were being held firmly in place by a biker-chic corset-top.

"I swear to god, Jack…"

Her voice took a deeper masculine tone with the second threat. She stopped to turn to the burly 6'8 red-skinned mutant beside her; who had a face like a blowfish wielding holding a nasty looking sledgehammer. He was wearing a black sweater with the word 'TOWER SECURITY' in thick white font across the chest. He shrugged at the woman with a blank expression.

"Maybe he's high, L."

The woman pinched the bridge of her nose and held herself back from banging a third time and began to reach in her pocket.

"Of course he's fucking high. He and his peeler bitch were blasted on powder when they rented the place! This is what I get for taking cash payments from junkies after hours."

The mutant blinked twice without moving, his very human-sounding voice was now higher with curiosity.

"He was smashing a Peeler? That's nasty, how torn up was she?"

She sighed.

"It's not like I watch these people fuck, Grady. They could have just been scoring together. And she was a typical peeler, greenish glow, eyes like mothballs. Some folks are into all that."

Grady said nothing and blinked once more.

She finished rummaging and pulled out a set of keys on a large ring and began flipping through them when Grady began to tighten his grip on his nasty looking sledgehammer weapon and stood in-position to swing. "I have keys for a reason, Grady. Relax."

"Yes Landlady, but I'm ready to bash his head in if he tries anything stupid," Grady reassured, with his knees slightly bent in a stance ready for action.

The Landlady found the key she was searching for and pushed it in a steel keyhole indent located in the middle of the door, "Ready or not, Jack…"

With a click of the lock opening, she kicked the door open with a shattering force, with Grady bursting through to take point. The both of them began searching the inside of what was a very cheap looking apartment. A vidscreen on the wall was hissing from a channel of pure static, and the smell of bodily waste and red powder hung high in the air. The walls were a rusted brown metal or pale grey concrete. There were shell-roaches the size of a fist darting around the sticky half-carpeted floor in search of leftovers and safety.

Grady halted to acknowledge a dead body on the floor. A female blight stripped down to her underwear was motionless and non-glowing in a fetal position. Her stiff fingers were clutching an empty vial.

"Landlady, the Peeler is here, I don't see any injuries," Grady said grimly while scanning the room.

The Landlady sighed again.

"She overdosed on powder, couldn't you tell by the damn stink?"

"I don't have a nose, Landlady."

The Landlady rolled her eye and stepped closer to the body and shook her head in jaded disgust, before moving to the slightly ajar bedroom door.

"Hey L, there is actually a condom next to-"

Grady's discovery was cut short by the small explosion of a gunshot.

A round fired through the bedroom door and missed both of them by a half-inch whizzing past their sides. The Landlady immediately leaped back with inhuman speed behind a portable fridge in the open kitchen and Grady ducked behind a nearby couch. Another gunshot cracked loudly, this time missing wildly and slamming into the fridge door.

"There's Jack," Grady stated calmly.

The Landlady drew her own weapon, a large gold-and-silver-plated automatic pistol, it was a restored classic. Grady grinned as she cocked it and began to fire back at the door while yelling at her assailant.

"You *fucked up* Jack," she yelled over the sound of her gunshots before ducking back into cover. "This has gone way beyond a late fine now!"

"No, **fuck you,** Clarissa, you killed her you **fucking bitch!"**

The screams from Jack behind the bedroom door were that of a clearly tilted and unhinged man, she could even hear him coughing tears as he spoke.

"I didn't kill her you fucking idiot. She overdosed, that's what you junkie dipshits tend to do, and don't fucking call me that!" The Landlady snarled before busting off two more shots at the door.

"Don't call you what: Bitch or Clarissa?" Grady snarked while getting more comfortable in his cover position. The Landlady stopped firing to give him the middle finger. Right before a bullet punched through the couch, tearing through to just escape past Grady's large shoulder.

"It was a **fucking HOT DOSE!** Your boys sold it to her!!" Jack cried spitefully, "We were always careful...fuck..."

The sobbing was getting louder and the voice was getting more enraged, Jack's footsteps could be heard as he was getting closer to the bedroom door.

"We were gettin' fuckin' married tomorrow you heartless fucking cunt!! You **took** her from me!! **I'll kill you!"**

The Landlady shook her head in confusion before ducking at the sound of two more loud gunshots and turned to Grady who looked even more puzzled at what he heard. He peered over the couch to inquire with the distraught man.

"You were really going to marry a *peeler*, Jack? How much powder were you doing?"

The Landlady sighed and shook her head slowly, knowing what was coming next.

"HER NAME WAS *GLORIA!*"

The bedroom door splintered open with violent force and the tormented tenant came rushing out. His completely naked body was covered in sweat and his mouth was foaming. Messy strands of greasy black hair partially covered his wild dilated eyes, and his track mark-covered arm swung in wild motions wielding a large kitchen knife. The Landlady darted to face him head-on while Grady flashed a wicked smirk.

"You stupid fuck," she stated coldly before weaving her upper body to dodge two wild slashes of Jack's knife.

Jack's snarling face was that of someone under the influence, his eyes showed someone truly hurt. The Landlady was able to acknowledge the emotional agony before making the pain very physical. She countered his knife attack by smashing the butt of her pistol into his nose, which caved in instantly with a crunch. Grady winced at the sounds of crumbling bone and gargling blood that was retching from Jack's now disfigured mouth.

She grit her teeth and struck him two, three, four more times before his face was indistinguishable from fried bug meat on the Folsom market. His shrieks of pain slowly turned to doomed whimpers before dropping the knife and attempting to grab Clarissa, despite being now completely blind by her assault. She halted her pistol-whipping to place the barrel of her gun at his stomach before firing two lethal shots, blowing a pair of holes straight through him.

Jack's naked, blood-soaked body looked like a crude anatomy lesson, his face an unrecognizable cavity and his insides dangling from his gut wound. He was somehow still alive; in a state that was far outside any normal concept of suffering. Gripping his torso, Clarissa spun into a shoulder throw position and swung him round her body before launching him out of the fairly large kitchen window. Screaming with rage, she hurled the man to his death; from 14 stories high.

"YARRRRRRGGGGHHHH!!!"

Even through a busted face, Jack still managed to give an audible scream during his 14-story freefall before splattering across the main parking lot. Grady rested his large sledgehammer across his shoulder before peeking out of the window.

"Eviction notices never work anyway," Grady commented flatly. "Thought these windows were stronger though,"

Clarissa wiped the blood off her pistol with a kitchen rag before holstering it inside her jacket, "I was going to get them replaced anyway."

She began to look around warily. The stench of blood made her dizzy, causing her to lose a little balance. Her mutant ally ran to her side to catch her, with a very serious look of concern on his face. His voice matched his expression.

"Landlady, there is too much blood here; you're breathing this shit in."

Clarissa looked at Grady with her sole eye dizzy and unfocused. Her mouth opened, bearing a very large set of sharp canines that she ran her tongue over several times before stabilizing herself and responding.

"Yeh...yes, the blood-stink..." She slurred as she found her feet underneath her. "But Jack said **our** boys were dealing them hot doses, which means Cook's dealers...what the hell are they up to?"

Grady threw the Landlady's arm over his shoulder and led her out of the apartment swiftly, crushing broken glass and slow bugs under his boot on the way. "L, as long as you owe them money, they are gonna do what they want in your towers. It's how it's always been."

Clarissa's strong face dropped into something more vulnerable and sullen before nodding softly. She allowed her full weight to lean on Grady in a way that only a true recipient of trust would. She perked up a little once they were away from the stink of the apartment. "Grady, Cook's people have been doing weird shit all month, I think it's finally time we do something about it." Clarissa declared firmly before cracking her knuckles.

Chapter 9: Tee Total

Iggy had decided to refrain from drinking anymore Root-water. It wasn't his favorite beverage, but he realized that his tolerance probably wasn't as high as he thought it was on a mostly empty stomach. So, he focused on the Hare-Jerky which was satisfying enough to sate his current appetite.

The group's conversation had now drifted to more general small talk, and they found themselves talking about how bored they were of hunting Plentipedes and how they needed to upgrade their weapons. Malkin told Iggy that he drove a Class B vehicle called the **Dresden Dune**. It was a reconstructed 4×4 jeep that he wanted to equip with a gas-powered harpoon launcher once he could afford it. He spoke about how that investment would make hunting mutated animals almost too easy. Iggy wanted to listen to the wide-eyed car talk all night but his fatigue was catching up with him.

Better get some sleep, I'll catch up with these guys tomorrow, they seem cool.

"Okay Jake, I need to hit the mattress, it's been a long day. You got any rooms left?"

Iggy yawned as he spoke.

"Sorry kid, got some Mercs staying here tonight, they bought up all the rooms maybe you can try th-"

The sound of smashing glass pierced through the bar and Jake's sentence with deafening effect. Iggy and the group could only turn their heads fast enough to see a bald bloodied man land painfully on the floor around a mess of shattered window glass. A good half of the bar turned to observe while the rest just carried on drinking. Penoli took a long drag of her 2nd cigar and shook her head slowly with mild annoyance.

Iggy's shocked face slowly turned to the saloon-style entrance which got his attention with their signature creak and gulped as he saw an extremely burly mutant enter the bar with another figure behind him he couldn't quite see but heard clearly speak.

"I ain't seen one standard of profit, Rafka! How long were you running that shit in the towers!?" The figure with the powerful female voice stepped out into plain view, hooded violet jacket, corset top, black jeans and metal-capped boots along with an eye patch across her face. Clarissa the Landlady and her enforcer Grady had entered the Iron Knuckle.

The burly Grady didn't have his sledgehammer with him, but he was not much less intimidating without it. With a huge grin on his fish-face, he walked closer to the downed bald man who was writhing in pain before turning to Clarissa.

"You really like using windows to make a point, L. Hope Jake has insurance?"

Jake held up his hand before giving a loose shrug. "Forget it, Grady...I was meaning to get that one replaced anyway!"

Grady, Jake, Malkin, and Clarissa all erupted in laughter at the comment along with a good third of the bar, while Nails and Penoli scoffed leaving Iggy silent in confusion.

Is this shit normal at the Iron Knuckle? The man called Rafka on the floor was writhing in the shattered glass, further injuring himself and whining fairly loudly in pain. Clarissa stepped over and gave him a quick kick to the midsection, which made his cries go silent as the air was knocked out of him.

"Landlady…I didn't know it was against the rules…ugh…just needed some extra cash…" Grady grabbed the man and lifted him effortlessly off the floor with one hand.

"Yeah okay Rafka, I think she gets the point. You can show your apology by paying her 4000 standards by the weekend or I'll squash your smooth head **without** using the hammer, alright?"

With that demand, Grady flung the man back through the broken open window like an empty soda can for him to be the problem of the street outside. He dusted off his hands and gave the entire bar a thumbs up, which they returned with a happy drunk cheer before quickly getting back to their business.

"Jake, me and L will have a double Backstab on the rocks, no spice," Grady said with a friendly tone.

Jake smiled at Grady and up-nodded to Clarissa; who was a little ways behind him. The Landlady kicked shards of glass out of the entrance space while shaking hands and waving to some of the patrons. He reached behind the bar to grab the necessary mixers and placed them on the bar.

"I take it you've had one hell of a night, you usually order soft-neck drinks, Grady."

Malkin turned toward the two huge mutants and gulped his root-water curiously.

"You know Jake, I don't get why you call us **soft-necks**. Like aren't we basically soft all over compared to guys like you and Grady?" Malkin queried.

Nails folded his arms and made a 'tsk' sound before interrupting.

"Not all Mutants are big fuckas, Malk. Don't be generalizin'."

I've never seen a Male Mutant below 6'5, but then I guess size must be relative.

Malkin shrugged to him before silently watching the Landlady approach the bar next to Grady. She leaned against the counter before taking a scanning everyone around the space, her single eye lingering on Iggy a second longer than the others. Iggy's chest went hot picking up on it, right before she spoke.

"Before anyone stockpiled weapons out in the Big Waste after the skirmishes, Blights would fight anyone and anything hand-to-hand. Wandering humans were their main targets; they would just snap their necks and rob their corpses. Because it was so easy, they were referred to as 'soft-necks' right at the bottom of the food chain."

There was a considered silence after the explanation. Iggy decided to break it by addressing her, "Uh, I take it you don't find that term offensive then, miss?"

"Miss?" Clarissa asked in mild surprise. "I'm the Landlady, and why would I take offense? *I ain't human.*"

Grady began to chuckle slowly followed by the rest of the group as if they were waiting for permission to find amusement. Clarissa flashed a grin at Iggy revealing her extra-long, sharp canines.

They look like Sil's! But they are longer. And she doesn't look like a mutant at all. So, what kind of non-human is she?

Grady eyed Iggy for a couple of moments before scratching his chin. Finally, he turned back to Jake grabbing both the drinks he ordered and handed one to Clarissa.

"Um Jake, why's your friend got a Citadel accent?" Grady asked bluntly while pointing at Iggy.

"Cause he's a Citadel driver, Ignition from the Derby League, he's in the top #15"

I must have dropped in rank after leaving Athens and missing the seasonal. I worked hard for #4.

"That so? I don't have much interest in cars, rather watch Orc fights in the Cit-Pits, I have a short attention span you see."

Grady chuckled before taking a swig and Iggy nodded at him before yawning loudly. Clarissa's ears pricked up and she moved closer to Iggy, her eye narrowing as she looked him over carefully. Iggy was taken aback by her burning stare. With her wild pink hair and seemly infamous reputation, he couldn't help but feel that familiar mix of excitement and fear.

"You're a driver? I don't watch derbies either but…" The Landlady looked Iggy up and down like a snack before licking her fangs "I'm guessing top #15 means you're pretty hot shit, right?" She asked in a curious tone.

Iggy was stunned by a combination of exhaustion and fascination. Jake piped up and spoke for Iggy, which he appreciated in his state. "He actually just got here today Landlady. Blanch has his vehicle and he's gonna go on some bug-hunts tomorrow with these lads."

Clarissa chuckled mockingly, with her eye fixed on his face. "Fuck bug-hunts, I got a real job for you, Crasher. Plus, I'll pay you more than you'll earn squashing Plentipedes in a week, you down?"

Iggy's face went hot as she made her fairly enthusiastic request. But he had to rub his eyes as tears began to gather from holding them open for too long. He wiped the excess away and responded as respectfully as he could.

"It sounds interesting, but I'm gonna need a few more details…plus I've been up a while and still haven't found a roo-"

Clarissa cut him off sharply. "It's sorted, you'll stay in my tower, I got rooms available. We can talk details on the way there. Sleep on it and then make a decision."

Grady rubbed the back of his head with uncertainty and piped up. "Uhh, L do you really think he should be staying in that room after Jack and the peeler…. you know?"

Clarissa shook her head and ran a hand through her floppy mohawk. "Not *that* room Grady, he can stay near my quarters on the top floor. Can't be certain some ganger won't snatch him from one of the lower floors and use him as a powder bag." She turned back to Iggy quickly. "So, are you in? Room is free of charge for the night but I'll want a decision before sunrise."

Iggy's mind drifted back to when Sil made him take her along; a comforting but bitter memory. But at that moment, he couldn't take his eyes off this 'Landlady'. She was clearly older than him, but she had a laid-back easiness to her which contrasted with her striking appearance. Once again, he let his desires lead his decision.

"Okay, I won't sleep too long; I take it the morning sun is a pain for you as well then?" Iggy said, trying to be relatable.

Grady, Jake, and Malkin all chuckled while Nails and Penoli did their signature head shake. Clarissa smiled, baring her canines slowly."Yeah, the morning sun is a pain...I am a *vampire* after all."

What.
The.
Fuck?

The trip back to the towers seemed longer than it was. Mainly due to Iggy's mind running a mile a minute, trying to evaluate the risks of not only his future but his present situation. He was in a van, picked up from a bar by a strange pair, for a job he knew nothing about. He also wasn't completely sober.

Grady drove while Clarissa was in the passenger, puffing on a large cigar similar to the one Penoli had back at the bar. She was humming under her breath as she filled the vehicle 2nd hand smoke, which caused Iggy a few chest coughs. They were five minutes into the journey but Iggy hadn't said a word. He had questions but they were so numerous it was if they were log-jammed in the front part of his head and none could make it to his mouth. Luckily, Clarissa broke the tension when she decided to speak, though it was to Grady.

"Do you think that bald idiot you threw is going to survive the night?"

Grady scoffed as he responded. "I'm pretty sure you threw him first, L."

"He was still conscious then. He wasn't moving when we left," Clarissa said.

"I think he's gonna get robbed, and then miss a very important payment to whoever is supplying him," Grady said.

"Yeah well, it'll be a reminder to the other dumbfuck powder pushers who knew him." Clarissa snarled before a long cigar drag. "They are getting ballsy to move like that."

"That can be solved, balls can be removed," Grady said dryly.

"**Maim-Creek** is pretty far though…hey Crasher,"

Iggy lifted his head to the name she decided to call him despite being told his preferred title by Jake.

"What's up?" Iggy asked, trying to sound like he wasn't somewhat disturbed by their violent conversation.

"You drive a Class A, right? What's her top speed?"

The info shot to Iggy's tongue instantly, he could recite the specs in his sleep. "On dry flat land the Blockgain can hit 210 mph without boosting, but I usually boost if I can."

Iggy spoke through a smile, briefly thinking about that hot wind on his face that a top speed drive gives him. Grady slowed the van to a halt as they approached the parking lot of the Towers. The two dizzyingly high apartment blocks flashed with hues of pink and purple in an off-beat rhythm as the neon signs at the top flickered back and forth. The left building's sign said 'Shock' and the right building was 'Vertigo'. Iggy couldn't figure out if they were pre-skirmish or post, but stopped wondering once they all got out of the van and Clarissa and Grady moved closer to him.

"We are here, tell me more about your car when we get inside," Clarissa said firmly, keeping her voice as neutral as possible.

She turned to Grady and nodded, pulling her pistol free of its holster without pointing it in any direction. "No guns on the top floor, Crasher, 'cept mine of course." Grady took one step closer to Iggy, his pitch-black eyes almost looking through Iggy for the truth.

No point in lying.

"I've got an Elephant Revolver, it's empty though," Iggy said while slowly lifting his shirt and turning around.

He wanted to be as co-operative as possible at this point. He knew they had no reason to kill him and he wanted to keep that way, at least until he knew what they really wanted. Grady snickered with a gentle hand wave of flippancy.

"Fuck you got an unloaded shooter for? Good fortune?" Grady sneered as he nodded towards the revolvers handle. waving the Landlady over to remove it.

Clarissa came up behind Iggy placing her hand softly on his waist before taking his gun and stowing it in an unknown part of her coat. She leaned in close to his ear, her breath was scalding hot. The similarity to Sil's made his neck tingle with that same fear and excitement that he hadn't quite gotten used to yet. She spoke under her breath with a whisper to him.

"I'm not going to find anything else under there am I?" Her hand moved down from his waist and towards his rear, giving it a tiny pinch. Despite the teasing Iggy's mind was fixated on the reveal of her large fangs and self-description.

Is she really a...?

"Don't worry crasher, I don't drink," she whispered menacingly, her hot breath leaving a sweet tingle on his neck.

Clarissa and Grady laughed at the young driver's stunned expression before escorting him into the left tower, whistling a haunting tune under the mixed light of the moon and neon.

Chapter 10: Risk Factors

Grady and Clarissa parted ways in the lobby. The statuesque vampire left for the surveillance room while the burly Grady took Iggy with him in the elevator. The poorly built lift climbed the many stories of the tower while stuttering on its ascent.

Grady took the time to ask more about Iggy's experiences in the derbies, mainly interested in which gang members he had competed against. Iggy tried to lay out his achievements with as little ego as possible, despite having an impeccable record on the circuit and totalling many top drivers with ease.

Iggy became more aware of his Citadel accent with every sentence he spoke, feeling like he stood out more in the gritty Shell. Grady's tone was consistent, aloof and snarky. Iggy started to wonder if this large henchman took anything seriously and was curious about his relationship with Clarissa. He paused his answers to risk asking.

"So, you been working for...or working with the Landlady a long time?"

Grady's voice was unchanged but his face dropped a little as if he was caught in a brief state of reminiscence. Because he had no pupils Iggy couldn't tell where he was looking exactly, but he felt like his black eyes were fixed on him.

"Well, I suppose it'd be 40 years now, so pretty long for a soft-neck...no offense."

Iggy waved his hand to show none was taken, he was getting used to it now.

"Hang on, 40 years? You two grew up together?" Iggy said as he attempted the math in his head quickly.

"No. I was a kid when she found me dumpster-diving in a scrapyard. I have no idea how old she was at the time, but in 40 years she doesn't look a whole lot different."

"Is that because she's a-"

Grady narrowed his pitch-black eyes.

"Vampire, yeah. She's old enough to know a shit load about the skirmishes that even the grandappys around here don't. She doesn't go out in the sun and I've never seen her have garlic bread with her Plenti-pizza."

Grady couldn't help but chuckle at his own words. Iggy fought to hold back a smile but failed. "I'm only going on what I know from pre-skirmish fairy-tales, but Vampires drink blood right?" Iggy questioned curiously.

Grady's neutral expression finally changed, his black eyes widened and his leathery red skin began to droop around his cheeks as his thick-lipped mouth became a fairly apparent frown. Iggy's heart once again skipped a beat at the sudden face change.

Grady's voice dropped an octave that more closely matched his hefty build. "She told you she doesn't drink, it's a choice she made." He declared firmly "I've not seen her take a drop of it in all the years I've known her, and she's had plenty opportunities with all the people she…we've killed. But she abstains, and that's that."

Iggy nodded carefully, instantly knowing not to push the issue any further. Iggy was convinced of Grady's loyalty to her, and the refusal to drink blood as a vampire was clearly a sensitive subject. Iggy had more questions regarding her ability to sustain herself, but he decided to stay silent. For the rest of the elevator journey, Iggy tuned out the sound of scraping metal as they reached the top of the tower.

The hallway that greeted Iggy was surprisingly clean and pleasing to the senses. Apart from a few loose wires and patches of graffiti, the design could almost be mistaken for a high-end penthouse in the center of a Citadel. A soft scent of mint-roast was about the air, and it instantly calmed Iggy's nerves. Grady, still not speaking, sped up to overtake Iggy before swiping a white card against a scanning device on a door aways in front of him that opened with a loud beep.

"You're in there, Daredevil. Get some rest."

Grady didn't turn around to address Iggy but instead disappeared around a corner at the end of the hallway. Shortly followed by the sound of a terrified, pleading man filling the entire floor.

"**Graaaaady!** Please man…I didn't think anyone would be up here **today…Graaady!!**"

Iggy shook his head and decided to opt-out of hearing the next part of that incident. He hurried up into his room as he was so tired at that point he just wanted to collapse.

Luckily, the quality of the room matched that of the rest of the floor. Apart from the dark purple decor, lava lamps and multiple flickering vid-screens it wasn't too different from his home back in the working stacks.

The recognizable atmosphere worked towards Iggy's body powering down. As soon as he found the bedroom a few feet past the main kitchen area, he dropped to the mattress to let his bruised and filthy body rest. The muffled screams of the unwelcome guest that Grady found in the hallways were the last thing Iggy heard before sinking into a total slumber.

Swirling lights were the backdrop for a highlight reel of significant events in Iggy's life. Spectacular car crashes, running through the slums as a child, the sound of obnoxious dance music playing on ad-vids at the betting shops, the strong stench of whiskey on his grandpa's breath and the feeling of a pit groupie's hair as he pulled it during a drunken romp. All of his senses were hyper tuned to this revolving door of memories, it was so pleasant he didn't want it to end. Iggy was so mentally and physically exhausted from his first day in the waste that he would have quite happily never woken up.

The sound of beeping cut harshly through his peaceful daze, dragging him all the way back into consciousness like a deep-sea piranha being reeled out of the ocean. It was so unpleasant to his ears; with every beep like a high contrast bullet being hammered into his skull. His eyes swung open with a disturbed rage to see an alarm clock. Without even checking the time his body went on autopilot, punching the clock silent and swinging himself off the bed to find the shower.

Like a confused zombie, he managed to strip down and wash his body in the dimly lit cubicle. The superfine water-jets peeled dirt from every inch from his body in seconds without even making him very wet. A luxury feature for all cleaning devices outside of the slums. Deciding to forgo his bloody and dirty clothes, he rummaged in the bedside wardrobe for something better.

He found some underwear, socks, and a pair of heavy-duty motocross pants in the bedside wardrobe. It was what he saw stunt bikers wear in the locker rooms of death runs. The motor-cross pants were a sporty pattern of black and dark gold with a logo of a devil's face on the side-legs. After rummaging again and finding boots to wear with it, he got dressed. He finally found himself back on the bed, shirtless and not really awake or asleep.

Shifting to his side he idly gazed out of the window. His eyes drank in the spectacle of the night sky from the perspective of one of the tallest towers in Folsom.

Barely aware of anything around him, all 5 of his senses turning on and off as he started to re-approach his deep slumber. He didn't hear the lock clicking in the apartment door or the footsteps approaching the bed.

But he did feel the very cold hand on his bare shoulder.

"Wake up Crasher, six hours is long enough."

Iggy did his best to force himself back into the brutal realm of consciousness as his skin prickled and his labored breath inhaled sharply. The tone was, warm, encouraging and gentle. But the voice was unmistakable – it was the Landlady.

"Only halfway dressed huh? Or do you not like shirts?"

The second sentence was in a more playful tone causing Iggy to roll over to face her. One eyebrow raised and both eyes squinted in fear of any brightness as they adjusted to the low light of the room. Drenched in the sensual hue of the lava lamp, Clarissa looked more radiant than ever.

Subtle dark blues made her skin look like a smooth blanket of midnight and her Mohawk was looser than ever, looking more purple than pink in the colored shade, with her eye retaining its gold-green shine. Still as ferocious and piercing as ever but with a touch of familiarity and the small amount of trust that comes with it.

She was now wearing a loose T-shirt that was branded with a logo that Iggy couldn't make out in the light. Even the shadows couldn't hide the curvature of her large bust. The shape contrasted with her very toned midsection and legs, which were covered by a pair of matching sweatpants that cuffed just above her calves. She looked like she had just gotten out of bed herself and Iggy's barely sentient mind couldn't make sense of it.

"Urgh...what is the time...?" Iggy yawned weakly.

"It's Four-thirty, Crasher. Sunrise will scare me away soon enough, but I had to speak to you before your job...you probably wanted more details, right?" There was a coy quality to her voice.

Iggy grumbled a little as he tried to will his mind out of its waking spiral. "You didn't sleep much?" Iggy asked.

"These are my waking hours, I sleep when the sun is up, I'm sure Grady explained all this to you?" Clarissa said firmly while crossing her pale arms.

Iggy rolled his way into a half-seated position before nodding. Trying to look serious and keeping his eyes wandering around her figure. "I've actually been up all night watching you, Ignition." She cackled frightfully watching Iggy stir at her revelation.

"M-me?"

"Ha. Not in this room, idiot. I was watching archived footage of your Derby highlights over the last five years. I had no idea that you totaled **Reinbeck** of the South end Lead-Slingers last year."

Iggy groaned a little as his acute memory played him back the event clearly. "He was ranked #19, I think he was the betting favorite, a lot of his gang were in the audience."

Clarissa smiled devilishly. "His gang couldn't have been happy he had to have both his legs amputated. You turned that tuner of his into a beer can." Clarissa said, holding back some excitement at the violent details.

Iggy lowered his head grimly. "It's just part of the sport. I never tried to hurt anyone."

Clarissa leaned forward, phasing out of the apartment neon and into a shadowy angle that obscured her face, leaving her golden eye to shine through like a laser. "You tried to hurt those Cookers after your cargo this morning, didn't you? The cleanup crew had to bring that driver back in 3 separate bags. That Scar-Buggy looks like modern art now. Was that part of the sport too, Crasher?"

She knew!? How!? And they've been cleaned up?

Iggy jerked backward in genuine fear as the Landlady continued to lean forward, her eye flashing with all sorts of evil discovery. "It was self-defense! They were shooting at me!" Iggy protested, trying to keep his voice from cracking.

Clarissa waved her hand dismissively. "You took a shortcut through their territory, right past their outpost. They were a guard patrol. Bandits generally don't fuck with delivery boys without a good reason. I wouldn't have heard about it otherwise."

Iggy's face went cold with the new information as if it was splashed on his face. His ears throbbed and he felt a rushing motion as he replayed the battle with the bandits in his head.

They were guarding their outpost, I instigated...without realizing. And she knows everything.

Clarissa licked her lips and placed her hand on Iggy's quivering thigh.

"You don't just have a 10K bounty on you from the Citadel; you also got a Cook outpost asking about your last known location. They signaled me an hour ago while you were dreaming of your pit groupies or whatever".

Iggy was frozen as she poured out all of her info, not being able to think or react. He was fully awake now as the feeling of doom started to creep up his back and toward his neck like a few dozen skirmish-spiders.

I'm trapped here…

Clarissa held her position without speaking or moving as her eye darted around the sight of Iggy's blood-drained face. "I didn't tell them where you are, Ignition. You're no use to me floating through a sewer system with all your skin removed." She paused to chuckle. "I need you in that vehicle, I have to get to Maim-Creek in 24 hours, and your Blockgain Chaser is the only whip that will get me there on this short-ass notice."

Some of Iggy's blood returned to his head as she relieved him of the threat of imminent death. But he was still very much shocked. Despite the details sparking immediate intrigue, he forced his throat to spit out a question.

"What and where is Maim-Creek?"

Clarissa leaned back into the visibility of the light, somehow looking even more gorgeous with a softer expression. "Maim-Creek is outside of this zone, in what some might call the badlands. It's one of Cook's hideouts. You remember his music career? The band he was in?"

Iggy nodded steadily. "That song...*'Carpool of Waste'* used to be my entrance music, they only released one album or something right?" Iggy asked while scratching his hair.

Clarissa pressed down on Iggy's leg a little before letting go. "Exactly. They were too busy running a syndicate to keep up with their recording. His bandmates from 'Well-Done' are his step-siblings: **Frye, Baker, Grille** and **The Boil**. I'm not proud of it, but Baker loaned me the start-up money for these beautiful Towers you find yourself in."

Iggy's eyes managed to pull themselves away from Clarissa's darkened image to scan the room while he pondered the implications of her ownership.

"That's impressive," he said flatly.

"What's impressive is how long I've put up with being in debt to that gang. I get a fuckload of interest on a building loan, plus I pay a couple of different taxes. Not just to them for cracking heads on Cook's turf, but also to the bloody Shell of Folsom, this gig ain't easy, Crasher."

Something in Iggy clicked, his brain began to switch on despite only being semi-awake.

"So, what do you need me to do? Why do you need a derby driver?" Clarissa smirked grimly at his question, licking her lips with excitement.

"I'm gonna clear this debt, it's early but I'm going to deliver this last payment to Baker directly and get myself out of this contract. No more dealers. No more bullshit."

Iggy rubbed his eyes in mild confusion. "You don't drive?" he inquired.

Clarissa snorted under her breath. "Time is of the essence, I have to get to Baker while he is still in the zone. Otherwise, I have to wait 'til pay drop next month. I would have killed every dealer in this tower by then. Your Blockgain can get me there in under 24 hours, that's all the time we have."

Wiping a sleepy tear from his eye he nodded gently, trying to visualize a full day journey in the waste. "Wait, you said Cook's gang know about me, and you want me to drive directly to their underboss?" Iggy asked.

"You're not on his radar. Outpost business wouldn't reach that level until your bounty was seven figures," Clarissa said. "Even then, he ain't gonna pull the trigger himself. He'd outsource the job. Nothing to be scared of, Crasher."

Iggy tilted his head a few times, deciding that made enough sense. He could only imagine how many targets and rivals that gang had. "24 hours...no stops?"

"No stops, I've already paid Blanch to fill your car up, repair any damage and install backseat blockers for the ride," Clarissa said with a hard expression.

Iggy's head reared back in slight disgust in response. "Backseat...*what!?* She did what to my car!?" Iggy snapped, with a fully awake face.

I only asked to have it stored, they've been messing with the Chaser without telling me?

Clarissa chuckled dismissively. "Calm down Daredevil, they are sunlight blockers in the backseat section. This might shock you, but vampires don't do too well in sunlight," she said with a grim smirk. "Even with the blockers up I still get quite weak. But they will stop me from burning alive in your backseat."

"I suppose that makes sense," Iggy replied softly.

"Yeah me staying alive does make sense, don't think you'll last too long out here if something happens to me, I'm cargo you can't afford to lose," Clarissa informed with a razor-sharp grin.

Point made.

"Alright. I can do it. How much?"

"Twenty thousand, enough cover your bounty and buy some new rims or whatever."

Pay off the bounty, just like that?

Iggy sat there stunned, taken completely off guard by her offer.

"What's wrong Crasher? Don't you want to go back to the Citadel? Ain't much in the waste for you is there?" Clarissa asked with tightly folded arms.

An image of Sil jumped into his mind, triggered by her sentence. A flash of her hungry eyes when she killed the gecko and saved him. Another flash of her curious eyes in his vehicle when she mounted him. And finally, a third flash of her eyes with strange anger and sadness when she ran out on him.

Where did she go…and why?

"I'm not going back, Landlady. I left that place for a reason. There was no freedom in that cycle of life at all. I crashed cars, made money and spent money on repairs," Iggy stated with painful conviction.

Clarissa tilted her head in surprise. His tone of voice caught her off guard as he continued.

"The only time I ever felt anything was when I was driving, I didn't realize it at the time but I was always thinking about driving fast, to break out the arena and into the wide world outside of it. Competition of the derby is exciting, but I was just going in circles. I don't want that anymore."

Iggy was surprised at himself, his stream of thoughts pouring out from him so neatly as if he was ready to say this years ago. He contorted his face with embarrassment once he stopped. But was taken aback from Clarissa's face, which seemed just as sincere as he felt.

"Break out into the wide world…make your own life…" she muttered softly.

Iggy raised his eyebrow, just as wary of her softer demeanor as she was of his stronger one. He felt different, he wasn't sheepish and unsure anymore.

"You don't need Folsom, build a life somewhere you don't answer to anyone, no one should be taxing you for running things your way, Landlady," Iggy said firmly.

The Landlady's single golden-green eye flickered curiously like an expensive candle about to go out. Her lips parted softly to make way for a single exhale that was perfectly silent but was felt on the air between them. She brought both of her legs closer to her to make her seated position on the bed a suggestive kneel, letting the weight of her bosom bring her heaving breasts into partial view in the dim light.

What did you say, Iggy, what did you do?

His chest was filled with a cocktail of confidence, fear, and primal vitality, he had never felt this way before, suddenly everything became clear and the Landlady's jagged beauty was amplified by his new focus. He had no words, but he felt like he was being interrogated in silence. She then broke it in a hushed but deliberate tone.

"*Do you want to fuck me?*"

Wha...?

Strange quivering noises came from Iggy as his mind struggled to process what he heard. His chest tightened and his neck boiled a satisfying heat that rose and settled in his ears. He wanted to speak but he couldn't, his tirade of confidence was gone as soon as it came.

She spoke again, this time more clearly.

"Even in the dark, your stiff is pointing at me accusingly. We gonna do something about it or not?"

A flush of hot breath exhaled from Iggy's lips, as he acknowledged the fabric of his racing pants pushing back and resisting against his private pulsations. Shockwaves of guilty arousal were coursing through him like a steady heartbeat and his back ached with a surprising new tension. There was no more use for words.

Disregarding any sense of smoothness or grace, Iggy crawled towards Clarissa hungrily before she snatched his face forcefully with one hand and took his lips into hers.

She wasn't quite as physically powerful as Sil, but it was clear her strength was not that of a normal human. Iggy's rational mind was sending him multiple warnings about her blood-sucking fangs, but his primal urges drowned them out easily. She kissed hard, but he kissed hard back. He let his pent-up desire for her power his actions and boldly grabbed one of her large breasts. As he squeezed it with a lusty intensity, his hand was almost swallowed by its soft pillowy texture. She hissed with pleasure as he began to knead and explore it with his hot-plate palms. Ice cool fingers clasped around his waist before smoothly gliding towards his stomach and finally dropping towards his bulge.

Iggy's breath rushed out in pleasure and surprise as she navigated his zipper and underwear to grip and release his throbbing member from his pants, stroking and turning in sensual but deliberate motions, which set Iggy off in an explosion of titillation. This taller, much stronger vampire was pulling him firmly, causing him to gently rock his hips in whichever angle she tugged him in. His groans of ecstasy were muffled by her soft lips and overwhelming tongue. Her free hand crushed his buttocks with depraved force.

Iggy was completely under her control and he loved every second of it. Yet her body remained cold as if she had just returned from a walk in the waste at night without a duster. Iggy could feel his warmth clashing against her frozen skin. He was too wrapped up in his urges to consider it substantially. After she was done pinching his rear, she moved her hand to her own pants, pulling them down with slight clumsiness assisted by Iggy peeling them off with her with his non-groping hand. She paused the kissing to pull away from his face and look him in the eyes before giving him orders.

"Make sure you cum inside me, I want to feel all of it."

"Yes...yes, I will," Iggy responded gingerly.

Not sure why, but don't care. Don't question it, Iggy.

Feeling Clarissa's ice-cold thighs clasp around his waist woke his body up to an even more alert state. She was as slick as a well-oiled engine. There was no gentle period of working in, and he penetrated and sunk all the way to the hilt with one thrust. She let out a soft cooing sound in response and began kissing him again, working her way from his neck to his chin to his mouth.

Iggy found a nice thrusting cadence that worked for them both, and her powerful hips were grinding in a way that seemed to be setting the motion for him. Although she was physically larger than Sil, she wasn't as overwhelmingly powerful. Whatever superhuman strength she possessed she clearly had learned to keep it in check when fornicating with a human. Her deep entrance was a little warmer than her skin, but still much colder than anything Iggy had felt with previous women. Her internal muscles squeezed him eagerly as if desperately wanting to milk him of his seed.

Iggy felt familiar sexual pleasure, but also something more. He respected this woman; he respected her desire for freedom. He feared her a little but also felt closer to her than he should have. With each thrust, he felt a bond strengthening, and the closer he felt, the louder her whispery moans became. It's as if she was feeling something too.

"I'm **close**...Crasher... don't fuckin' stop!"

Iggy's sweat-slick body was bucking inconsistent rhythm and bringing the proud Landlady close to her climax, her massive breasts heaving in hypnotic step with the slapping of warm flesh against cold. Resting her brisk feet on his calves, she curled her toes to indicate the orgasm was imminent. She held his face and struck with a thousand-yard stare before she roared in deep relish as her peak seized every nerve in her shaking body.

Iggy felt a wash of pure pride. As he sustained his hammering hips, he was only a few seconds behind her and was determined to give her what she asked. Narrowly dodging a drop of sweat from his forehead, Clarissa's head rose up to Iggy's neck, noticing a throbbing vein. It was pumping large amounts of blood in its current state and Clarissa's eye would not leave it. She licked her lips and got closer and closer, not fully in control of her body anymore…

"Arrrrgghhh"

Her head was pushed back to the mattress by Iggy's collarbone as he shouted in tandem with his climax, pumping heavy rounds of ejaculation deep inside her as he was told. Her eye rolled back and her mind left his artery, soaked in the invigoration she felt from what he poured within her. Her body tingled with it, mixed with the aftershock of the orgasm. The sensation had the raw kick of a near-lethal cocktail of powder. Her senses were pushed to the point of losing consciousness but she held on to savor. Iggy's face dropped into her soft breasts gasping for air. With an easy smile across his face that slowly turned to a gasp of confusion.

She's getting warmer?

His mind dwelled on the strange sudden temperature, before enveloping in comfort and dragging him back towards the sweet darkness of slumber.

Chapter 11: The Clutch

Iggy's eyes flinched open to stabbing sunlight, defeating any chance of him laying-in for the morning. His arm flopped over in search of the vampire he sexed just hours prior, only to find an empty bed sheet.

He felt even more out of place when he glanced around the room, he was in. It was made all the more strange by the sunlight, revealed in its full state. The room had a lot more wires, monitors and electronic clutter than he noticed in the dark. The decor of the room was that of pre-skirmish luxury, but Iggy suspected the room was also used as a 'control room' of sorts. This didn't surprise him considering how knowledgeable and savvy the Landlady came across.

Iggy's thoughts were halted by the click and creak of the front door, followed by heavy steps that could only belong to the burly Grady. Springing off the bed with a spritely freshness (which was no doubt due to his time with Clarissa), he found himself in front of the large mutant who looked the shirtless driver up and down curiously.

"You need to do more sit-ups, Crasher. L is with your Blockgain at Blanch's. You're leaving immediately. I don't need to tell you what will happen if you fuck this up."

Grady's black eyes widened with serious intent as his powerful leathery hand crashed down on Iggy's shoulder in a shockingly painful patting motion. His point couldn't be made any more clearly.

After throwing on a tank top vest and a motor jacket to match his new pants from the room's wardrobe, he took the elevator downstairs with Grady.

They didn't talk much at all aside from Iggy clarifying the location and path to his destination. Grady warned him about increased bandit presence, along with bigger and badder creatures of the waste. Iggy resolved that as long as he stayed driving fast, he wouldn't be in too much trouble. The Blockgain was a marvel of the big waste with very few equals and even fewer superiors. Grady gave Iggy a couple of standards to grab something to eat from the market and told Iggy to meet him and Clarissa in half an hour.

The rusty, decrepit shell of Folsom looked especially ugly in the daytime. The damage to the structures was jarring against the exotic decorations and colorful graffiti. Wisps of smoke were pillowing the air in various shades of white and grey, mostly emanating from open bug barbecues and poorly maintained vehicles.

The scarred, scabbed and filthy inhabitants of the shell were fully revealed by the morning light; armor-clad ruffians wondering in and out of traffic like zombies. Looking for their next powder fix, blights chased human teenagers through the markets and leather-clad mutant dominatrix figures, performed lewd acts on their customers in front of the public. The only ones breaking the image of the chaos were stern-looking men and women in dark grey riot armor which read FOLSOM WATCH across their backs. All of them were armed with Shotguns of various models and quality. Iggy could see how someone could find a warped charm in this insane place, but it really wasn't for him.

Just as he tried to follow his nose to the least-disturbing food scent, the flash of a body flew past him and crashed into a nearby Cactus soup stall. This caused a large spill of scalding hot broth to splash a few bystanders who reflexively screamed in agony. Iggy's head snapped to see the Iron-Knuckle bartender Jake rubbing his fist before rolling down his dirty white sleeve. Before Iggy could gasp Jake smiled and greeted him.

"Morning soft-neck! Just doing a bit of market patrol, I get free food from basically everywhere as long as I knock around a thief or two!" Jake said with a cheery tone. "That little bastard was trying to steal death lobsters from the seafood quarter. If he's lucky, they might just break his arms, otherwise, the owners will feed him to some live lobster to make a point...get a good rest at the towers?"

The burly Orc-mutant whose skin was visibly bright blue outside of the dingy bar seemed to be wearing the same apron as last night. Though Iggy couldn't be sure, he doubted Jake had slept at all himself.

"Oh, hey Jake, yeah I slept pretty good," Iggy said modestly. Iggy tried with every fiber to not smile but he felt a tiny grin crack from the side of his mouth.

"She's a fine host, Ignition," Jake said with a knowing smirk.

"Y-yeah, well. Grady sent me to get something to eat, any suggestions?" Iggy asked before turning to the twitching thief in the stall wreckage. "I'm guessing soup is off the menu."

Jake snorted out a chuckle. "Don't pay for this shit. Here have some crow wings and black turnips. I'm not going to finish them anyway."

Jake handed a takeaway bag with a logo of a mutant chef holding a trident-sized fork covered in blood. The scent from the bag wafted something tasty. Fried bird and crunchy veg was not a bad meal to start the day with. Iggy took the bag and began munching immediately while thanking Jake through a full mouth. Jake wiped his slightly bloodied knuckles on his apron and turned to street corner before waving down a piss-yellow cab car.

"Oh, Malkin and the lads were looking for you," Jake muttered on his way into the cab which looked too small to hold him.

Iggy swallowed down the meat of a juicy crow wing before responding with a cocked eyebrow,

"Oh yeah, them from last night, they say what it was about?"

"Something about a big hunt, something much better paying than the usual Plentipedes shit, you'd have to ask them though!"

Maybe they wanted my help...or just wanted to hang out, it's a shame I gotta leave for this job so soon, it would have been nice to socialize a bit more.

"Ah, well I got to see the Landlady now. Job is on a timer," Iggy said with a friendly wave.

"Go easy on her!" Jake laughed before the door shut.

Iggy rubbed the back of his neck with minor embarrassment before walking past the messed-up stall and growing crowd to head to Blanch's. While munching heaps of his wings and turnips, his heart was light and giddy. He was having an enjoyable meal and was about to be reunited not only with his car but his recent sexual partner, Clarissa.

Iggy's good mood carried him all the way the Blanch's garage with no mind paid to the various ruffians and punks he passed on the way over. There was an assortment of Class C vehicles parked near the single gas pump and a few drivers both human and mutant were arguing over parking spots. Before he could eavesdrop on the conflict the familiar friendly voice of Blanch cut through the rabble.

"Hey, sugar! You get anything good to eat for breakfast? Take the side door into the auto shop. Your friends are all here!"

Iggy followed the welcoming but croaky tone of the Blight mechanic to a rusty latched door at the rear of the main auto garage, his stomach tightened as he pushed it open.

Wonder what they've done to my Blockgain….

The room was almost pitch-black, all the windows had been very thoroughly covered by sheets of black shutter metal and the smell of oil and burned rubber sat in the air with a bloated density. In the dark, he could make out the large figure of Grady who was drinking a hot beverage, the tall frame of the Landlady in a leaning position, the glowing eye goggles of a small person who he didn't immediately recognize. The shape that stood out to him the most was the beautifully familiar body of his beloved car. He could only really make out the exterior but it didn't look any different which he was grateful for.

"I can smell crow wings on your breath, good protein for them sit-ups I told you to do," Grady snarked before sipping his drink carefully.

Iggy didn't even respond and walked over to his car to run his palm along the hood. "She's a real marvel! Not much I could do to improve on her with what I have here, but I tightened up her brakes and fixed your auto drive and transmission. You should have a nice boost to your acceleration and handling, sugar".

Blanch's unmistakable drawl came from inside the car, as she tinkered with a few parts on the dashboard. "You're too good Blanch, thank you," Iggy said sincerely. "Are the window blockers in?"

"Just fixing them in now, Darlin', there won't be any performance difference, they are just to keep our Landlady from getting an unwanted tan!"

Iggy looked over to Clarissa's silent figure and nodded to himself.

"They threw in a bonus for you Iggy, one that I wanted, so you better be grateful."

The voice of the small person with the goggles jogged Iggy's memory and he realized it was the unassuming hunter, Penoli from the group he met at the bar the night before. Her voice was even but laced with a hint of resentment.

"What? What bonus?" Iggy asked.

Blanch's croaked laugh shot from the inside of the car, followed by a deep snigger from Grady. "Oh, darlin' I was going to surprise you when we turned the lights on, the Landlady dipped into her deep pockets and bought a gas-powered harpoon attachment for your beautiful vehicle here, handy tool! Penoli will have to wait until I order in one next month haha".

Iggy's fists balled as his voice wretched. "You put a weapon attachment on my car?! No one thinks to ask me first?"

Iggy noticed as Grady set his cup down and was reminded to watch his tone before Clarissa finally spoke. "Your -wonderful- car has zero in the way of weapons, and I can't exactly lean out of the window to drive-by on motherfuckers, can I?" Clarissa stated in irritation.

"B-but a roof attachment weapon is heavy, it will mess with the weight distribution on tight chicanes and alter the top speed on a-"

"Then adapt! You're a Top 20 Derby hotshot, figure it out. I'm not going to be outgunned in the Big Waste so you can steer smoother," Clarissa cut in bluntly.

Penoli, Blanch, and Grady all snickered as Iggy shut his mouth with great frustration, fists still pathetically balled up. Penoli began to walk to the side door and pulled the goggles off her head.

"Okay, Blanch I gotta go. Malkin and Nailz will be back later, so I'll begin the paperwork at the bounty office," Penoli said with a little more enthusiasm than normal.

"No problem honey, the supercharger I installed for them should give them the speed to keep up with that creature. Let me know how it goes when they get back!" Blanch responded.

This must be the big hunt that Jake told me about.

"Too bad you're stuck with a long day job with the Landlady, Ignition. This legendary hunt's bounty is 280,000 standards. We would have split it with you if you joined us, but you got the harpoon so I guess that balances it out," Penoli declared.

Iggy didn't really care about hunts but the prize sounded pretty good even after being split between them. He shrugged as Penoli left the auto shop and then waved her goodbye.

Grady finished the last of his drink and walked over to the Landlady as she pushed off from the wall. Grady towered over his boss but lowered his head in respect to her in a rare moment of poignant silence from the snarking brute. Clarissa placed her hand on his shoulder and lightly leaned her forehead against his chest.

"Alright, you're in charge of the towers now, you gonna be a good landlord?" she said with a voice that was trying to hold back emotion.

"I got it under control L. Focus on Baker and that payment. I'll be here," Grady said with a tone that was also trying to hold back his true feelings.

They are close, like family. This can't be easy for either of them knowing the danger.

"Alright fuck it, let's go. Crasher, your weapons are in the car. Your Elephant Revolver is loaded in your glove box and your bat is in the passenger seat. We added a console near the steering wheel for the harpoon. I'll talk you through it on the road," Clarissa said.

"Twenty-four hours or less, let's get this done," Iggy said with a determined tone.

Clarissa climbed into the back of the Blockgain and pulled down the sun blockers around the windows from the inside. Iggy thanked Blanch once more before entering the driver's seat. Grady paid Blanch a large number of standards before walking around to the driver's window. The garage door began to open and light slowly revealed Grady's trout face grinning with a disturbing look in his black eyes. But Iggy had no time to respond to a taunt.

He was focused on the task at hand because Clarissa the Landlord was counting on him. Iggy hit the ignition and felt his car roar to life with a new level of health. Not to mention a smell clean of all the gunpowder, sex and blood from the night before. Pressing the gas softly he pulled out of the garage into the sunlit Folsom and headed for the front gates.

His passenger Clarissa remained unseen behind the blockers, trying to stay calm and alert despite how 'close' she was to the deadly sunlight. Leaning in the makeshift speaking box, she called to Iggy.

"Crasher, Blanch do a good job? Blockgain feels good don't it?"

"Really good, can barely feel the weight of the harpoon, we should be fine."

"Ain't no 'should be' about it. We have to be. Don't fuck it up."

I WON'T. NOT THIS TIME.

Chapter 12: Amazon Chaser

The sky was clear and the sun was beaming. Iggy and his new passenger were only an hour and a half into their journey, but the amount of ground covered was significant. The landscape was a different appearance, there was far less sand and more earth-like soil. It was discolored with patches of brown grass intermingled with cracked pavement and occasionally broken telephone poles. Bent and rusted guard rails stretched sporadically alongside the beaten road and half wrecked cabins made up the atmosphere around their path.

Whatever was left of pre-skirmish civilization was a lot more recognizable out here. Iggy's delight in tearing through the waste in his Blockgain was offset by his uncertainty with his fellow traveler Clarissa.

She hadn't spoken much since leaving the garage aside from a few general directions and she was hidden from his view with the sun blockers installed behind the front seats. Iggy didn't know how to feel. He slept with her and he felt something pretty strong. He felt like he understood her in some way. And now he was with her for the duration of this mission in the hope to get to know her better. But she was showing no signs of returning that curiosity and it was making him anxious. He chose to break the relative silence with a conversation.

"Landlady, what exactly did you do before you were a…. Landlady?"

Iggy asked flatly.

There was a moment of silence before her muffled response seeped out through the voice box.

"Been a long time...even before the Folsom towers I was running freelance security. Some called me a 'problem solver' of sorts."

I got a good idea of what that entailed.

"But before that?" Iggy pressed.

"Before that, I was a fucking full-time **vampire,** Dumb-ass." Clarissa hissed bitterly. "I pounced on weak homesteaders and nomads who were stupid enough to wander the scrap yards after dark. Never a shortage of moron soft-necks out here."

Iggy picked up on this being a sensitive subject but he was curious, and Grady wasn't here to glare at him for it. However dangerous she was, she was currently completely helpless in a backseat box protecting her from the lethal rays of the sun. Iggy felt confident to keep pushing.

"But you stopped, you don't do that anymore?"

"I don't drink blood these days, I still happily kill idiot humans who don't watch themselves," Clarissa growled with growing annoyance.

"But how exactly does that work? Don't vampires need blood to survive? How can you just 'quit' something that sustains you?"

Iggy heard a sigh from the voice box.

"I-I'm different. My genes are strong. Something to do with my parents, I don't really fucking understand it."

"Genes? Different from other vampires?" Iggy asked.

Clarissa paused for longer this time, exhaling long before responding. "Maybe...I don't know. Never met many vampires...."

Who is she really? That doesn't seem right.

Iggy's mind was front-loaded with so many questions they didn't come out right away. But he put his curiosity when he heard the loud buzz of a nearby engine.

The first thing Iggy noticed was the healthy gargle of the vehicle. Not the same sound of perfection that came from his own Blockgain, but certainly a class B vehicle at the least. Peering to the west he could see it in the distance. It was a large-medium dark jeep covered in an array of hood ornaments and spikes. It was a custom model for all-purpose uses. Not something you'd see in a derby but a top pick for a death run's obstacle course. It seemed too expensive to be a bandit vehicle but Iggy wasn't sure what it was doing, speeding out in waste at such a speed.

Peeling off cracked tarmac path, Iggy veered a little closer to get a better look at the vehicle and what it was up to. He noticed the 4×4 began to veer closer to him, making the waving driver just visible enough to Iggy in the glaring sunlight.

"Ignition! I didn't know you'd be leaving this early? Did Jake tell you about our big hunt?" The voice was unmistakable, it was Nails. Iggy assumed that the other hunter from their group, Malkin was in the passenger seat.

Iggy rolled down his window and yelled to respond.

"Yeah, Penoli told me it was a big payout, but I'm on a job for the Landlady."

"We are closing in on her now, Ignition!" Nails replied with excitement. "Malkin shot her with his crossbow. Blue Gecko poison-tipped bolts, means she can't run too quick for long, probably behind one of these wrecked cabins."

She?

"Why is the hunt such a big deal? Rare creature?"

Nails heavily studded face pulled into a manic grin.

"The rarest in the zone! Fenrir was all but a legend until she killed the last band that was hunting her, that plus her fur is invaluable."

"What kind of a name is Fenrir?"

"Uhhh same grandpappy told me an ancient civilization had a giant *Wolf-Monster* that could kill a god named Fenrir, has a nice ring to it, I guess."

"Wolf Monster?"

"Not as big as the old legend, but she's easily the size of this car, and runs nearly as fast as it, been told she looks about eight feet on her hind legs, beautiful coat of silver fur too, never seen anything quite like it...you sure you don't want to change your mind and get in on this hunt?"

Silver fur? No...no way.

Iggy paused a little before his next question.

"She...Fenrir is close?"

The 4×4 began to speed up and the Blockgain matched it easily.

"Malkin tagged her about five minutes ago, with all these old structures she could be hiding or still running around cover, I know we are close though. What I'm driving here is the **Dresden Dune.** It's a beautiful machine but it's still a Class B, help us out and we'll cut you in, Ignition."

I have to know.

Iggy rolled back down his window quickly and leaned into his voice box to speak to Clarissa.

"Slight detour, Landlady. Just gonna see if I can spot a monster for these guys, we are still basically on course anyway." Iggy tried to explain.

"Who the fuck is paying you, Crasher? You're on an escort job with my time limit, you can buy your drinking buddies around after you come back." Clarissa stated with annoyance.

Iggy felt the pressure, but there was no way he was going to change his mind, he gulped his fear and responded with a cold conviction.

"I can take 10 minutes to help these two and we will still get to Maim-creek with time to spare. If you want to get out and sunbathe while I do that, be my guest."

Clarissa grumbled under her breath, while Iggy exhaled his bold bluff energy as quietly as possible. "Ten minutes Crasher, I'm setting my watch."

Holy shit.

Rolling the window back down, he shouted back to the other car.

"Okay I'm in, I'll help you spot. I'll pull ahead on the west flank of this row of road shacks."

Nails nodded enthusiastically and Malkin leaned over past him, brandishing his crossbow for Iggy to see.

"Good to be hunting with you Ignition. You point 'er out and I won't miss!" Malkin yelled happily as if he was celebrating a birthday.

The Blockgain Chaser accelerated past the 4×4 and shifted off the worn path to the cracked bumpy soil of the off-road. The suspension balanced the vehicle easily, and the Chaser's all-purpose tires clung to the ground reliably. The area they were in looked to be some sort of very old pre-skirmish farm town, just based on the mostly wooden half structures that were in immediate vision. Iggy slowed down to begin scanning the area once he got to the angle that covered the widest field of view.

The high sun created narrow but thick shadows behind some of the larger wood structures which Iggy was diligently checking for movement or sounds. The old town was getting harder to drive through as he got towards the heart of it. Large barns and wells became obstacles to veer around and Iggy worried there were too many hiding spots for him to check from the car at any speed, knowing he couldn't risk leaving it.

Not keeping his eyes in front of him, the Blockgain smashed into a small wooden sign that read: 'Welcome to Carnaby' that bounced off the car. Iggy thought nothing of it, but Clarissa spoke up.

"I heard a yelping sound. Southeast I think," she said with a tone of flat indifference.

"You sure? I'll spin around," Iggy said with haste.

"Take all the damn time in the world. Crasher."

Iggy ignored her quip and braked into a near 180 spin, kicking up a healthy amount of dirt in the skid. And then he saw it, almost as a stream of silver.

At least 7 feet in length and 5 feet in height on all fours, the majestic beauty of the creature came into view from a side angle of its rear as it ran. Its glossy bright coat hung tightly over a network of thick complex muscles that seemed the most heavily woven at the upper legs and back. Its light grey tail looked like a stream of glistening smoke, only adding to its fascinating appearance. Iggy felt drawn to it immediately and slammed on the gas to chase it, its silver-grey coat keeping it in clear vision against the dull brown of the waste landscape.

There was no more time to weave through the cabins. Luckily for Iggy, the Blockgain was more than strong enough to plow through old wooden houses as if they were made of stiff cardboard. But the impact was still felt by Clarissa who was feeling the fierce turbulence in the backseat. Iggy fought through the obstacles to get alongside the darting 'Fenrir', gaining steadily and surely. The screaming buzz of the Dresden Dune engine tore into the atmosphere as it broke through an old corral gate to join the chase, approaching its top speed.

"IGNITION! Too much cover for me to get a clear shot with the crossbow! Hit her with your harpoon, or just knock into her, we can clean the coat after and still get a good price!" Malkin yelled from the approaching vehicle.

The surroundings began to blur, both cars and the Fenrir were approaching breakneck speeds, only hindered by the semi careful navigation of some of the more solid-looking structures in their immediate path. Iggy rolled his window halfway to respond.

"Hasn't she already been shot? You said she would slow down!!"

The wolf turned to Iggy's car as they reached parallel formation as if to respond to him. The first thing he saw was the eyes, ice-cold white, almost otherworldly. A handsome face of a powerful wolf; bearing a set of jagged fangs with a mouth being pulled back by the sheer speed of movement. Around its neck was a neat mane of cobalt grey-blue and a piece of fabric that caused immediate déjà-vu.

It... can't be! No!!

The cloth was a light brown blanket that fit snugly below the wolf's neck below the mane. But around a humanoid's neck, it would most likely fit like a **loose poncho.**

The icy eyes fixed on Iggy, there was no discernible emotion aside from that of recognition, familiarity, and slight *surprise*. Iggy's stare was broken when the Blockgain smashed into another unknown wooden piece of debris. Slowing the car down a little.

"Ignition! She's fast but she's limping, the poison will work! We gotta get her now while she's still a beast. If she dies after shifting, we won't get paid!"

A cold ache hit Iggy's stomach like a fist made of solid ice. The feeling raced up his chest and thumped into his head.

"Malkin, what do you mean shift?"

Please, please don't say it.

"Fenrir is a shifter! It's only occasionally in beast form, apparently, she sometimes turns back to a more human shape when she weakens…never mind I've got a clear shot. Get on her flank."

It's her.

Flashes of Sil's bright eyes appeared in Iggy's mind like floodlights revealing the truth. He felt her hot breath, her mouth over his leg wounds, her insides as she took hold of him in passion. The memories swirled around him like a cyclone. His trip down memory lane broke when he saw a crossbow-wielding Malkin leaning out of the Dresden lining up his shot.

I'm sorry fellas…I'm truly sorry.

The Blockgain Chaser swerved heavily into the 4×4. Despite it being slightly smaller, the weighty impact slammed it into a brief fishtail and nearly caused Malkin to spill out of the window. Nails had to pull some hard counter-steering not to spin out.

"What the fuck Ignition? Watch where you're going, buddy!" Nails yelled in confusion.

The voice box flared up with Clarissa's disapproving tone.

"Crasher, this isn't a derby, why the hell are you ramming cars!? Get back on track, this hunt is over."

Iggy ignored Clarissa, knowing that there would be a lot of explaining to do later. As Nails drove back up in position for the now visibly banged up Malkin to take another shot, Iggy began to notice the Fenrir slowing down. Every 4th step was like a hopping motion. The poison was taking effect.

"Nails, Malkin, abort this hunt! You can't kill her!"

"**Her!?**" Clarissa barked from the back.

There was a look of shock on Malkin's face as if he heard a new language for the first time.

"We **can** kill her, Ignition. It'll just take another shot or two, Penoli told you how much we would make, right? We are so close!" Malkin explained desperately.

"I... I know, but as Nails says, this is a shifter that is a person, we can't kill that person for money, it isn't an animal."

Malkin's face dropped into a blank state of disbelief. Nails yelled in his place.

"Person!? This is the fucking **Big Waste** you silver-spoon Citi-boy! We, you, everyone kills people for money all the time! I don't know what powder you snorted in the morning, but we are collecting this hunt, and if you ain't going to help, then you need to *back the fuck off!*"

The Dresden Dune screeched into an aggressive turn and banged against the Blockgain as a warning. The jolt sent knocked Iggy upwards knocking his head into his car roof with minor impact. He knew there was no turning back. He took a deep breath, ignoring the heavy stream of cursing from the voice box and rolled up his window. Nails did the same. Minds were made up, there was no turning back.

The Blockgain pitched a hard right towards its new enemy. But there was less impact than Iggy had hoped, not enough room for a full charge side swipe. The 4×4 recoiled and swung back, bashing Iggy and Clarissa around their respective seats. The weight difference between was real, and the town obstacles and uneven ground gave little opportunity for free swerving. Iggy was reminded of the regional Derby qualifiers in the dirt arena on his 25th birthday, a brutal run.

An ancient horse carriage was obliterated as Iggy unknowingly plowed into it, splintering wood flying off around him and the crunching sound whetting his appetite for vehicular impact. He hastily tried another shunt, but lost speed as the Blockgain's left tire hit a bump, causing him to miss. He was now at the Dresden Dunes' rear and saw a bloodied Malkin lean out again with his crossbow. Fenrir was dashing valiantly but was visibly in no shape for any agile maneuvers. Iggy knew she was an easy target for a veteran hunter like Malkin.

It's not happening, not today!

Iggy slammed the gas pedal and grit his teeth, purely focused 4×4 like a homing missile. The Blockgain's engine screamed in sync with its driver's raw determination. It peeled through the dusty air closing in on the hunters.

There was a ***thwip*** sound followed by a heavy ***clunk***, and then an ear-piercing ***squeal***.

Malkin had managed to get off one shot with his poison-tipped weapon before being rammed by Iggy's Blockgain roughly. The squeal came from the Fenrir when the bolt meant for her head slammed into her back leg instead. Dark red blood began to spurt from the leg of the speeding wolf, splattering all over the windows of both cars.

"She's gonna die! I'm out of time!" Iggy growled in helpless anger.

He heard the majestic wolf cry in what could only be pure agony. She was pushing herself beyond any normal limits to outrun a Class B vehicle, while her weakening system was gripped by whatever powerful venom, she just got a double dose of. Iggy skid out of the way of a stone well only to hit at a broken outhouse. The Blockgain lost more speed and fell further behind the charging hunters. Malkin appeared out of the window once again, lining up another shot.

Iggy desperately scanned everything around him, as his experience estimated the time and distance. He knew he couldn't speed up enough to interrupt this next shot. His ringing ears went into overdrive, and finally began to tune-in Clarissa's constant threats and rants from the voice box; catching the tail end of one sentence.

"I didn't buy you those upgrades for this shit!!"

Upgrades...not the engine......

He spotted it immediately, the console on his dashboard that was out of place. He took no notice of it until now. A grey panel with a large yellow switch, with two functions for up and down: 'LAUNCH" and 'RETRACT'. It was currently set to retract. Iggy had never seen or used it before.

Harpoon is on the roof; I need them square in front of me....

Veering a little to the right he managed to pull behind the 4×4 until he was mostly in the slipstream. He hit another bump that knocked him out of line just a little. His head seemed to be pumping with its own heartbeat. All he could taste was metal. He placed his hand on the switch and gulped cold mucus.

NOW!!

The sound of the Harpoon-blast was like an imploding flak-cannon mixed with an old shotgun. Iggy could even feel his car being pushed back slightly by the recoil. The 'claw' of the harpoon was a nasty looking instrument that looked like a giant fish hook made to catch a Landshark. It propelled through the dust-filled air and smashed right through the trunk of the 4×4, snagging the interior with its sharp prongs and clinging to it securely. Malkin fired his crossbow, but the new impact was just enough to make him shoot wide and miss Fenrir by a half foot. The hunter almost fell out of the window once again. But with steely refusal to give in, he began to string another bolt to his bow.

Iggy was morbidly impressed with how determined these hunters were, it's as if they were willing to die as long as they could see the death of this creature to the end. He resolved that their passion for this couldn't be too different from his own all or nothing attitude towards the demolition of car combat.

All or nothing.

With the harpoon affixed to the back of the 4×4 Iggy buzzed through options of what to do next. He wondered if he could try and drag the car away like an angry Dogbull on a leash, maybe a hard break to stop it in the tracks.

I'm not sure how secure that hook is, it might slip off the back if just keep tugging, but I have to end this chase.

The option settled in his mind and he took a breath before leaning into his voice box and giving Clarissa strict orders.

"If you want to live long enough to kill me for this Landlady, you are gonna have to brace for impact! Strap in tight and hold on to the dummy bars…this is gonna hurt."

The enraged vampire said nothing and Iggy could only hope she took what he said seriously, as he moved one hand over his booster trigger and another over the harpoon switch.

There would have been other hunts, fellas, you should have left her alone.

The whooshing eruption of the Blockgain boosting blended with the searing buzz of the tires ripping through the land. Iggy flipped the 'RETRACT' function on the switch simultaneously. The effect was the Chaser surging forward while the mighty harpoon yanked the 4×4 back. Though a fine vehicle in its own right, when colliding with the Blockgain chaser from the rear it didn't stand a chance.

The sound of pulverizing impact shook the earth, all of Iggy's senses turned off for a split second. The shockwave of the brunt blew the nearby Fenrir off her feet, and to the side of the collision. The Dresden Dune folded like a cheap can. The glass burst and the metal gave way as the frame crunched inwards.

Malkin was cut in half from the torso, his upper body flying forward as his legs sandwiched within the pressed backseat and the corpse of

Nails' shattered body.

The mangled scrapheap of the vehicle tumbled out of view after the harpoon hook snapped away from it. The wrecked jeep bounced harmlessly behind the Blockgain as it braked into a hard skid before stopping. Iggy's forehead was bleeding with a messy but shallow cut. Clarissa's super strength kept her almost unscathed when she gripped for impact. Both of them panted heavily in unison over the voice box before Clarissa spoke up.

"Crasher…. are you going to tell me what the **fuck** just happened?"

"I will Landlady, I'll tell you everything…but first I gotta find her."

Chapter 13: Canis Canem Edit

The search for the Fenrir was brief. A mostly intact cabin a few feet from where he parked had a large smashed open hole, which was most likely from the impact of a giant creature crashing through it. Iggy stepped in carefully, hoping that the 'Fenrir' creature was as hardy as she looked. But inside the rotting wood structure, there was no large wolf creature to be found. Only the much smaller, human-sized woman he found in the Big Waste.

*It **was** Sil.*

She lay still and mostly silent apart from short haggard breaths which told a very serious tale of discomfort and illness. Her ashen grey skin had faint but noticeable blotches of dark blue, and she was covered head to toe in dried blood. Her now tattered poncho was mostly dark red from soaking in blood. Iggy ran to her in panicked horror, scooping her up in his arms before dashing back to the Blockgain. He shuddered when he felt how *soft* her body was and how relatively light, she was to carry, a very jarring experience to the superhuman killing machine he watched in action just the other day. He was scared but still touched with the relief of being reunited with her.

"You better have the best explanation in the fucking world Crasher. Why am I in a car that isn't moving? Why hasn't this car been moving for the last 20 minutes? What the hell happened to Nails and Malkin?" Clarissa shouted from inside the car.

Clarissa's voice was scratchy from the near non-stop yelling before and after the collision. But Iggy had his priorities, he wasn't thinking about Clarissa's mission right now.

"I had to save someone. No explanation will satisfy you so I won't even bother," Iggy said with a new tone of seriousness. "But this person is seriously hurt and until I can do something about that your mission is on hold, got that?"

Clarissa's fire and fury blasted out from the inside of the backseat as Iggy opened the front door to lay the battered Sil inside; long ways across both seats.

"You **stupid Citi-simp, softneck-shitstain!** What the fuck am I paying you for!? I don't give a shit about some dying bitch. Twenty randomers died in my towers last week! You have a fucking job to do. You drove for 20 mins before deciding to play rough and tumble with your drinking buddies, and, **where are they?!"**

"They're fuckin' dead, I warned them and they didn't listen. I feel bad, but not as bad as *you* are going to feel if I open that back door while the sun is still out!" Iggy snapped with a sinister tone in his voice.

Clarissa paused for a moment, taking in the seriousness of Iggy's tone, before responding in a much flatter emotionless timbre. "Blue Gecko poison right...? That's what Malkin hunts with, there isn't any real cure for it. If you're strong enough to withstand the fever and paralysis, some have been known to make a full recovery with high-end round the clock type treatment... but it's not a sure thing."

Iggy gulped with panicked despair and ran his hand over the cheek Sil's pained face as her quick breaths became like whimpers. "She isn't strong enough to beat the fever, she got shot twice and she's badly injured, I think she's lost quite a bit of blood too. We got to turn around back to Folsom, maybe-"

"You fucking moron, I was giving you the diagnosis for **one** Gecko bite, two crossbow bolt shots can be as powerful as **four bites**. If she's in the state you say she is, she won't last half an hour regardless of where you take her, Folsom doesn't have shit in the way of medical facilities anyway. Whoever she is, you need to put her out of her misery. This is one of the most painful deaths anyone can experience." Clarissa stated with grim empathy.

Cold anguish gripped Iggy's chest like a snare. He looked at Sil's agonized expression, and coughed into a teary splutter as he dropped his head on her lap.

She's...in so much pain...and it's my fault. I should have been faster!

Iggy's mind tried to push it out, but his eyes hovered over to the glove compartment, where his fully loaded elephant revolver was. In her current state, Iggy resolved that despite her superhuman durability, a shot to the head with the revolver would be a quick and painless end. Shaking his head hard, hoping to rattle the thought free from his mind he looked at Sil through blurred eyes filled with tears.

"Sil...tell me what to do..." Iggy spluttered

Clarissa spoke softly over the voice box, acknowledging the depressing situation.
"Don't be selfish, no one deserves to die like this, finish it."

Iggy's shaking hand began to reach for the glove box as he turned his head and forced his eyes closed. His body felt like it was being torn in two ways. Despite the constant near-death situations of his life in the derby and more recently the trials of the waste, he had never felt as helpless as he did now.

Then he heard the faintest whisper, a croak of speech.

"N-Nish...in...took me *home*," Sil uttered with a mere fragment of the powerful bark he was used to hearing from her.

"Yes Sil, you're home," Iggy said with a crushed resolve.

His hand was finally in the glove box and reluctantly feeling for the gun. His heart lifted ever so slightly with the bittersweet knowledge the last place she would see is the car she feels at home in.

"She saved my life...Clarissa..." Iggy sobbed into the voice box as he took shaky aim with his weapon.

Killing that reptile right before it would have eaten me, hitching a ride and forcing me to drive around with my leg injury, then saving it with that clear-wet...

"CLEAR-WET!!"

Iggy's veins pumped fire, a fire that set his nerves alight, a fire that burned through his head and set all cylinders of his brain on overdrive. A fire that burned away his tears, fire which hit the ignition key in his guts. Just like his beloved Blockgain, his engine roared to life.

Everything became clear, he slammed the pistol back into the glove box and shut it, never wanting to see it, let alone hold it again. He carefully lifted Sil into the passenger seat so she was sitting up, but reclined it enough to give her what little comfort he could. He scrambled into the driver's seat and turned the engine on as Clarissa spoke through the voice box with bewilderment in her speech.

"Crasher? What are you-"

"Cactus! Clarissa, where can I find a cactus, where do they grow?!"

Clarissa went silent as she pondered the implications of her driver losing his very sanity. She was jolted when he yelled again with the most intensity, she had heard from him.

"TELL ME NOW!"

"Ah-fuck what kind? Plenty of regular ones around the Sivander Creek west of-"

The instant she gave an indication of a direction, the Blockgain peeled out into a rocket start, knocking Clarissa around the backseat unprepared for the inertia. Iggy was gritting his teeth and squeezing his steering wheel as if he was hanging on to life itself. The Blockgain Chaser seared off west at top speed, tearing through everything solid that it could run over or smash through.

Iggy's eyes were darting between the scenery in front of him; his speedometer that was pushing 200mph and Sil, fighting a losing battle against the poison silently. Despite the world around him whipping by in a screaming rush, his eyes saw everything; every boulder, signpost, wreckage, rodent, and corpse as he flew by. He wasn't going to miss anything. His ears suffered Sil's whispery breaths turning into yowls of agony. Her dark skin blotches were becoming more pronounced and uglier, and her blue veins becoming visible under her grey skin.

"Keep fighting Sil, **stay alive!!**" Iggy yelled through clenched teeth as he tore into a new part of the landscape that seemed to have more grass and plant life than the barren ground before it.

He managed to catch the sight of a few people in long duster coats and mining masks wandering around, presumably looking for scrap, most of them turned when they saw a dark, class A muscle car barrelling past them at 210 mph, but Iggy wasn't going to waste time asking for directions, he knew he was close, the lakes, the trees, they were familiar enough to him from where they found the first cactus near the pool.

And with the immediate sight of a green looking lake, Iggy's vision registered a plant that looked enough like it. Short, wide, bright green and not too prickly.

It has to be, has to be it....

Swinging his car into an emergency brake which skewed the entire car sideways and almost backward as the wheels shrieked to a halt, Iggy grabbed his barbed wire bat and jumped out of the car and ran towards the plant that he was wishing as hard as he could that it wasn't a mirage.

Almost tripping up on his own feet he dashed and landed in front of the cactus, a thick green beacon of hope that he prodded with his bat. He was convinced instantly.

This is it! I did it!

His planned move back to the car was cut off by the lock and tumble of what could only be a firearm. Looking up, he peered down the barrel of a rifle, which was in the hands of a scavenger girl, no more than 18 years old. Behind her was a boy of a similar age wielding holding a shovel.

The girl's face was covered by wasteland goggles, and her sandy blonde hair fell over her right shoulder in a braided pony-tail, her mouth a non-nonsense frown. The young man behind her had a face of shock and fear, dark brown bangs covered his bright blue eyes and his jaw was a quivering mount for his gaping mouth.

I got no time for this shit…why didn't I bring my revolver?

"Don't move! I'll...shoot you! I swear I will!!" said the rifle-armed girl, her voice was tomboyish and rough but clearly nervous and uncertain.

"He has a dark muscle car…odd clothes I think it's him…" the quivering young man uttered; his voice even shakier than his gun-toting companion.

They know me!?

"I don't know who you are or who you think I am, but I'm scavenging this plant here, nothing else! I've got no quarrel with you two!" Iggy shouted, half demanding and half pleading.

"Citadel accent! Listen, it's him! The Kill-Driver!! He murdered Uncle Novi!" the young man cried.

"Uncle Nov-who?" Iggy queried.

He was met with the response of the hammer of the rifle being pulled back, ready to shoot.

Nov...Novak and his wife...the scavengers that Sil...got rid of.

Iggy was taken back to the incident with the nomads that he and Sil ended up fighting, he remembered their eyes of fear when they realized the extreme force of nature that Sil was.

She was merciless. She tore them apart and ate most of their bodies. Iggy himself reluctantly salvaged most of their equipment for himself. It was brutal, but they started it, and Iggy knew he was technically in the right. Even if he didn't want Sil to kill Novak after he got cold feet and surrendered, he rationalized it as part of the way of the Big Waste.

"Wait a minute! I can explain! It's not what you think, please I need this plant!" Iggy babbled desperately.

He was 4 feet from the cactus, but they had the drop on him. If she pulled that trigger, not only does he die, but Sil and Clarissa do too. He raised a hand in passive surrender.

The girl's grip on the rifle is shaky, uncertain. She keeps it trained on him but she doesn't shoot. There was a murmur from her throat before she blurted her words.

"They were homesteaders! Just looking to support a convoy! You sick murdering fuck!!" she shouted accusingly.

The young man cut off her yelling with a panicked warning.

"Joely, he has a pet too, a rabid bitch that's more Dog than Woman. Had her eat the bodies after he slaughtered them!!"

Sil? She was doing most of the killing, I just shot the Tin-Man. Who told them this story?

Iggy's alert eyes caught Joely's finger moving to the trigger and tensing up to squeeze, he closed his eyes and thought of his actions up to this point, swearing to have no regrets.

No... regrets? Regret nothing, own it.

Iggy rose to his feet as if the rifle trained on him didn't exist, and looked at the two assailants up and down. Assessing them as the panicky teenagers they were. Iggy's face became a vindictive scowl, and his mouth curled in a cruel smirk.

"You're shaking, just like Novak did, right before my partner tore him in two with one swipe," Iggy recalled coldly, with a guttural tone. "He watched his stupid wife's skull get popped like a sludge-melon. I think he shit himself at that moment, right before I blew his cheap Tin-Man's head clean off."

"Y-you...bastard! Y-you demon!" the young man sobbed. Iggy watched as his upper-body began shaking like a washing machine as tears squeezed from his eyes.

"**You COWARD**, killing good people with a crazed mutant dog!" Joely said with equal parts fear and conviction.

"You stupid kids, she's not a mutant, or a dog or a bitch. My partner is the **Fenrir,** and she's in my car now, hungry as ever...listen." Iggy declared with a cruel smile.

The pained cries from Sil continued from the car. When they both were silent enough to hear it, their faces drained of all color, as if they became the living dead.

"FENRIR!!! IT'S HERE!!!"

"IN THE CAR!? FENRIR?!"

Iggy had never seen anyone scream so loud or run so fast in his entire life. Not only the two teens but a few of the masked scavengers in the surrounding area made a hard break for it when they heard the name of the wolf monster being repeated.

Joely had dropped her rifle before she turned heel, and Iggy instinctively took it with him. It was a bolt action rifle known as a 2-2: a popular model for guards and hunters on a budget. As Iggy watched the Nomads sprint for their lives, he felt different than normal but similar to how he did with his night with Clarissa. He exhaled all of the fire out of his spirit and shut his eyes to refocus.

Alright, clear-wet, time to do your thing.

The cactus was incredibly tough, its thick skin was like battle armor. Iggy couldn't even pierce it with a pen-knife. He had to spend a bullet from his new rifle to blow a few smaller chunks off. Iggy estimated they should be small enough to put into her mouth, hoping that was how it worked.

Iggy marched back to his car with two hands full of cactus chunks. His uncertainty made the 5-second walk back to Blockgain feel like an hour.
After sliding back inside he cradled Sil in his lap, stroking her hair as he held a wet chunk of the cactus to her nose, desperately expecting she knew what to do with it. Iggy wasn't 100% certain that the strong-smelling plant he held was the same as what she used on him before. Neither was he sure this would cure her of the ridiculously powerful venom in her system.

"Sil, wake up, I found the Clear-wet...here," Iggy informed gently.

When Sil's eyes flickered open, she looked like death. Her skin wracked with blemishes, her neck was an almost transparent window to her failing arteries, and her eyes were bloodshot dark red. Her dry tongue snaked over her dry lips as she forced out words.

"C-clear…wet…Nish…in?"

A tear fell from Iggy's eye onto Sil's forehead as soon as he heard her wild interpretation of his name on her breath. He held the cactus chunk a little closer to her face. Willing her to do whatever needed to be done with it.

Please…

Her swollen tongue ran over the glistening hunk of moist cactus, first as a sort of test-taste and then again as if to savor. She craned her head weakly to move her mouth closer and took the softest, slightest of bites. Iggy's heart skipped with a slight twinge.

"C-clear-wet.," Sil uttered with the slightest more conviction.

She followed with a larger bite, this time drawing the juices from the chunk like a human might with a peach or an orange. Iggy could hear gulping sounds from her quivering chest. Slowly as ever, she was eating more enthusiastically, until finally took the whole part in her mouth and devoured it.

With haggard shaky weakness, she pulled herself to a seated position with her arms locked around Iggy, finally turning to him to meet his gaze. Licking her lips as the dark blotches on her face began to fade, she grabbed another chunk of cactus from the seat and bit into it heartily.

"Mmph…more Clear-wet, *Nishin, more!*" She said with a half-cocked, hungry grin.

Iggy threw his arms around her and sobbed long and loud. His grip around her tightened and his face buried deep into her shoulders as she continued to munch. His tears streamed down her chest and towards her hips.

We did it…

Chapter 14: Lore and Infamy

Iggy had so much to explain, he felt bad that Clarissa had to interpret everything that happened, blind in the backseat of his car. The sun-blockers were keeping her in the dark as much as they were keeping her alive. He was able to give her a very brief summary as he walked back to the car and carried more chunks of cactus to Sil, but he knew he probably left her with more questions than answers. But he first had to catch up with Sil. He wanted to know why she left him that evening but thought that he better explains the 'new guest in the home first'.

He climbed into the car with Sil who was feasting on a huge chunk of the cactus. She was still looking poorly but her skin had cleared, she was recovering fast. After turning the engine on, Clarissa spoke up.

"Don't leave me in the dark, what the hell happened? Did it work?" Sil turned to the voice box and with a look of unhappy surprise and began to growl. Clarissa sighed deeply in response. "The Fenrir, she's coming with us, isn't she?"

Iggy turned to Sil with his palms up, trying to keep her calm.

"Sil, this is Clarissa, she is in the backseat of the...home. I'm driving her somewhere. She needs the house to get where she is going."

Sil growled lower, looking like she understood. "Rissa...not live in home?"

"No, she's just traveling with us to Maim Creek and back, not staying."

"Rissa...not staying…"

Sil's eyes began to droop and her words slurred, after taking a large bite of cactus she chewed it slowly, swallowed and then fell asleep dropping the rest on her naked lap.

"Sil!? Oh no, wake up!" Iggy said startled as he jumped to grab her.

"Crasher, she's just survived one of the deadliest toxins known to the Big Waste in the space of a few minutes. A soft-neck, hell even a mutant would take weeks before they could move around. Let her rest, and start driving," Clarissa ordered calmly.

Iggy pulled away from Sil and left her to her seated slumber in his passenger seat. He turned the ignition and reversed to take the beaten road west. He was determined to make up for lost time.

"Yes Landlady, we will get there…sorry about all of this," Iggy said weakly.

"Why don't you start from the beginning? We got a lot of miles to catch up on and you got a shitload of explaining to do," Clarissa said with acid.

In the next hour of driving Iggy was able to cover everything since he left Athens to do the cargo run. He explained his meeting Sil and everything about her behavior, from her wild animal instincts to her attachment to his car. The sexual encounter was the only part he omitted, not being sure how it might be taken after his own experience with Clarissa. He also explained in greater detail what happened with Malkin & Nails and why he had to do what he did, along with his wicked boast to the teenagers to call their bluff.

Clarissa stayed silent through most of it, only asking for minor clarification mainly around Sil's abilities an appearance, as she still hadn't seen her. When Iggy stopped to take a breath, she offered her insight.

"I think your Fenrir girl is a Werewolf. I had my suspicions when I heard about the hunt, but it makes sense."

"W-werewolf? You mean like the fabled monster? Really?" Iggy said as he processed the possibility.

"Yes Citi-boy, you were attacked by a lizard the size of an Alligator and you're currently speaking to a Vampire. I should hope a Werewolf isn't too much of a stretch for your imagination," Clarissa said.

She has a point,

"I just never seen or heard of them outside of scary folk tales, I assumed a wolf monster was just a highly evolved form of mutant," Iggy said.

"No, they aren't mutants, in the same way vampires aren't. We all existed long before the skirmishes," Clarissa said. "But you're right, there haven't been any reliable reports that I heard of either, only rumors and tales. Scarily strong, shifting into beasts at the full moon and all that, that's why she ran out on you Crasher."

"Last night?"

"It was a full moon last night, you said you saw her face change with aggression? She couldn't control the shift under that moonlight so she ran from the car, for your own safety."

Why didn't I notice the moon? She ran out to protect me from her beast form?

Iggy looked over at Sil, the sleeping werewolf girl and quietly thanked her. Before quickly spotting a road sign for Maim-Creek. "We are back on the road, Landlady. I think we can still get there with time to spare. Tell me more about vampires. You said you didn't know any?"

"Fucking finally! Better hope I don't have to dock your pay and uh…well…" Clarissa paused before divulging. "I don't know any **living** vampires but I did have a family. We lived along with some other families. I guess you could say it was like our own nomad convoy, except we traveled less, mainly just to get to a new cave-"

"To stay out of the sunlight?" Iggy interrupted enthusiastically.

"You're a fucking genius, aren't you!?"

"Sorry, carry on."

"My dad told me once the skirmishes started, vampires couldn't blend in with humans because society got militarized and everyone was being watched. So those of us that weren't killed had to flee. A lot of them starved out. Weren't able to find easy blood outside of warzones, and then you were just as likely to be shot or blown up as anyone else," Clarissa said.

"But not you? You don't drink blood and you are still sustained?" Iggy asked.

Clarissa sighed before gearing herself up to respond. "All Vampires are different, some have different abilities, different levels of strength. Mother called it 'the dark gift wrapped in different ways. Our family apparently descended from vampire lords, near immortals who controlled human society in something called the 'Renaissance' period, but I don't know what that is."

"Near immortal? As in can't die?"

"As in incredibly fucking hard to kill, growing back limbs, rising from graves. There was even a rumor some of my ancestors could briefly walk in sunlight. But the biggest gift was being able to survive without blood. They would crave it, but they would never starve as if they were running on something else."

Wow, Clarissa…

"Sounds like you inherited some impressive powers," Iggy said with a dazzled smirk.

"I can't access most of them. I can stay alive without blood, but my body parts don't grow back, my eye is still gone as you saw. I'm not anywhere near as fast as I would be, I can't fly, I'm aging…"

Fly?

"Hold on, **how old** are you?" Iggy asked, not placing her physically any older than forty, but remembering what Grady said about her not looking any different when he met her.

"I'm Eighty-Eight. Did it feel good sticking your cock in a senior vampire citizen?" Clarissa asked with a chuckle.

Eighty-Eight? No way!

"How are you aging? You don't look anywhere near that old!"

"You're too sweet Crasher, but I look a hell of a lot older than I would do if I was drinking. It's just part of abstaining." Clarissa said with her voice dropping into something melancholier.

"But **why** don't you drink? Especially when you could have all those benefits, those powers?"

Clarissa gave a lengthy pause, exhaling before clearing her throat. "I think that's enough questions, Crasher. Just focus on not wasting any more damn time chasing animals through the waste and taking us off course. I need to get some sleep anyway. Daytime is not my active hours."

Iggy sighed with minor frustration of being kept in suspense but did as he was told. He drove quietly while Sil and now Clarissa both slept in his car. Looking out of the window he saw more barren wasteland race by him. Fewer plants and more steel wreckage.

What have you got for me now, Big Waste?

Chapter 15: Limited Dreams

She tried to count back from a thousand this time. She did so quietly, so as not to bother her father upstairs. But when she got to 843, she stopped. This is not something she wanted to do anymore. It was *boring*. This of course made no sense. She can't get *bored*. She wasn't made that way, she was made to complete tasks, no matter how mundane, or simple or dull. But despite the lack of sense, it was still the truth. She wanted to do something else. Anything else. No more counting in the dark.

Her father was upstairs, tinkering. So many parts and components to put together; a complex network of circuitry and mechanisms. It'll take a lifetime to finish to completion, and he barely has the end of his own life left. But it kept him busy, it kept him happy. It gave him purpose. His daughter needed legs, after all.

To Dr Francis Hughes, the Tin-Men are not tools; they are prototypes, blueprints of the future. The idea of making synthetic intelligent machines only for them to be doing the most basic, factory-like jobs known to man, disgusted him. The untapped potential of sentient androids was wasted during the skirmishes and forgotten when it was time to rebuild. Humanity let Dr Hughes down in so many ways, but unlike many other Blights, his response was not to indiscriminately murder every person he laid eyes on. He wanted to *improve* on humanity. Preserve everything good about them while correcting everything awful. For the Doctor, his was the destiny of the artificial, to make it into something humanity *should* be but never *could* be.

His life was reaching its end. He would spend more time sleeping and every morning was more of a struggle to rise than the last. But he had his personal creation, his magnum opus, his daughter. He would make sure she had none of the flaws he had come to hate in people; the cruelty, addictions, bigotry, insecurities, selfishness or *chaos* that humanity inherited. His daughter would be perfect, in his eyes at least.

She lay quietly in his basement, with only a portion of her body attached to her head. A curious but bored mind tried to find ways to pass the time without having to count numbers. Later that afternoon, her father would attach some legs to her torso chassis. He promised he would get around to synthesizing the rest of her skin to make her beautiful. She trusted him, after all, he had gotten this far.

Unable to speak, she would listen to him tell stories in the workshop, mainly about his role in the Skirmishes. How he as a 19-year-old engineering student was drafted into frontline maintenance, fixing sentry guns and fixed view turrets under the constant hail of enemy fire.

He spoke about his first kill. It wasn't an enemy soldier, but a 33-year-old mother of 5 who had been drafted as a grenadier on the southern front. Hughes had to shoot her in the back when she abandoned her post. He was later told that she went insane and wanted to 'quickly run home to check on the babysitter'. He also told his daughter about being caught in the fallout of the 'bright' and the catastrophic effect it had on his body. He told her about his first wife leaving him after his skin began to peel, and his service record being erased around the end of the skirmishes.

Hughes did not tell her about his actions during his time in a Blight outpost. Despite his disdain for humans, he took no pride or pleasure in the things he engaged in over that 30-year period. He didn't want his daughter to think less of him, or worse to think that anything he or the other Blights did were justified. He wanted her to be better than himself, better than everyone.

After working tirelessly on some other body parts, Hughes decided to call it a night, kissing his daughter on the forehead before retiring to his room upstairs. He kept his house in immaculate condition, stepping inside was like entering a time capsule of pre-skirmish suburbia. High-quality steel, mahogany furniture, plastic cutlery, paintings of many famous sports vehicles and preserved castles. Hughes insulated himself from the bleak reality of the Big Waste by maintaining the small house and garden around him to an unheard-of standard-of-beauty.

Once he snuggled himself in his large oak bed, he reached for his reading glasses and cup of cocoa while he turned to page 104 of his favorite graphic novel series; *'City of Maximum'*. After letting his tired body find its 'groove' in the warmest part of the bed it finally started its long countdown to falling into the perfect sleep. But he would be interrupted by his ringing phone. Nearly knocking over his cup of cocoa, he angrily reached for the buzzing device while trying to keep the exploits in the comic book firmly in his mind.

"Yes...hello?"

"Doctor Frank Hughes, sorry to disturb you at this hour, this is Con Rayko from the Athens Export Cargo Delivery Depot."

"Oh, yes. Regarding my package? It didn't arrive this evening..."

"Yes sir, we are sorry to say that your courier; Randall Gainsborough has failed to report back to us, we are assuming the package has been lost."

"Oh my, well that's a shame indeed. No matter, I can make another order to..."

"Doctor Hughes, we at Athens Exports take our customer service very seriously and hold all our employees both freelance and permanent to the highest standard. We have called to inform you that we will be tracking the courier in question down for full recuperation of payment and pending charges of breaking our regulations."

"Well if you think that's necessary…but in regards to my order, can I make another?"

"Sadly, that item was very limited and we ran out of stock earlier today. We will be processing you a full refund along with the first claim to the courier's repossessed property. We feel it's only fair before it is put up for auction."

"Repossessed? Does that mean you have-"?

"Very soon. He is being tracked and our reclaimers are on the way. If he knows the whereabouts of the cargo, we will get the information from him."

Hughes paused before responding, rubbing his hand across his torn face.

"Well…thank you for your diligence, but such measures are not necessary, a simple refund would suffice."

"Not at all Dr. Hughes, you are one of our most cherished customers, we will be in touch once the courier is apprehended."

Hughes thanked them and put down the phone before returning to his book. He briefly considered what it might be like to be caught by a 'reclaimer' and shuddered, before putting the thought out of his head immediately.

"Randall Gainsborough? Hmm.*"*

Chapter 16: Nature's Path

Sil and Clarissa both slept peacefully as the sky went from a deep grey to blood-orange. The sky was clear, and the air was becoming cold. Iggy looked around the Big Waste with a yawn, acknowledging how long the journey really would be before taking a swig of his water canteen. Although the shell-like industrial area he was driving through was fascinating he found himself constantly looking at Sil, initially to check up on her, but quickly to admire how fast she had recovered, her skin was almost completely free of blemishes and a few of her moderate-sized wounds had closed completely in the space of 6 hours. He wanted to feel protective of her, but that instinct came into direct conflict with his awe of her survivability. To think that this legendary werewolf was this hard to kill was equal parts terrifying and remarkable.

"Hmm, the sun is nearly down, Crasher. I can feel my stomach cooling," Clarissa said with a waking groan. Iggy looked out of the window to see the last fraction of the sun begin to tuck itself away behind the horizon. Iggy yawned again a little louder, realizing he would have to rest soon himself.

"I can see a pretty big lake to my right, do you think the water is clean enough to wash in?" Iggy responded while rubbing his eyes.

"We will never know if we drive past it, pull over. I need to get out and stretch my legs anyway."

Steering gently towards the large body of water, Iggy scanned back and forth for any dangerous-looking wildlife while it was still bright enough to do so. After he parked a few dozen feet from the edge of the lake, he was sure to take his revolver and bat with him as he stepped out. Breathing in the cool evening air, he pondered his current situation while finding a seat on the soft earth around the water.

She's back. A legendary werewolf of the waste that incites fear with her name alone. And for some reason she thinks the Blockgain is her home, I still don't even know how she views me. I drive the car so am I a roommate or something? I wonder how she will react to the Landlady when she wakes up, they haven't even seen each other yet.

As if summoned by his thoughts, Sil walked out of the car, stretching her arms. Her now-healthy, but blood-covered skin was bathed in the dark orange of the sunset. It gave Iggy the perfect portrait of his companion; wild, beautiful and always in proximity to violence. Saying no words, she jumped into the water in front of him, covering Iggy with a heavy splash and began to clean herself giddily.
"Ha, you feeling better, Sil?" Iggy asked as he wiped the surprisingly clean tasting water from his face.

"Clear-wet is good! Nishin feels. Sil feels!" Sil said with the happiest tone he had heard her speak, the rough edge to her voice was all but gone.

"You-you were shot with Blue Gecko poison; do you know what that is? I wasn't sure if you were going to make it…"

"Clear-wet is good, saves legs, stop poison. Good for anything."

"You were being hunted when you were in your…wolf form, I had no idea that you were worth such a high bounty. You are going to need to be more careful if they start using more poison to catch you," Iggy warned.

Sil turned over in the water, her clawed hands rubbing her hair with a perky enthusiasm, trying to rid it of all the blood that had crusted into it. She looked up at Iggy with a slightly more serious face.

"Humans...always hunt Fenreer, Sil cannot hide Fenreer in bright moon, so Sil is hunted," Sil explained as best as she could.

Iggy ran a hand through his soaked hair in thought. "You're a werewolf," Iggy said flatly.

Sil locked eyes with Iggy as she submerged herself in the water down to the neck as if to confirm. "So, what are you going to do now? Anywhere there are humans there will be hunters, and the more you escape them the higher the bounty will be. I almost couldn't protect you this morning."

Sil began scrubbing a shoulder with her claws. It looked painful, but her skin was so strong it had the effect of a rough loofah sponge. She looked up at the dark sky as if she barely listened to Iggy's concerns before speaking. "Sil has home, Nishin moves home fast, home will save Sil and Nishin. Nothing else to think about," Sil declared with calm confidence.

Despite her limited vocabulary, she sure has a way with words.

Iggy's rational risk-assessing mind was quickly overpowered by the romantic idea of dashing through the wastes with reckless abandon with nothing but his beautiful werewolf companion and his beloved vehicle. It was so simple but so alluring. It was freedom.

"Nothing else to think about..." Iggy quietly repeated back to her while she dived underwater for more washing.

"She's got a nice body, I can see why you were so desperate to save her now," Clarissa said, emerging from the shadows.

Iggy looked up to see the tall vampire landlady standing over him, her voice was a sneer but her face wore a gentle grin. She was happy to finally be out of the backseat and stretching her legs after a short but pleasant nap.

She sat down next to Iggy near the edge of the lake and removed her duster coat before outstretching her arms with a yawn. Her large breasts rose and fell with her stretch, sitting comfortably in her loose olive-green tank top. Clarissa noticed Iggy noticing and she smirked.

"Do I say 'Good-Morning' or 'Good-Night'?" Iggy scoffed before returning her smile.

"You say 'thank the Waste-Gods we aren't too far behind schedule or the Landlady would have shot me in the face', Crasher."

"We doing good for time? I've been cruising at about 170. Blockgain can do a lot faster but I didn't want to wake either of you."

Clarissa bared her fangs with a wicked grin.

"Wanted me rested and recharged Crasher? Energized?"

She moved her hand over his leg before pulling him in for a deep kiss by his shoulders. Iggy was surprised but had no intention of pulling away from it. Their tongues coiled hungrily until a deep low growling interrupted them. Iggy snapped his head towards the sound to see a freshly-clean, snarling Sil, halfway out of the water with her eyes fixed on Clarissa. Someone she had never seen before now.

"Sil! It's alright, calm down," Iggy said with a slight panic, pulling off of Clarissa and standing up in one motion.

Clarissa held a very confident smirk as she discreetly reached into her duster pocket and grabbed her trusty pistol, pulling the hammer back behind her.

"Enjoy your bath, puppy? How about some lead biscuits?" Clarissa hissed with deadly intent.

"Clarissa, **no!**" Iggy ordered with the most commanding tone he could muster before stepping in between Sil and Clarissa with his palms up.

Clarissa rose to her feet and took a few steps back, her black and gold automatic pistol swaying by her side. Iggy took note of it before walking closer towards Sil, blocking any possible bullet path with his body.

"Sil, this is Clarissa, she was the voice in the backseat, remember? Just before you fell asleep you heard her."

"Rissa...was in house? Rissa **take house?**" Sil growled with growing volume.

"No, she's just traveling with me. I'm taking her somewhere, using the house to move her, yes?" Iggy said.

Sil's pale eyes flicked between Iggy and Clarissa as she processed the information. Her wet body glistened in the evening light, with her heavy breathing lifting her bare chest in a hypnotic rhythm. Iggy had no idea how she would react but her appearance had his heart racing and his vision unfocused, staying calm was impossible.

"Sil hungry. Fish in water," Sil grumbled.

The naked werewolf launched in the air backward from a standing jump to dive back into the lake. Her form perfect upon re-entry into the ravine, followed by a graceful ripple after the splash. Iggy exhaled with relief before turning back to Clarissa, who was still gingerly swinging her designer pistol back and forth. She licked her fangs and stepped towards Iggy.

"Cute. Now, where were we?" she said before clasping her lips around his for another deep lusty kiss.

The recent series of events perplexed Iggy but the sedative-like quality of her powerful tongue made him too weak to question.

Before he knew it, the Landlady was dragging him back to the car, stripping him of his clothes as they frantically kissed while walking.

"I'm going to fuck you into the car floor, Ignition. Hope the suspension can take it," Clarissa teased ravenously.

Iggy responded by gripping her buttocks with a new intensity and used the grapple to guide her into the car from the rear. By the time they scrambled in the front seat, both of their pants were halfway off, exposing the eager lower regions to each other once again.

The Vampire began by running her cold fingers under his shirt, before lifting it up to press her lips against his quivering chest. Iggy gently cupped Clarissa's face in his hands as she made her way to his navel, letting her hefty bosom press into his groin. Iggy lifted her vest off in one motion and let his fiercely hot erection nuzzle itself between her cool breasts.

"You like that, Crasher? Do they feel soft and smooth on you?" Clarissa hummed as she pushed her female flesh around him with each hand.

"Cla...rissa...ah..."

Iggy panted while writhing, rhythmically thrusting upwards, his tip just grazing the chin of his vampiric mistress.

"Careful, daredevil, don't let that go too early," Clarissa said as she slowly pulled herself away from his penis, placing a small kiss on its head before crawling towards him.

"I want you, Landlady...I want you now..." Iggy said as she was preparing his rigid organ for entry, climbing over him excitedly to straddle in the front seat.

Even with Sil back in his life, he was no less attracted to Clarissa. It wasn't just her body; he liked her commanding-but-lurid voice. He liked her long hanging pink hair and her single cat-like eye that seemed to probe him as he spoke to her.

Her advanced age seemed like a poor joke. He cognitively believed her claim but couldn't see an 88-year-old in her neat, appealing face. She certainly didn't fornicate like a senior person either. She wailed in pleasure, gripping her breasts while throwing her head back, mouth wide with vampire fangs on full display. Leaving Iggy to have to trust that she had truly given up on blood while being pinned underneath her.

She was attempting to drain fluids from him in a different sense.

Knowing that her strength was diminished due to abstinence from blood left him to wonder in mild horror how strong she really could be during sex. It was already somewhat painful having her forceful hips slam into his pelvis, and he still got the feeling she was restraining herself a little. But above all else, her skin was still cold, unnaturally cold in the body-heat roasted car that Iggy sweat in. But he had no time to question, he leaned into her long torso to get a mouthful of her breasts while approaching climax.

"Crasher! You're close? Fill me up! Cum inside!" Clarissa gasped in between panting breaths.

Just like before, a really big deal for her...but why?

Iggy had no time to fully contemplate it as his prickly orgasm surged through him, seizing his body viciously as he expelled his heated solution inside of her while groaning with severe pleasure. He managed to look up at her delighted face, past her huge breasts to see her golden pupil dilating. Her open mouth stretched wider than a normal human should be capable of as if she was about to feed.

But once again the strange after effect kicked in. Her hard, cold body began to warm up, slowly, like the roast of a campfire on a chilly night. Her temperature didn't quite match the standard human heat post-coitus, but it was significant enough to be noticed.

"That was a good load, just the kick I needed," Clarissa said while climbing off of Iggy's lap abruptly.

Iggy, too fatigued to pull his pants up, lay in his seat slightly shocked at her dismissive tone and departure from intimacy.

"That really means a lot to you? When guys er...finish inside you?" Iggy asked.

Clarissa smirked while buttoning up her pants, her eye telling a tale of elation and amusement. "Well it wakes me up, decent buzz," she said curtly.

"You mean the sex does? I'm talking about the finishing-inside-you part."

"I'm talking about your spunk, Crasher. It's like a shot of espresso, nice when I wake up," she scoffed.

What the fuck? Espresso?!

Pulling her tank top back on she sat sideways on the passenger seat. Leaning her back against the car window and shaking her head like a concerned teacher, but with a half-cocked grin as if she were in on some clever joke. Iggy finally lifted his pants around his waist, with an expression knowing he wouldn't like what he heard next.

"Ha, I guess you fell asleep last night before I could tell you. Human semen stimulates me when I absorb it. Feels nice too," Clarissa said with a smirk.

"Absorb? Do I even want to know how that works?" Iggy exclaimed, visibly cringing.

"Crasher, I don't drink blood. But Vampires naturally crave all human fluids; tears, sweat, saliva...all of it kicks our hormones into gear, whets our appetites to feed. Blood is the only true sustenance, but there's nothing like a hot human load getting me to feel very alive for a few minutes." Clarissa's eye widened with desire as she spoke.

Which is why she warms up after, it's like she tricks her body into thinking she's feeding.

"So, you're milking me for a quick buzz, what about the...sex?" Iggy uttered, trying to hide his feelings of insecurity.

Clarissa threw her head back and began cackling wildly before forcing herself to stop and finally met Iggy's hurt gaze.

"Oh well, I mean my clit still works if that's what you're asking. You are okay for a *human, I guess...* maybe even above average. I just usually prefer mutants for the because of the size," Clarissa said while running her foot up Iggy's leg. "So, want to go again?"

"**No!**" Iggy shouted while pushing her leg away from him and pulling his jacket back on.

"Squeeze your next fix out of a sperm bank or something! I didn't want this! I wanted...I mean...I thought."

"What?" Clarissa snapped. "You thought I was going to make *my hired driver* my new pet lover? Did you want to take me on a romantic walk through the barren wasteland and hold my hand? Should I pump out a few dhampir kids for you Crasher?"

Iggy was filled with embarrassment, the blood rushing around his head made his face feel itchy with shame. His throat jammed and he could muster no sounds other than a pathetic grumble as Clarissa continued with her lashing rant.

"No wonder you're in **love** with that *Fuck-Puppy* in the water out there. She doesn't have enough of a grasp of human language to tell you anything you don't want to hear. Humans have sex for gratification, you're in no position to bitch when a vampire takes what she wants!" Clarissa said while leaning forward, her face twisting into a cruel sneer. "So, if you can't muster your average dick for a second-round you can either eat me out or fuck off."

Iggy sat there stunned as if he had just been hit in the chest with a shotgun blast, all confidence seeped out of him rapidly like his last breaths from such a wound. His defiant stare transformed into a series of awkward floor glances. With a heavy breath, he opened the door of his car.

"I'll go check on Sil," he muttered quietly before leaving Clarissa in the vehicle. Almost feeling like he wasn't worthy to sit in the Blockgain after what he heard.

Clarissa exhaled and let her feelings of disrespect and irritation leave her. After a few minutes, she grabbed her communicator and tried to call Grady, only to be met with a busy signal. She was slightly concerned that he hadn't called her yet, considering it had been over 7 hours from when she left.

"I hope Cook's boys are behaving themselves…" Clarissa muttered to herself before pulling out a pre-skirmish Cigarillo to smoke.

Back outside Iggy paced around the edge of the lake, watching Sil as she repeatedly dived into the water. Catching a large mutant piranha to eat in two or three bites only to dive back in and catch another.

Iggy's low mood was countered by the simple amusement of Sil throwing discarded piranha bones toward him as a gesture of leftovers. As a dozen mostly devoured fish carcasses collected around his feet, Iggy considered what Clarissa had told him about Sil, and wondered how much truth there was in her words regarding his relationship with her.

Sil has always been honest, I think honesty is all she knows, but what do I know? I've only known her a day.

Sil's lithe but powerful body surged out of the water like a hidden missile, splashing Iggy quite a bit and bringing his thoughts back to the real world swiftly. She held a wriggling predator fish roughly the same length of his barbed wire bat and bit into it, taking a huge chunk out with every chomp.

"Nishin, eat!" she yapped happily while holding the longfish to his face.

Does she expect me to eat it out of her hand? It's raw too…

"Ah no, Sil, I'm not hungry," Iggy lied with his hands up. "But you go ahead. We should get moving again soon though, it's starting to get pretty dark."

Sil engulfed the rest of her fresh catch with three bites before leaving its bones in the pile with the piranha remains. Her eyes locked on to Iggy as she stepped closer towards him and began to sniff around his torso. He didn't even bother recoiling, he was curious.

What now?

In one motion she dropped to her knees and pressed her face into Iggy's crotch, taking larger huffing sniffs, making a curious guttural noise in the process.

"What the hell, Sil?" Iggy said while stepping back. Although he wasn't fully rested, he became hard instantly at the feeling of her hot breath at his groin, combined with the sight of a naked Sil on her knees again. Sil rose to her feet, with her bright eyes peering deep into his.

"Nishin…push?" She asked while tilting her head to glance at the Blockgain Chaser behind them. "Nishin…push with Rissa?"

Iggy felt an immediate invasion of privacy, which was followed very quickly by embarrassment for feeling private at all. He awkwardly pulled back, not being able to muster a clear answer.

What the hell did you expect Ignition? To keep it a secret from both of them in the same car?

Before he could blurt out a non-answer, Sil's face had shifted from a nonchalant gaze to a primal snarl. Her deep growling sounded like a small volcano bubbling up before eruption. Her pale eyes were quickly forming a blood-red outline, and her neck and shoulders were bulging with raw muscle. Iggy wondered if his lack of response angered her, right before realizing she wasn't looking at him, but *behind him*.

Turning around slowly, he heard it before he saw it. A gurgling clicking sound, somehow an even lower pitch than Sil's growl, along with the sloshing slick sound of wet mud. He couldn't see it perfectly clear at night, but he instantly recognized the creature standing only 3 feet from him and Sil.

Krokadilikus...*here?!*

Chapter 17: Food Chains

Standing on its rear legs at 9 feet tall, and covered in midnight black scales, the mutant crocodile **'Krokadilikus'** is one of the most feared predators in the Big Waste. Not only for its ridiculous size and strength, but it's cunning and stealth. Usually moving almost-silently through thick mud and water.

Iggy had seen them from afar once before, being used as obstacles for a swamp-based death run. A hazard for any car that crashed or slowed down too much in the drudge, a fully grown Krokadilikus would rip the doors off any vehicle and snatch the driver in its jaws within seconds. Its eyes shine a medium blue that glows in the dark, and alongside many jagged teeth, its long mouth would hold a long sticky purple tongue. Despite being a warped product of post-skirmish mutation, the massive reptile had a ferociously impressive look, like a work of horrific art, come to life.

So silent. Snuck up on me and Sil, using mud to mask its scent. Clever animal.

The Krok had its eyes fixed on Sil, sizing her up. Although it was literally double her size, it recognized her as a predator, holding still and carefully reading her moves out of savage respect. Iggy was in petrified awe at the living embodiment of wasteland death towering over him, trying to figure out his next action. He was armed, but he knew his nail-bat would be useless against the scaled armor of the Krok. He was tempted to draw his revolver and fire, but at this range, the huge reptile would snap off his head and shoulders before he could pull the trigger. Sil made the decision for them, howling like battle horn before charging right at the black reptile, like a silver cannonball fired at close range.

The impact of the tackle sounded like a small car collision, the explosive super-strength of a werewolf smashing into the thick hide of a mega-predator nearly made Iggy drop his revolver. Circling away with his gun drawn he prepared to back up Sil anyway he could. The Krok violently tangled with Sil in the mud, too close to bite or scratch but strong enough to nullify and counter her attempts to wrestle into a top position. Sil managed to lash out with her claws twice, but only for them to glance off the Krok's tough skin. The combined hissing, barking, growling and gnashing of both predators was enough to scare off any other living creature within 30 feet. Iggy being the lone exception, now locked in place by adrenaline and fear. He tried to aim his heavy gun, but could not get a clear shot at the Krok as it writhed with Sil. He wanted to save her but knew he needed help.

"Clarissa!!!, There's a Krokadilikus out here!!" Iggy screamed at the car.

But there was no response from it. The door didn't open, the light in the car wasn't even on. Iggy wondered if she could hear him with the door closed. Keeping the fight in his view he screamed again while backing closer to the car.

"CLARISSA, KROK!"

"Crasher you fucking idiot! I know that! I was going to sneak up on it!" Clarissa yelled emerging from the shadows with Iggy's recently acquired 2-2 rifle trained on the scuffle.

Iggy gasped, trying to make sense of how she got there without him noticing. Her golden eye glistened with awareness and intimidation at the massive beast.

"Your wailing just is gonna bring the other one over, didn't you know Kroks hunt in pai-**AHHH!**" Clarissa's explanation was cut short as a black tail lashed her from her feet and sent her tumbling towards the lake. It was the thick, scaly appendage of a *second Krokadilikus.*

The smaller, more agile, Krok, that was walking on all fours seemed to jump out of the shadows just like Clarissa. Snapping and hissing wildly in triumph after landing its tremendous attack. Iggy called out to Clarissa again as the predator chased her to where she landed. The now snarling vampire had drawn her pistol and let off two shots before it closed the distance between them. One bullet catching it in the shoulder and causing it to roar in pain before tumbling on top of her. The wounded animal was flailing with what seemed to be a broken limb from the gunshot. Clarissa screamed in rage as she repeatedly pistol-whipped the weakened shoulder with unnerving strength and accuracy, causing the Krok to scream even louder than Sil's howl.

Holy fucking shit Landlady...

Iggy watched with fear and uncertainty as both of his companions wrestled with these rare, dangerous beasts. As a popular derby driver, he had been in the occasional bar fight, but combat outside his car was not his forte. His arm refused to stay steady as he aimed back and forth between Sil and Clarissa's struggles, confused at where or when to fire first.

"Crasher!!! Sil is losing her fight! **Do something!**" Clarissa shouted while slamming the butt of her gun into the beast for the 20th time, while narrowly avoiding it's snapping jaw.

Iggy stepped closer to Sil's brawl to see her indeed getting handled with steadily greater ease by the much larger Krok. The huge monster threw her down multiple times, catching her with wild swipes of its own claws along with blunt strikes from the backhand. Sil was fighting back ferociously but with a clearly diminished amount of speed and strength.

She isn't fully recovered, and that thing is literally twice her size...she...she needs to...

"Hey, Sil! You need to turn into the **Fenrir,** now!" Iggy desperately ordered the werewolf as her face was smacked down by another swipe of the giant

"Need.... time...too...tired," Sil responded with weakened barks.

Iggy yelled out in panic as he watched her recoil under more blows from the Krok, Iggy realized the beast was not trying to kill her quickly. It was trying to dominate the fight. Breaking her will along with her body, as if *it had something to prove.*

"Arrrghhhh!!!" Clarissa screamed as the younger Krok bit down into her shoulder. She was bloodied and gasping for air as she continued to smash with her pistol, too close to the animal to shoot it.

*Do something **Randall**, they are going to die!*

Throwing all caution out of his mind, Iggy grit his teeth and let his instincts take over. Reaching for his barbed bat he dashed towards Sil's opponent and began to swing into the Krok frantically. Beating as hard as he could while spitting and cursing at the beast, his spirited attacks were having almost no effect. Each time the bat made contact with the hide of the beast, it bounced off. It was a similar feeling to hitting an off-road tire, and the Krok continued to thrash Sil, paying no attention to Iggy.

"Look at me when I'm **beating you,** Krok!" Iggy snarled with desperate aggression.

He followed his demand by holstering his revolver and cocking his bat back as far as he could with both arms, (thinking briefly of the blood-toad that he burst with the same swing) as he let loose with all his might aiming for the Krok's face. The wood shattered on impact, with parts of the rusty metal and splintered wood lodging into its mouth and eyes. With a gargled howl of shocked pain, the Krok had finally acknowledged Iggy.

Shoving itself off of the thrashed Sil, the irritated beast turned to face Iggy as he continued to curse and taunt it. The Krok raised to its hind legs and began to tread towards him steadily but deliberately, letting the soft earth beneath it feel the powerful impact of its heavy advance. Its gaping mouth panted hungrily as it scrutinized the human in front of it with its glowing demonic eyes. Iggy threw what was left of his broken bat while skipping backward towards the Blockgain until the moment he was sure the Krok was clear of Sil.

"Sil! **Get up!** Save Clarissa! I'll handle the big one!" Iggy demanded as the big Krok began to pick up speed towards Iggy.

Sil's guttural screech was like the burnout of tires on the citadel asphalt as she lifted herself from the mud in response to Iggy's cries. Fighting her animal instinct to re-engage with the hefty Krok, she turned to see the smaller beast violently overpowering the weakened vampire. Dazed, bloodied and much slower, Sil charged into the fray with a desperate roar, slamming into Clarissa's opponent hard enough to break the snare of its bite. The two women managed to sync their assault on the monster. Stomping, slashing and beating the smaller Krok down, like a mugging victim in a Folsom alleyway. They were both wounded, so their attacks were slower, sloppier, and nastier, taking primal pleasure in returning the pain.

Fuck yeah, girls!

Iggy smiled at the intervention before refocusing on the ten-foot-tall fiend which was chasing him faster than he could retreat. Its face was mostly obscured by the darkness, but Iggy saw the killer intent in its illuminated eyes. Hastily drawing his elephant revolver, Iggy let off a shot at the center of the Krok's chest, hoping to wound, or at least slow it.

The heavy boom of the gun blast startled Iggy's already shaky aim but the target was so big and close it was almost impossible to miss. The lead slug pierced into the thick hide of Krok with a splintering crunch but it didn't hinder its advance at all.

Shrugging off the gunshot wound with a moderate snarl, the bleeding reptile burst into a much higher speed and lunged at Iggy with a clawed fist, knocking him through the air in a half spin before thudding on the hood of his trusty Blockgain and dropping his not-so trusty gun in the process. The dark night was spinning around him. The audio of squelching mud footsteps, superhuman punches and kicks slamming into bodies and combined cries of living creatures fighting only added to his sensory disorientation.

Coming to his senses just in time, Iggy rolled off the hood of the Blockgain to narrowly avoid a half-blind punch from the Krok that left a large dent into the bonnet.

My engine! This thing needs to die!

Roaring with pain and anger Iggy desperately scrambled to his feet and dashed to his car door reaching for the handle only to feel a wet scaly hand clasp around his ankle. He turned to see the half-smiling Krok open its terrifying jaws ready to snap-down on Iggy as he screamed.

Then, a blistering crunch of another bullet slammed into the giant, but this time from its back. Clarissa had found a brief moment to fire the rifle at the larger Krok before the smaller one clocked her again with a lash of its powerful tail. It still very much in the fight and rising to trade blows with the exhausted Sil.

Iggy pulled his ankle free of the recoiling Krok and scrambled into his Blockgain, knowing exactly what to do next. Gunning the ignition, the engine sputtered to life and the headlights illuminated the massive predator in all its terrifying glory. Face mutilated and heavily bleeding, it was still advancing towards Iggy. Now trying to climb on to the hood of the Blockgain, leaving large smears of blood across the paintwork.

Get off my car, Krok.

Iggy activated the roof-mounted harpoon and gas-powered cannon expelled the hook right at the Krok's face. Tearing past the side of its head and ripping off a large chunk of jaw, gums and its already damaged eye. The beast yowled painfully and backed up off of the car. He prepared to run right over the beast when the disfigured Krok howled at an ear-splitting volume that caused Iggy to hold his head in pain.

Breaking into a desperately fast dash away from the car, the Big Krok surged towards its smaller partner's fight with Sil and Clarissa, who, despite their combined assault were running on fumes. Their killer instinct faded with fatigue along with the grim realization that these Kroks were just *too tough* to beat up. Iggy's headlights illuminated the looks of doom on both their faces right before the Big Krok made contact, tackling Sil into the lake with the smaller Krok jumping in right after them.

"NOOO! Clarissa **get her out of there!**" Iggy yelled desperately from his car, gargling blood and tears, as he drove to the edge of the lake before climbing out.

Clarissa shakily aimed at the water with the rifle, only seeing the torrent of splashing and sloshing where the struggle was taking place. With blood streaming down her face she turned to Iggy in desperation.

"I-I c-can't see shit…. I haven't got a shot! I-Is she winning?" Clarissa stuttered with a voice of panic Iggy hadn't heard until now.

Iggy dropped to his knees and wailed in rage slamming his fists into the squishy mud. His mind stabbed him with images of the brutalities being inflicted on Sil under-water.

Clarissa and Iggy both knew that as powerful the Krokadilikus is on land, their savage agility and strength in the marine is unmatched, known to casually hunt and kill schools of sharks solo. Superhuman or not, a wounded and exhausted Sil who wasn't fully recovered was about as unfavorable as could be. Clarissa shook with angry fear, dreading facing two Kroks after they were finished with Sil.

Turning to Iggy with tears streaming from her single eye, she dropped her rifle and walked over to him grabbing his arm.

"Gun the Blockgain, Crasher, we have to get out of here while there is still time!!"

"No way!! She's still in there! We gotta kill tho-"

A bright flash of pain jumped at Iggy's face as Clarissa's palm struck it forcefully.

"She's **dead**! I don't like it any more than you do, but we are throwing our lives away waiting to be killed next. Get in your fucking car!"

Iggy cried long and hard, choking on his own voice and slowly pulling himself to his feet. His vision completely blurred and ears ringing like bomb alarms. His guilt and despair threatening to drag him down further than the deep mud he was in ever could.

Clarissa hoisted Iggy to his feet, trying to ignore the increased sounds of splashing and gargled pain coming from the river which signaled the last frantic signs of life. Quietly thanking the werewolf for bravely fighting alongside her.

Then the sounds stopped, the splashing subsided and the lake was quiet. Clarissa yanked the still sobbing Iggy towards his car door, yelling and cursing him to open it before the resurfacing of the Kroks. But Iggy didn't open the door in time.
Bursting out of the water, the larger Krok's face flew towards him, followed by the second. Clarissa gasped, and Iggy closed his eyes, thinking of Sil.

But there was no biting, no attack, and no danger.

The flying Krok's faces were **severed heads.** They both bounced off the hood of the Blockgain Chaser before rolling harmlessly into the mud. Both with eyes wide with terror, brutally mangled and tongues hanging out of their gaping maws.

Clarissa and Iggy stayed still and silent, trying to process what they saw. Eyes twitching and lips quivered. Then, the water exploded once more, a mini-wave gushed out from the lake and drenched them both completely. The beam of two glowing white eyes cut through the mist of vapor and the howl of a legendary wolf creature followed.

"Fenrir…" Clarissa stated with disbelief.

She did it, she turned!

Standing on her hind legs, the Fenrir seemed much taller than when Iggy saw her running on all fours. Her shoulders looked broader and powerful. Her mane, fangs, and eyes looked majestic as ever. Stepping towards them both she growled under her breath with some half-healed scars of battle becoming more visible in the yellow-white glare from the Blockgain's headlamps. Iggy was paralyzed by fear and happiness as the legendary werewolf approached him, finally rushing towards her with delighted relief.

"Sil! You made it, how di-" Iggy cried with joy before being knocked to the ground by the snarling wolf's shoulder as she charged him with a small nudge. Dropping to all fours over his body she bared her fangs and her glowing white eyes blazed with primal savagery. Iggy heard the familiar click of Clarissa's pistol from the right-hand side of him along with her weak hiss.

"She's gonna kill you, Crasher, she's a wild animal."

"No…wait, if she wanted to kill us, we would have been like those two Kroks before we even saw her, she's not doing anything."

Looking in the face of the snarling wolf, Iggy remained calm and still, showing no signs of fear or aggression. The Fenrir, without changing her primal expression just watched him, completely ignoring Clarissa who still had her gun trained on her. Iggy gulped softly and his mouth fell into an easy smile. The eyes of the wolf narrowed in response.

"Sil, you did it. You saved us," Iggy said tenderly. The Fenrir's growls became louder but higher pitched. The harsh glare became dimmer.

"You're tired Sil, let's go home...let's go **home**." Iggy continued softly.

The Fenrir dropped to her side, flopping next Iggy writhing in the mud back and forth. Her growls became higher and higher until getting closer to her humanoid tone. Clarissa pocketed her pistol and stood over them both in surprise. "She's...changing back, Crasher."

Iggy looked up at the night sky and smiled wide as he lost consciousness, his lack of sleep and exhaustion finally taking its toll.

She always comes back.

Chapter 18: Homebody

The screeching death of the bandits was louder than ever, matched only by their pathetic car being severed by the mighty Blockgain Chaser. This time with their faces clear as day to see. The stretched out dead faces of screaming men who were torn asunder by a vehicle collision hung in view. Joining them was the face of the nomads. The smug, reckless wife and her reluctant husband both torn in two by the Big Waste's most dangerous werewolf.

Laughing, drunk faces of Malkin and Nails, slurping booze and telling stories became crumpled gory meat that joined the others. Finally, two Krokadilikus heads with open mouths and hanging tongues appeared with the rest they began to shift around in dancing motion. As if they were held up as some sort of deranged puppet show. Finally, the face of Randall Gainsborough joined them, a face of clenched teeth and grim determination shifting to one of deathly fear, before corroding into a dry white skull.

All faces then screamed at the top of their lungs.

Iggy awoke to a thick blanket of darkness, eyes straining to make out the world around him. His sense of touch and smell quickly locating him inside his beloved vehicle. But he was in the backseat, and it was *moving*. Iggy scrambled around making panicked sounds until the voice box in front of him crackled on.

"Crasher, shut up. You're fine." Clarissa said bluntly.

Iggy controlled his breathing as his mind fully woke up, bringing with it the sore pain of several bruises and scratches.

"You're driving?! Why am I in the back?!" Iggy asked hotly.

"Because I've got a damn schedule to keep and it's still dark out, you were only out for two hours. Plus, I think Sil wanted the company, she fidgets too much to have her up in the front."

Iggy turned to see Sil in human form with her legs up against the front shutters, completely silent and watching Iggy with unblinking pale eyes.

She's okay!

"W-what exactly happened Clarissa?" Iggy asked with a cooler tone.

"Sil passed out right when you did, after turning back. I don't know how she pulled it off, but considering her injuries and poisoning today I'm surprised she's alive. Any living thing shifting form like that takes so much energy you usually need a day's rest before attempting again." Clarissa explained.

"You seem quite knowledgeable about shapeshifting."

"Well, I used to turn into a vampire bat-thing."

Ah.

"You can drive the Blockgain okay then?"

"The engine is a little choppy but we are on a proper road now so it's smooth, we are probably two-thirds of the way there now."

"Okay, sounds good," Iggy said before turning to Sil to acknowledge her. "Sil, how are you feeling? Did you sleep much?" Iggy asked with concern.

"Sil still tired," she answered flatly.

She was fully naked having lost her poncho. Slowly she shifted her slightly damaged body over Iggy, watching him for a moment before smelling his crotch once again. Iggy didn't recoil this time, realizing she was brought over by his waking erection.

"Nishin...push with Sil?" she purred eagerly while softly running her clawed hands through his hair. The affection she was showing was in much more of a 'human' manner than last time. It seemed as if she was making some sort of effort.

"Hahaha, I forgot to tell you, she was saying your name in her sleep while I was dragging you both in the car. She was having a 'Nishin' dream, so she's gonna need some attention, Crasher," Clarissa chortled.

He felt his gut turn sour at Clarissa's voice, recalling what she said to him after their last session of intercourse.

"You sure she wasn't just telling me what I wanted to hear, Landlady?" Iggy snapped resentfully, not fully reciprocating Sil's advances.

Clarissa sighed over the voice box before responding.

"Listen, Crasher, I can get a little ruthless when I'm buzzing off a human load. I had no intention of belittling you."

"I can take it, Landlady. I didn't want to think I was overstepping with either of you."

"You're not, I don't just fuck every soft-neck who offers you know, I'd never get anything done. You did good back there, I know a lot of mutants and humans alike who would have jumped in their cars and shot away at the first sight of one Krok, let alone two. Sil sees that too, for sure." Clarissa explained.

Iggy felt the soothing reassurance of Clarissa's words wash over him completely, all resentment and insecurity were gone. He gazed over Sil's toned body in the dim light, his concern for her tiredness quickly being erased by his carnal desire for her. Running his hands all over her chest, he firmly gripped her breasts which drew out a very small whimper from her as she leaned into him fully. Pulling her face to his he once again attempted a human kiss. It was a little awkward but her tongue finally found the sensitivity and rhythm to follow Iggy's lead as their mouths enveloped. Iggy pulled away momentarily, acknowledging the voice box.

"Uh Clarissa, you're gonna still drive while we.... well, you know the voice box doesn't have a mute function...." Iggy said sheepishly.

"Why the hell would I mute this? I've been curious to hear you two fuck around! Give Sil what she needs, Crasher. I know what I'm like when I wake up," Clarissa said with a chirpy tone.

Iggy couldn't help but chuckle and turned back to Sil to see the slightest of grins on her face; as if she picked up on the jist of what was being said. "Nishin...did...good," Sil whispered to him before taking Iggy's face into her hands and continuing the kiss, her technique improving every second. Pushing her back against the side window, Iggy realized the enormous loss of strength her body had, easily being able to lay her in the direction he wanted.

She's eager. Hell, I am too. But she's probably running on fumes by just being awake, neither of us has the strength to go all the way, especially not in the way she likes to.

"Sil, lay still, I want to try something okay?" Iggy said softly.

Sil nodded as Iggy arched his back and lowered his face to her waistline, noticing a few light battle scars he began to kiss them gently, a symbolic gesture for saving his life from the Kroks. His kissing became heavier and quicker, planting them on the way down to her hips, and then in the inside of her thighs. Her skin was smooth but strong, Iggy felt he could bite and it wouldn't even leave a mark.

But she was reacting to the sensitive affection small whispers of arousal resounding from her mouth.

As Iggy kissed closer and closer to her lower lips, Sil held her primary instincts back to jump into wild intercourse and surrendered to his lead. She went silent as he parted her hips wider and began to stimulate her more directly. This was completely new to her, but she let Iggy continue with his oral favors. Soft waves of indulgence throbbed through her body when his tongue made contact with her clitoris. Iggy's tongue was soft, and his motions were gentle. Everything Sil knew about sex was being turned upside down, and she was starting to enjoy it.

"Ahhh...Nishin...mouth...nice." she cooed.

Emulating the gentle approach, she placed one of her feet across his back as she spread herself wider, the gentle bumps of the moving car were causing a perfect level of mild vibration for maximum stimulation. Iggy began to turn his licks to laps, kissing to sucking as his confidence grew along with Sil's moans of encouragement. Clarissa had to constantly refocus on the road as the sounds of the cunnilingus and arousal were causing the vampire to stir in her seat. Prickly heat gripping her from her lap as she drove. Iggy was aware of the effect on both of the women and he felt his sexual appetite fill his weakened body full of vigor.

Sil was now crooning at full volume, head back, chest forward and legs fully apart with her hips swirling in the motion set by Iggy's head. Clarissa was panting as her body temperature cooked her alive in the driver's seat, her acute hearing giving her the full blind detail of the carnal acts behind her. Iggy pulled her legs over his shoulders and brought his hands into the mix. One hand to assist his mouth in pleasuring the now-screaming werewolf the other to grip her breasts as her torso shuddered with the approaching climax. Her skin was so strong it was like groping chainmail, but Iggy found some extra sensitivity from her nipple, causing the pitch of her cries to jump an octave as the slow eruption of her orgasm hit her like a flak gun.

"**Aaaaauuughhhhh!!!**" Sil howled ecstatically while gripping Iggy's hair so hard, he feared losing his scalp.

Smiling to himself proudly for his achievement, he leaned over her to her face, bringing it level to his to see her pleasure-soaked expression. Staring deep into her glazed eyes he whispered, "Thank you."

Sil breathed slow as her body began to power down and embrace much-needed sleep. She gripped Iggy's face and gave him the most human, sensual kiss she had attempted thus far. Her eyes fixed on Iggy's shocked eyes and said "Thank...you...Nishin..." before drifting back into slumber.

Before Iggy could fully process her unprecedented human response, the voice box crackled on with Clarissa's panting voice.

"Crasher, if you want one standard of the money from this job, you better eat my pussy like that next time, got it?"

"Of course, Landlady I only aim to please," Iggy said with an easy smile.

I wonder if -next time- will continue on after this job...

BEEEEPzzzzzBEEEPzzzBEEEP!

Iggy's inner thoughts were wrecked by the alarming sound of his communicator ringing. The device was connected to the vehicle and the sound shot through the entire car on the loudspeaker, causing both Iggy and Clarissa to jump but with no reaction from a peacefully sleeping Sil.

Who the hell could this be? Only the Citadel has my signal...

"I think it's Grady, though I don't know why he's calling your car..."

"You gave Grady my car's signal? I'm trying to keep private." Iggy stated in irritation.

"He...we paid for your car's maintenance and all the upgrades including that trusty hook you are starting to love. Plus, I need a back-up form of communication with him on a long journey like this...Hello?" Clarissa responded as she answered the call, exhaling to cool her body down.

The communicator crackled with an unfamiliar voice.

"Am I speaking to Randall Gainsborough?" the voice said. Iggy's gut jumped as his real name was casually uttered by the strange voice. It was a scratchy male voice that spoke with an academic citadel accent.

Iggy leaned into the voice box with morbid curiosity.

"Only a few people know me by that name, and I have no idea who you are," Iggy said sternly.

"Forgive me, I was told you also go by the moniker 'Ignition'? I'm afraid I don't watch the derbies much these days for me to know all of the-"

"You still haven't told me who you are!" Iggy shouted in paranoia.

"Apologies Mister Ignition, my name is Francis Nolan Hughes, I was the one you were delivering cargo to the other night, and I believe you've lost it?"

A broth of hot embarrassment simmered in Iggy's face stirred and mixed by the bumps in the car as Clarissa took the Blockgain over the rugged off-road. Despite putting the cargo delivery and the incident behind him, he acknowledged his failure to do the job assigned to him, the job that he sought out. Nonetheless, he was a fugitive from the citadel and he had no desire to turn himself in, failure or not.

"I apologize, Mr. Hughes, I was attacked by bandits and barely managed to survive. I woke up after being injured and.... the strongbox of your cargo was gone," Iggy explained as respectfully as he could. "I regret not being able to retain it but I'm…not returning to the Citadel."

"It's quite alright, I've been granted a free re-order from the company, and there was no great urgency for the delivery anyway. I've contacted you because there is something, I want to discuss with you, Mr. Ignition. Would you be able to visit me now?" Hughes responded.

"Sorry Frank, Ignition is on another driving job and we've had enough pointless detours already, no offense," Clarissa bluntly parsed.

"Not only that, but you've been in contact with the depot, and you could be leading me into an ambush. I don't really know you, Mr. Hughes." Iggy seconded.

"I understand your concerns, but in this instance, I'm actually trying to lead you away from an ambush."

"Explain!" Clarissa shouted, while her hands gripped the steering wheel with mild panic. Iggy pressed his face up to the shuttered windows, pointlessly trying to listen out for any assailants.

"The Citadel poachers, they already know you're here in this zone, they called me to update that they would be apprehending you soon," Hughes explained with slight urgency.

The poachers?! Now!?

Iggy started breathing quicker, hearing Clarissa's fist slam the dashboard in anger.

"My bounty is only ten..twelve thousand? Why would poachers be after me this far out of zone?" Iggy questioned.

"Mr. Ignition, as of now your Citadel bounty is 224,000 standards, just enough for a lower end poacher to go out of his way," Hughes responded.

"But all he did was lose some damn cargo? That don't add up at all. He could have only jumped six figures by murder, and he ain't killed any Citizens." Clarissa barked with hurried breaths.

"On the contrary, he was recently reported for the murder of **Corey Malkin** and **Abdul 'Nails' Sah**. They were Citadel warehouse workers who moonlit as hunters in Folsom. This was apparently made possible by their floor supervisor, **Joni Penoli**," Hughes revealed. "Nomad witnesses described the vehicle that attacked them as the 'Dark Kill-Car', later confirmed to be *The Blockgain Chaser*."

The car was quiet for a few long seconds apart from the mild rumble of the drive.

Nails and Malkin were from the Citadel? How could I have known?

"So, they've been tracking us since those kills. They know our path?" Clarissa asked, slightly defeated.

"If my timing estimation is correct, you should be approaching some very large jagged rock formations and cliffs. I think they are called the Hangman's Hills? The poachers are waiting for you there." Hughes warned.

With a few sweeps of her eye, Clarissa silently acknowledged the described rocks in the distance. When Iggy heard no protest, he took the claim to be true, watching the sleeping Sil and thinking about how he was going to keep her alive.

"So...we can avoid this ambush by coming your way? How far is it?" Iggy asked, having to wonder Clarissa's reaction to this without seeing her face.

"If the stories I hear about your machine's speed hold true, then it shouldn't take you longer than an hour. Probably less." Hughes said with creeping enthusiasm.

"Why are you doing this? Just to talk to Ignition? Never thought to come to one of his groupie meet-and-greets in the pit?" Clarissa snickered.

"I see he keeps humorous company," Hughes said flatly. "This is in regards to a possible family member: Alana Gainsborough"

Alana? I feel like I heard it before…

"I don't know any family apart from my Grandpappy, Oren Gainsborough," Iggy said sourly.

"Well, then we might both learn something more about the family. I'm sending my home coordinates to your car. I hope you make the right decision." Hughes said before ending the call.

There was a click and then a buzz that faded out against the temperamental bumping of the car. Iggy and Clarissa considered the options to themselves quietly before speaking into the respective voice boxes.

"We will never survive an ambush, Clarissa. Poachers drive **Citadel Interceptors**.
Superchargers, reinforced plates, mounted weapons, deadly gadgets…." Iggy paused as he was haunted by the memory of 2 interceptors chasing down a tuned-up getaway car near the south gates in Athens. It was a horrifically efficient massacre; Iggy had no delusions about their abilities after that.

"With my experience and the Blockgain's specs, my chances against one are about 50/50, but two or more…." Iggy said hesitantly before going silent.

"Okay, we are doing alright for time I guess," Clarissa said calmly. "I better get in the backseat; I don't want to catch the sunrise while driving." She slowed the car to a stop.

After climbing out of the car Iggy saw a few nasty cuts and bruises around the Landlady's arms and shoulders, with a fairly deep one right underneath her chin. She reassured him that while she couldn't grow body parts back while abstaining from blood her vampire healing was still incredibly quick for minor wounds. After sharing a quick full-tongued kiss with him, Clarissa inhaled a warning smell of the backseat, confirming the blood had dried.

Iggy returned to his driver's seat and promptly forgot all the pain and injuries he sustained just a few hours ago. He pressed the gas and felt his Blockgain growl to life beneath him. After hearing the approaching footsteps of what he could have sworn to be a pack of RaidLions, Iggy hit the gas westward leaving the unknown creatures and the Hangman Hills behind him.

Okay, Frank, let's see what you're about...and what you really know about...them.

Chapter 19: Surrogates

The detour led the Blockgain Chaser through a natural road that connected to a thick woodlands area. Trees were rarely seen in the Big Waste and almost never numerously enough to form a forest path like the one Iggy found himself navigating. The soil was firm but smooth, the bark of the trees was a very dark brown, and the leaves ranged from the colors of deep purple to bright red. Iggy had never seen anything like it. He was amazed at how beautiful some parts of the post-skirmish world could be outside of the Citadel.

Iggy described the scenery to Clarissa who took the time to dream about her future outside Folsom. She mentioned to Iggy she may invest in a rural hideout in an area as beautiful as the one he was illustrating. For the next 30 minutes, Iggy, Clarissa and the deeply slumbering Sil felt their most relaxed in the whole journey so far. But as the trees became scarcer and the road more defined Iggy found himself in an area even more alien to him than the last; a pre-skirmish countryside.

Few had seen this much lush grass outside of a pre-skirmish history journal. To popular knowledge, the toxic air of the waste had destroyed or deformed nearly all organic plant-life, so neatly manicured fields of green-yellow, dotted with daisies and bushes seemed impossible to the average Wastelander or Citizen. Clarissa couldn't see the beauty around her but she could smell the air. It was clean and delicious, almost soothing to breathe in, which she and Iggy did in gulps.

"Where are we, Crasher?" Clarissa asked with a voice full of wonder.

Before Iggy could even attempt to describe his current surroundings, the harsh buzz of the communicator ring cut through the relaxing moment. Iggy answered it immediately. "Ah I see you now, your vehicle truly is a marvel, and I'm not even a motor enthusiast. You built her yourself at the Blockgain junkyard in Athens, correct?" asked the voice of Hughes.

"Yes, I did, well mostly...are we in the right place?" Iggy responded.

"Yes, carry along the small road right, you'll see my house. The fields are quite beautiful, aren't they?" Hughes asked.

Clarissa spoke up while Iggy mused on their surroundings, a slight concern in her voice. "Hughes, do you have a garage or shelter for us to park in?"

"Ah yes to block the sunlight, yes I have an old barn you can park at the side which connects to my house, Ms. LaVaye," Hughes said with calm reassurance.

Clarissa almost jumped out of her seat with shock and leaned forward into the voice box curiously. "How the...that's my...**how!?**" she stammered. Iggy turned around in confusion at the unfamiliar name.

"Ahem, Clarissa LaVaye, am I pronouncing it correctly? I know you often go by the 'Landlady' or the 'Fangs of Folsom' but I never found nicknames fitting on a lady," Hughes said with slight amusement.

Before Clarissa had a chance to respond, Iggy told Hughes they would be approaching soon and ended the call. "I don't trust this at all, as wide as my reputation might be. My family name is not public knowledge. Who the hell is this person?" Clarissa asked.

"I don't know, I also don't know how he knew where I built my car, that's not public knowledge either. Everything about this place and this person doesn't sit right with me either. But we have to find out more," Iggy said.

"Ammo check, Crasher. How many rounds do you have left in that hand cannon?" Clarissa asked.

"Uh, three, I think. Yours?" Iggy asked.

"One clip left in my pistol, fifteen, and one in the hole. Rifle has four. This guy sounds pretty old and he sounds like he lives alone but I don't want to take any chances, especially in daylight. Keep your head on a swivel," Clarissa ordered.

"I won't take any chances," Iggy confirmed as he spotted the house which was hidden behind a small hill on a corner.

Much like the surrounding area, the house looked like an ancient oil painting. A moderately sized cottage, hand-built with cream-colored bricks and chocolate brown roof tiles. The structure was surrounded by high grass and a multitude of colorful flowers and vines that Iggy had never seen before. The 'barn' connected to the house was tiny. Iggy struggled to think of what type of animals would be kept inside and for what purpose, as he drove closer to the entrance.

He parked inside the red-brown structure and honked his horn once to announce his arrival. Before he could get a good look at the mostly wooden interior, an automated shutter began to close behind him and the space around the Blockgain was covered in pure darkness. Iggy gulped audibly as he pulled back the hammer on his revolver, hearing the click in chorus with Clarissa doing the same with her own firearms. Once the shutter closed Iggy confirmed they were out of the sun and they both stepped out.

"This is no barn, Crasher. I can't smell the traces of any animal shit. This is a workshop." Clarissa said while scanning the place with her darkness-attuned vision. Iggy turned about a few times, his human vision not being able to make out anything more than shapes and it was frustrating him.

"Is Sil still sleeping?" he asked in a whisper.

"She is, but leave the doors unlocked. If she hears something important enough to wake up, then we will probably need her help," Clarissa whispered back.

After a few more seconds of searching, Clarissa found a door which she assumed led into the house. She turned the knob slowly with the pistol trained on the door only for it to be pulled open for her. With the dim light coming from outside of the room, a shadowy figure appeared in the doorway. The figure raised his hand and waved before flicking a light switch next to him. Illuminating the 'barn' in yellow light. Iggy blinked and Clarissa squinted as the man in front of them came into view.

He was a Blight, typical in every way apart from his clothes. The rotting yellow and green skin on his gaunt face clashed with his high-quality sky-blue shirt and the dark brown sweater vest covering it. He wore academy slacks and beige loafers to complete the outfit. Iggy thought he looked like a zombie professor and wondered if he was ever going to get used to looking at Blights.

"I assure you Miss LaVaye, you don't need a pistol as fine as that to kill someone as fragile as me, you could shove me down these two steps and save a bullet," the Blight said to Clarissa, his rough but eloquent voice confirming him to be Hughes. The vampire lowered her pistol and stood still, unsure of how to respond, as her single eye still scanning the shack around her.

"You wanted to talk to me?" Iggy asked, taking a few steps forward towards Hughes.

"I do, Mr. Gainsborough. There is quite a bit to discuss and I inferred that you are probably limited on time, so please join me in my living room. The windows are quite small and I have thick curtains so Ms. LaVaye won't have to worry about sunlight." Hughes explained.

"Landlady," she said curtly. "Call me Landlady, and then you can tell me how you know my family name."

"Of course, Ms. Landlady. Come through."

The living room was something straight out of a storybook, oak furniture, a few bookshelves, ornate tea sets and large plush armchairs with patterns of deer and birds. With the windows blocked, the main source of light was a few scented candles that smelled like roasted chestnuts and grape juice. As suspicious as Iggy and Clarissa were, it was impossible for them not to feel comfortable.

After taking their places at three separate chairs, Hughes offered them tea which they declined in unison. After pouring himself a cup he took a gentle sip which looked strange to Iggy. A man that looked like a walking corpse with table manners fitting of a central Citi-zen.

"I know we don't have much time, even though I am curious how a former top ten derby racer came to be in the company of the most notorious leaseholder in the Folsom shell," Hughes said calmly with a sip.

"You said you recognized my family name. Who's Alana Gainsborough?" Iggy asked while folding his arms.

"I had someone...who I wrote letters to, you could call them a long-distance sweetheart of sorts." Hughes said as he lowered his ornate teacup. "She wasn't aware of me being a blight so I sacrificed the hope of seeing her in person to keep my...identity a secret." Hughes continued with a melancholy tone.

Iggy's gut pinched with guilt as he considered the reality of being a Blight in the Big Waste. Hughes' pale eyes made contact with Iggy's before taking another, slower sip.

"Like me, she lived 'off the grid' in a house out in one of the south zones...5th, I think. She was a kind lady, a foster mother of sorts. Used to take in runaway children and raise them as her own, even some mutants," he went on.

"So, she looked after mutants but you didn't want her knowing you were a blight?" Clarissa quizzed.

"Different levels of tolerance, Ms. Landlady. Mutants are only really looked down on in Citadels. Blights are hated everywhere, given our...history with humanity," Hughes said while trying to avoid looking at Iggy directly.

"This woman was Alana Gainsborough?" Iggy asked

"Yes, but I only found this out recently. She was going by the name Celia Cors publically, but when she hadn't written back in over a month, I got worried. Against my better judgment, I initiated a background check. Alana was her birth name."

"Background check? You said she was off the grid," Iggy said curiously.

"A lot of blights are ex-military, but for him to be able to pull background check in the present day means he must have been pretty high ranking. That's how you know my family name, right?" Clarissa declared assertively.

Hughes' nightmarish face stretched into a smirk. "Chief Engineer of R&D. If I stayed in the field, I probably would have been a Captain. But that was another century, back when I still had smooth pretty skin like you two," Hughes said with a tone of resentment.

"So, this Alana was hiding her real name? Why did she stop sending letters?" Iggy asked.

"I was hoping you could tell me that. I'm aware of the world we live in and the constant death that persists here, but when the poachers mentioned your surname I wondered if Alana meant anything to you," Hughes said. "Plus, the fact that the poachers are after you for losing some flowers didn't sit right with me."

"Losing some flowers? The cargo-?" Iggy couldn't quite wrap his head around that.

"Yes, sorry. The **sapphire vine** flower, an uncommon plant that Celia used to grow She said the scent made the children feel cozy and at home," Hughes explained whimsically. "So, in addition to having them growing in the garden, she used to make perfumes out of the crushed petals to spray the house with. So, a while after she stopped responding, I wanted to start my own sapphire vine garden, mainly for my daughter."

Those bandits nearly killed me over some fucking flowers?

"Sounds like she was a real saint, but living off the grid with a bunch of runaway kids outside the protection of a Shell or Citadel is a death sentence," Clarissa said bluntly. "Um, no offense Crasher."

"None taken, I never knew her. Could have been a grandmother or an aunt or something. How many did she have living with her?" Iggy asked.

"She spoke of at least a dozen in her letters but there could have been more. Some only stayed a day or a week, but her house was open to all. Which was dangerous of course, but the way she spoke of her home, it was like it had a soothing effect on everyone who came in," Hughes said. "She attributed it to the smell of the flowers. She actually sent me a perfume bottle years ago. The scent is quite potent."

"If this lady had a chemical that could tame runaways it's possible someone would have been trying to get it. Not difficult to see the value in that," Clarissa mused

Rising up from his chair he walked over to a nearby oak drawer, humming to himself as he rummaged through it. Iggy watched as

Hughes pulled out a pear-shaped bottle with a small amount of dark liquid inside it.

"A sample she sent me a year ago, still few drops left," he said while smiling softly, his mind very much on his memories of her.

Hughes sprayed the air around Iggy twice. Clarissa immediately covered her nose and mouth with her forearm in a defensive reflex. Iggy's curiosity led him to lean forward and inhale.

The scent was subtle, dry and fruity. It had the trace of fresh plants that Iggy never would have come in contact within the Citadel, but there was also something oddly familiar in the aroma.

With her face still covered Clarissa questioned Iggy with a muffled, but sarcastic voice. "Does it make you feel all cozy and at home?"

"Maybe if I was twelve," Iggy responded dryly. Hughes couldn't help but chuckle.

"Just based on what she told me in the letters, the scent had mixed results. But it did manage to calm down a shifter, a dangerous one at that," Hughes mentioned while putting the bottle in his breast pocket.

"Shifter?"

"A person that transforms. Celia had a very troubled girl who would turn into a large dog-like creature-"

Hughes paused with the shocked expressions of both of his guest's faces. Iggy's head felt cold and heavy as the scent lingering in the air became slightly more familiar. Clarissa turned to him with a similar look of surprise before looking back at Hughes. Before any of them could question further, the softest set of footsteps entered the living den.

"**Home**...I'm home..." said Sil in a tone of disbelief.

Completely naked and with a glassy stare in her eye, the newly-awoken Sil paced over to the middle of the room seemingly oblivious to everything around her. Hughes almost fell backward in shock before taking a longer look at the young werewolf in his house. He noticed that she was breathing deeply through her nose, smelling the air where he sprayed. His voice croaked with disbelief within seconds of studying her.

"Sylvia? My lord is that **y-**"

There was a sound that started as a loud crack of breaking the glass that ended with a heavy piercing of flesh. A bullet slammed into Hughes' chest violently, causing him to fly backward and crash into his own desk drawer. Multiple more cracking sounds rattled through the room breaking more glass and tearing across the room; grazing limbs of Iggy, Sil, and Clarissa as the latter dived to the floor hastily dragging the others into crouched cover.

"**Shots from the window, Crasher, get your gun!!**" Clarissa barked at the top of her lungs while drawing her own pistol and pointing it at a bleeding Hughes who was slumped and gasping for air.

"Friends of yours, Frank!?"

Frank coughed and sputtered as he tried to talk but no coherent words were coming from him. Iggy scrambled behind one of the sofas pulling Sil with him, trying to peer toward the direction of the bullets only to be met with a hail of broken glass exploding from the window.

"Do you hear that!? Those are *assault rifles!* They're fucking **Poachers!**" Iggy yelled over the hell-storm of gunfire.

Over the chaotic noise, a cold, emotionless voice of authority blared through the room, propelled by an amplifier.

"**Doctor Francis Hughes, you are guilty of aiding and housing a wanted fugitive; Randall Gainsborough. You have 5 seconds to exit the house and surrender...**"

The blaring voice spoke in tandem with the gunfire. Iggy shook his head at Clarissa while clutching one of his bullet-grazed triceps as he saw the bleak reality of the situation.

"Out of zone poachers...they won't take us alive...that demand is just a formality," Iggy stated bleakly.

Clarissa turned to Iggy and Sil with a look of pain mixed with desperation. Her leg had been hit as she dived, but her surging adrenaline was preventing her discovery of any other wounds at that moment. She saw Iggy's shoulder was grazed but Sil was left unscathed.

The most shocking thing for them both was Sil's demeanor. She was quiet and docile, still in a trance with the blank stare that she entered the room with. She was whispering "I'm home" to herself gently in a very soft human voice repeatedly.

Raising her pistol above the cabinet she was ducking behind, Clarissa let off a few shots of blind fire with her pistol out of combat instinct. Iggy covered his ears in terror.

He called her Sylvia?

Hughes fidgeted in pain, slowly twisting himself into a seated position before extending his hand to Iggy. His blood gurgling slowly forming into the audio of speech.

"Rand..al...my daughter...in the...base...ment. Save...my..daughter...she...can..help you."

Mouthfuls of very dark red blood seeped down his fine sweater as he spoke in labored rhythms. His pale blue eyes were clear windows into his fading thoughts; a century and a half of life on playback through his old mind. His extended fist dropped a set of two keys in front of Iggy before slumping backward desperately gasping for his last breaths of air.

Broken plates, shattered wood, wall plaster, and brick fragments rained over all three of them like a monsoon, and the jagged splutter of bullets assaulted their ears as if death itself was banging on their doors.

Clarissa cursed wildly as she raised her hand to fire over the cover, poorly trying to establish some level of offense in the gunfight. Only for a high-velocity bullet to tear into her exposed hand. Grunting in pain she dropped her trusted pistol and clutched her new wound, quickly discovering she was now missing her ring finger. Clarissa scowled at her new deformity and shot a look of panic at Iggy, who could only stare blankly at the grisly injury in horror as he covered his head from the cascading debris.

"**Fuck!** I can't see how many guns are on us! Get Sil up, we gotta fight!" Clarissa shouted at Iggy as a burst of gunfire chewed up a coffee table a few feet away from her.

"S-she's exhausted, I don't even think she knows where she is…" Iggy responded weakly before crawling over to the rapidly-fading Hughes and grasping the bloodstained keys from his hand.

"I'll get your daughter, I promise. But you know Sil, I need to know how!" Iggy demanded over the sound of gunshots.

"Save…my daughter…she…knows…mor-" were Hughes's last words before his breath gave out and his eyes rolled back far into his head.

His torso slumped forward and he didn't move again. Grabbing Iggy's ankle, Clarissa yanked him out of his exposed position and into cover with her. Both of them watched Sil curled up like a gentle baby. She was robbed of all energy from her last two transformations and still in the same daze since smelling the spray.

"I'm gonna get to the basement. I can't shoot anyway. If those really are poachers then we aren't getting out alive without help," Iggy said with hurried breath as he handed Clarissa his revolver.

"Unless he's keeping a Blight mercenary squad or another werewolf in the basement, then that 'help' won't count for shit!" Clarissa snapped back in an angry panic.

At that moment the gunfire stopped. There were faint sounds of clunks and clicks that Clarissa instantly identified as reloading, followed by the careful but deliberate footsteps of a slow flank.

"They aren't talking...must be silent orders through hand signals. Your poachers aren't fucking around..." Clarissa scoffed with a quivering smile. Iggy offered a smile in return before wincing in moderate pain.

"Door to the basement is gonna be in the kitchen, Crasher. I'll have better luck against these softneck soldiers once they are up close. Maybe Sil will find her nerve and join in the fun," Clarissa continued with forced optimism as she reloaded and cocked her pistol.

Iggy nodded slowly. He knew that despite being a vampire, her chances against multiple poachers after being shot in the leg and hand were almost non-existent. He held back tears with the realization that she probably knew it too. He inhaled long and deep before squeezing the keys in his hand in grim determination, before sprinting for the kitchen. He didn't quite have the nerve to look at Sil or Clarissa's face before turning to leave.

With her own pistol in her injured hand and Iggy's much heavier revolver in her 'good' hand. Clarissa propped her arms over a bullet-riddled cabinet that gave her a clear view of the front hallway. Her single eye was darting from the door to Sil to the stump of her missing finger that was bleeding quite heavily and coating her pistol all over.

"Anytime you feel like being a savage werewolf again would be great, Sil," she whispered in a chuckle.

Iggy was crouched low as he entered the kitchen. Despite the bullet holes across the milky pink walls and the various smashed cups and plates on the floor, the room still had a cozy feel to it. With the ever-apparent low chances of survival hanging over his head, he rationalized that this house wouldn't be the worst place to die. After a stabbing pain from his shoulder kicked his mind back into survival mode, he clenched his teeth as he scanned the room for an entrance to the basement.

The faint sounds of flanking footsteps around the outside of the house filled Iggy with dread. He knew that they wouldn't infiltrate the house until they had every exit covered, and Iggy guessed Clarissa's blind fire had the effect of making their entry a little slower with caution which bought them a little bit of time. After taking a crouched step that crunched a small teacup under his boot, he spun his head around in reaction to the noise. Only to find himself facing an open kitchen cabinet that a *draft of air* was whistling from.

Upon a closer look, he saw that the doors of the cabinet did not match the decor of the rest of the room. His gloved hand touched the handle and felt the wind rattling from behind it. As he pulled it open, he felt a gust of air that hit him in the face forcefully like a wave of hope as he realized he found the entrance to the basement. The cabinet was just large enough for an average-sized man to crawl through and the pitch-black darkness made that crawl a very nerve-racking descent further inside. Palming his environment blindly, he felt the studded metal sensation of folding steps which he used to climb downwards, carefully but urgently.

The Vampire was hyper-aware of the beams of morning light piercing through the bullet holes in the curtains, knowing that direct contact with that light could burn her to a crisp. But her main concern was the fact the stump of her severed finger wouldn't stop bleeding. Her supernatural healing ability had the power to seal it in seconds, but during daytime hours she was weak, sluggish and very mortal. Her pink hair was smattered against her face in wild directions, stuck to her temple and cheeks with sweat.

Clarissa was not convinced she would win this fight but refused to die by bleeding out. Holding her breath and bracing all of her nerves she moved her shaking, four-fingered hand towards one of the thinner beams of sunlight. After pushing a discarded tablecloth into her mouth to bite down on, she placed the stump of her finger to the light. Searing, stabbing pain hit Clarissa like a tattoo gun of lit cigarettes. The tablecloth was just thick enough to muffle her agonized screams as the searing sunlight cauterized the wound, burning the blood-flow dry.

She yanked her hand away the moment the stump was sealed and forced herself to pick up her pistol, trying to ignore the smell of her own cooked flesh which was now fairly thick in the air. A single tear pushed from her eye as she shrieked silently into the cloth in her mouth before spitting it out, choosing not to look directly at where her finger once was. She didn't have the nerve to treat her leg in the same way, so she hastily tied the cloth around the bullet wound as tight as she could before retrieving her gun and pointing it at the door.

Iggy's eyes started to adjust to the heavy darkness of the basement as he carefully descended the shrouded steps. From what he could tell the passage was a single person-sized cylinder that had the dark grey sheen of metal. Small slivers of pale green light protruding from underneath his feet as he reached the bottom of the step ladder. The minor illumination was just enough for Iggy to spot the panel of where they keyhole was. Droplets of sweat rained on the back of his hand as he hastily unlocked the floor hatch. There was a loud creak as he pulled it open and his eyes were hit with the harsh green light of the room causing him to stumble. He lost his footing and fell into the basement with a painful crash.

Fortunately for Iggy, it was not a long fall and he landed on his good shoulder. It was forming a regular-sized bruise but with nothing dislocated or broken. A large ceiling light was flooding the area around him with the sickly light green glow that caused his recent accident. It revealed the room, which was something between a crude laboratory and makeshift hospital room. The hot metal scent of power-tools and industrial machinery blanketed a more subtle smell of fresh blood. Clutching the 2nd key on the ring Iggy reigned in his curiosity about the room and resolved to find the daughter of Hughes, with the lingering confusion as to why she would be kept in such a strange room.

A large container was immediately visible under a mess of scattered papers and assorted wires. It was shaped like a bulky coffin with smooth edges with a faded set of characters printed across the lid. It read 'FH-MODE...' with some unrecognizable letters that may have been scratched off. Iggy's chest went tight when he spotted a square panel on the lid which had a keyhole roughly the same size as the one on the hatch.

You really keep your daughter in here, Hughes? In this locked chamber?

Iggy's moderate concern was replaced by cold terror when he heard the hard cracking of gunshots on the ground floor above him.

As Iggy turned the second key on the chamber, there was a series of beeps and flashes coming from around the room. It was as if he set off an alarm during a robbery. The lid of the chamber lifted open automatically, accompanied by the piercing hiss of trapped air. Clouds of white vapor obscured Iggy's vision as he reached for his 2-2 rifle in cautious instinct. Two red lasers of light cut through the mist and locked on to Iggy like a stare before he felt a slender hand reach past him and snatch his rifle away. In a split second, the vapor cleared enough for him to see the barrel of his own gun pointing at his face.

His heart was thumping against his ribs like a battering ram. To say he was off-guard was an understatement. One twitch of the trigger could end everything. But the gunshot didn't come. There were no sounds apart from the fading hiss of the opening chamber, and once Iggy blinked, the owner of the red laser stare and freshly taken rifle came into full view.

A young-looking female, slight of build and completely naked stood before him, holding the rifle at him with one hand. This drew attention to the fact she only *had one hand.* Her left arm was lowered to her side and stopped short at the elbow, with no forearm to speak of. But it wasn't just her arm, she was missing *some of her skin too.*

A portion of her face was that of an attractive young woman, her face shape was perfectly angled like a model from a video ad, with high cheekbones and thin but pouting lips that sat just beneath a pert nose. Dark, straight hair fell just past her shoulders, which had its true color obscured by the green glare of the room they were in. But these features were offset by the fact that roughly 40% of her face and body was missing skin, and revealing the true structure underneath: the metal and clear plastic of 'tin-man' machinery. Iggy discovered that Hughes' 'daughter' wasn't his biological offspring, he had built her.

Still pointing the rifle, her red eyes glowed brighter as her head tilted up and down with her intense gaze as if she was softly 'scanning' Iggy before her lips parted to speak.

"You are not Father, identify yourself," said the female.

Her voice was direct and with a slight hint of a metallic reverb. She had the dialect of an automated voice that could be heard in a high-end Citadel shopping center. It was both comforting and unnerving to Iggy to hear it from the most sophisticated looking human-machine he had ever seen.

"Your father sent me down here! He gave me these keys! Said that you could help us," Iggy half-shouted in panic, dangling the bloody keys visibly.

The daughter glanced at the keys before speaking again, not moving the rifle an inch.

"That's father's blood. Has he been wounded or killed?" she said with no discernable emotion.

"I-I don't know if he's still alive. He was shot by poachers; you can hear them upstairs now. They are going to kill all of us." Iggy said solemnly, forcing himself not to grip his shoulder in pain. He didn't want to make any sudden movements with a gun trained on him.

"Father wanted me to ensure your survival?"

"He...he said you could help, we are all out of options for survival," Iggy said.

The 'daughter' paused, before dropping her head slightly to examine her own body.

"Father attached my legs this morning, but I'm still incomplete." She said as he raised her missing arm to examine it. "I can kill. Let's engage them," she said with the slightest hint of enthusiasm in her cold voice.

She finally lowered the rifle but did not return it, choosing to rest it across her shoulder instead.

Guess it's hers now. She didn't take much convincing though.

"You're gonna help us fight them? Just like that?"

"Just...like that," she confirmed before taking a few steps back and looking straight at the ceiling hatch that Iggy fell through. "No more counting..." she continued quietly.

With no warning, she ran straight at Iggy with unbelievable acceleration. He instinctively raised his arms only to have her leap vertically towards him, high enough to step off his shoulder and further launch herself upwards 10 feet through the hatch as if gravity didn't apply to her. Iggy noted how light she was as she jumped from him. It was as if her body was hollow. She didn't even make a sound as she landed.

Guess her new legs work just fine, now how am I gonna get back up there?

"Don't hurt the Vampire or Werewolf! They are on our side!"
Iggy shouted as he searched for a way to climb back up the ceiling passage to the ground floor.

He heard the light patter of her metal and flesh feet as she scrambled up the ladder, Iggy knew it was up to her now.

Chapter 20: Artificiality

"No more counting, I'm finally living. Take human life to preserve humanity. Father knew best."

Her legs thrust her vertically up the ladder through the passageway. She moved with such force and balance that she didn't need to touch the grip the rungs with her single hand (which was firmly holding the 2-2 rifle by the barrel). The red glow of her eyes switched to green as she scanned the ground floor above her, attempting to get a position on all the living things before entry.

Clarissa cursed and spat at the two poachers who burst in through the front door as she blasted at them with double-fisted firepower. They were dressed like Desert Military – adorned in beige combat boots, pants and infantry jackets that matched their camouflage skin assault rifles. Their faces were covered with thick tactical goggles and dark brown bandannas. They were trained well, firing back in short controlled bursts at their vampire opponent, steadily pushing forward through the living room, making use of suppressing fire to cover each other's advance.

Clarissa's superhuman abilities were keeping her alive, allowing her to react and move quicker to avoid being caught out of position as she retreated. She was being especially careful to dodge all rays of sunlight that were beaming in through fresh bullet holes in the front wall.

Clarissa could hear other poachers circling the house. She was too disoriented to estimate the number. She noticed that Sil still had not moved from her original spot and the poachers were getting dangerously close to her. The dazed werewolf was becoming more aware of her surroundings but was still unfocused, not to mention exhausted.

The closest Poacher popped out of cover and fired at Clarissa as she ran behind a brick pillar, narrowly missing her head by inches. Wiping her sweat and blood-drenched Mohawk from her face with her wrist, she let off a few rounds of blind fire with her nearly empty pistol. Clarissa snarled with weak frustration as more bullets drilled the environment around her position. She knew she had enough bullets in both guns for one more quick volley of gunfire before she was out. Her mind was in the biggest tug of war with her spirit, between the acceptance and defiance of death. She took a deep sober breath, knowing it could be her last.

"Sil! Get up and fight! They are gonna take our home!" Clarissa ordered with fury as she let loose with both guns, blasting at the location of the poachers who were now aware of another hostile in the room.

Sil's ears finally picked up, and she pulled herself to her feet. "Rissa's...home...Nishin's home...**our home!"** Sil roared mightily and leaped from her crouched position bearing claws at the poachers.

Sil slammed one to the ground. The second turned his gun on her. Clarissa's final revolver round tore through his arm, knocking him to the floor and sending his rifle flying. The rifle skidded across the torn carpet and landed underneath a thick beam of sunlight.

"FUCK!" Clarissa shouted as she ran back into the room towards the downed poacher. A hail of bullets punched through the front wall from outside. She stumbled back as more sunlight filled the room and blocked her path to the poacher's end of the room completely.

Sil fought the poacher she pounced on with spirit and grit, but was so fatigued she could barely land a slash with her claws. Her swings were sluggish, her strength gone. The combat-trained poacher was able to block most of her attacks before driving a hard counter-punch into her chin, followed by a lifting knee to the gut. Sil's hard skin absorbed most of the damage, but her lack of balance caused her to stagger from the blows, giving the poacher time to aim his rifle at her head.

A new gunshot sound jolted Clarissa to her bones as she turned to witnessed the red explosion of a bullet-popped skull. The Poacher's headless torso fell to the floor beside blood-soaked Sil, arms still flailing wildly without any follow-up messages from the now missing brain. The android daughter had demonstrated the power of the 2-2 rifle on a human head, with one-handed aim.

Before Sil or Clarissa could react, the remaining poacher dove for his weapon upon hearing the gunshot and fired on the daughter from a prone position. She was already moving in a running jump. Launching herself so high in the air she was able to push herself off the ceiling to dive-bomb at her new opponent at a cutting angle avoiding all gunfire in dramatic fashion.

Clarissa's open-mouthed stare told the tale of someone who had never seen a diving tackle performed before, and certainly not by a naked half metal girl at that. Though her descent was swift, the impact was light. The daughter's agility was balanced with her almost weightless frame which wasn't powerful enough to disarm the rising poacher, who was able to shove her to the floor before training his sights on her to shoot.

Sil intervened with a hard swipe of her claws behind his knee, almost severing the leg with one swipe. The first audible scream was heard from the poacher, gruff and raspy as he hit the floor once again, and cut short when the lithe android sank a broken shard of one of the ceramic plates into his neck. Sil and Clarissa stared in awe at the mysterious female who had just eliminated two poachers in front of them. The daughter's gaze fell on the now very dead body of her father which she quietly acknowledged before turning between Sil and Clarissa.

"There are hostiles remaining, chances of survival for you are both slim," she said coldly.

Clarissa scowled at the tone, trying to hide her exhale of relief. "Speak for yourself, Tin-Girl," Clarissa scoffed as she eyed the smoking rifle. "But how did you get that gun?"

"I took it off him."

"By force?" Clarissa demanded.

"He offered almost no resistance," the daughter said coolly.

Clarissa balled her fists, stepping into the room but still well away from the sunlight. "Y-you...couldn't! he was wounded...he was…"

"Nishin!" Sil barked over Clarissa, motioning towards the kitchen.

Iggy hoisted himself out of the hidden cabinet, clutching his shoulder as he slowly found the floor under his feet. His eyes widened at the sight of the poacher corpses on the ground, before turning back to the daughter.

"You could have helped me out of there you know! Stacking those boxes to reach the exit took too long!" He complained as he simultaneously acknowledged that Sil and Clarissa were still alive.

"This is his daughter? She don't look like a Blightspawn to me," Clarissa snapped at Iggy.

The daughter ignored the comment and removed the jacket from the headless poacher before pulling it on. Iggy wasn't sure if she felt modesty for her nudity or it was strictly practical.

Sil slowly rose to her feet sniffing the air wildly around the daughter as Iggy picked up the two assault rifles, throwing one to Clarissa.

"Metal Girl...push Nishin?" Sil asked with a raspy grumble, followed by a loud chuckle from Clarissa as she cocked her new gun.

"No Sil, I just woke her up to help-"

Iggy's bashful explanation was cut short by a large explosion on the kitchen wall. Bricks, plaster, and dust propelled into the living room like a frag grenade, followed by a number of thumping footsteps and muffled yelling. The daughter saw straight through the dust and yanked a stunned Iggy into cover by the pillar before the gunfire filled the room.

"We need to get to the car now!" Iggy screamed as the group shuffled through the doorway into the garage. Sil paused with hesitation, sniffing around the house one last time before darting after them, narrowly avoiding the poacher's aim on her way out.

"I count 3 hostiles inside father's house, but I can't detect the remaining number outside." the daughter said calmly as Iggy opened the Blockgain, shuffling Clarissa into the backseat.

"They hunt in groups of 4, and I doubt they'd send more than two teams after me and Hughes. With the two you killed in the house there should be three outside," Iggy deduced as he waved Sil over, who scrambled in the backseat with Clarissa, who embraced her warmly as she entered.

"Nice arithmetic, Crasher, no better foreplay for a tin-girl than mathematics." Clarissa snarked, masking her physical pain with humor.

Ignoring the vampire, Iggy handed the other assault rifle to the android before climbing into the Blockgain with her and gunning the engine, just as the poachers burst in the garage, firing on the car.

"**HOLD ON!**" Iggy screamed as the Blockgain roared to life, exploding into acceleration which launched it through the garage door and out into the green hills. Clarissa held Sil tightly as she heard stray bullets slamming into the car, hoping that none of them would punch through the sun blockers that were keeping her from being incinerated by the daylight. Iggy swerved the Blockgain round a grassy knoll and back on the forest path he entered, hoping to lose the poachers but still get back on track to Maim Creek.

Chapter 21: Help Wanted

The thick canopy of the forest created a dazzling natural light show. Fractions of sunlight cut through the heavy network of leaves that partially lit the path to Iggy's escape as he swallowed large gulps of delicious tree-fresh oxygen, in mild disbelief that he survived an encounter with multiple citadel poachers. Beside him, the android daughter was attempting to reload the assault rifle with a spare mag that she pulled from the pocket of the poacher jacket she was wearing, though it was a somewhat difficult task with only one hand.

"Crasher! Are we out of there? I can't hear any more gunshots," Clarissa said into the voice box, once again blind to the world outside of the backseat.

"Yeah, I'm heading back through the original path through to Maim Creek, whatever ambush was waiting there came straight to the Hughes' house. I'm gonna cut through the mountains, we still got 3 hours," Iggy responded as the Blockgain shook with turbulence over the dirt terrain.

"You and Sil are lucky this job is nearly over. You gonna fuck around and get me killed with that bounty," Clarissa grumbled.

"I had no idea about Malkin and Nails, never thought citizens would be living a double life in a shell," Iggy protested.

"But if you did know, would it have made any difference? Would they still be alive?" Clarissa asked pointedly while stroking Sil's rough hair.

Iggy's mind played back the grisly result of his rescue. His stomach turned with guilt and horror of his capability to end lives with his vehicle. "They gave me no choice. They chose to hunt Sil, so I got involved," Iggy said with steel cold conviction. Sil was dipping in and out of consciousness, but she was still aware that Iggy's tone was serious.

The daughter slapped in the new magazine and cocked the rifle before resting it across her lap. Her head turned towards Iggy mechanically as he drove, her eyes focused but vacant, glowing the softest hue of green.

"You're Randall Gainsborough, twenty-seven years old, born in Athens. Human. Considered extremely dangerous operating a vehicle," the daughter stated as if she was reading a dossier.

"That sounds like my citadel Wanted Record," Iggy said nonchalantly. "What should we call you then?" Iggy asked as he glanced at her flesh and mechanical patchwork body.

The daughter's eyes lost their green tinge as she moved her empty gaze from Iggy's face to her handless arm as if she was trying to make sense of her own existence. "Father was going to tell me a name when I was complete. But I saw no label before leaving."

"The name on your container said FH-MODE with the rest of the letters scratched off, any idea wha-" Iggy began.

"Francis Hughes Model 1.0," she said, cutting him off. "But 'Mode' will suffice if you prefer."

Iggy shrugged as she ultimately named herself, thinking that it kind of suited her. When he took the 2nd glance, he began to appreciate her unusual beauty. Despite one half of her face being a dark grey metal that contrasted with the fleshy color of her skin on the rest of it, she was still striking, like a piece of chaotic art. The fact that her legs were mismatched based on the amount of metal and skin covering the surface didn't make them any less shapely or appealing to Iggy's eyes.

"Hey Tin-Girl, scan me. I want to see what my public files say." Clarissa asked from the voice box with noticeable snark.

"Clarissa LaVaye, Eighty-Nine years old, Birthplace unknown. Vampire. Armed and extremely dangerous. High authority in the shell of Folsom. Closely associated with the Cook syndicate." Mode said succinctly.

"Not bad! Birthplace was a long-shot though, I don't even know where I was born," Clarissa said with an audible clap

"I thought you said you were 88," Iggy asked curiously.

"Well my birthday was coming up sometime this week, hell it might even be today," she said with a snicker.

Mode's brow furrowed slightly as she turned around to look at the backseat as if she was trying to look right through it.

"What's wrong?" Iggy asked.

"No public files, accessing classified missing person's report…" Mode stated before pausing, leaving both Iggy and Clarissa in bemused suspense. "Sylvia, twenty-five years old. Birthplace Unknown. Werewolf. Also known as the Fenrir, exceptionally lethal. Avoid at all costs."

"Missing person's report? You mean that Sylvi- uh Sil leaving home was unexpected?" Iggy asked.

Mode turned back to Iggy, her disturbing gaze holding for a few too many seconds while she was silent as if she was processing some extra information. "I have no more information on her, Randall. In my incomplete state, I have limited access to data. How did she come into your capture?"

"Capture? No, Sil just sort of...found me. She feels at home in this vehicle so...she travels along I guess," Iggy said.

"Don't leave out all the hot sex you have with her, Crasher. I'm sure Tin-Girl's database logs all the details," Clarissa snorted.

"I..well...she..." Iggy stuttered.

"Yes, you've been having sexual intercourse with both the Werewolf and Vampire, I detected multiple traces of your semen on their bodies on-encounter."

"Hey...that's...oh god really?" Iggy said with a hot face.

"Guess I didn't absorb all of it!" Clarissa chortled.

"Father's programming left me with very little information on human relationships outside of established traditions. Do you plan to marry them both?"

This fucking conversation!

Clarissa's mocking laughter filled the entire car as Iggy's face swelled with embarrassment. "Sorry Crasher, I no longer have the finger for your wedding ring! But Sil could double up as a wife and the family dog, what do you think?"

"I... I think with any luck we can still get to Maim Creek on time, now that we are out of that forest, how is she anyway?"

Iggy felt he had to change the conversation, he had no desire to reveal his recent feelings about Sil **or** Clarissa to his new mechanical guest. "She's sleeping again, I think those last two 'shifts' really took

it out of her. She looked almost human back at the house…"
Clarissa paused, her jaw audibly clenched in pain and frustration.
"Fuckin' poachers, shooting off my damn finger. When this deal is
done, I don't want to even look at guns for another decade. "

The reminder of why they were traveling soothed Iggy's mind. She
never explicitly said it, but he quietly hoped that whatever plans
Clarissa had for the future, he would be able to keep in contact with
her. Her version of freedom had become a part of his.

"So, Mode, what happens now? I mean I'm sure you're upset about
your dad…" Iggy tried to say sensitively.

"I do not feel any sadness, Father was very clear that life in this world
is fragile and finite and that his was coming to an end. His existence
and words are all stored in my memory, clear as when he was living,"
Mode said.

Iggy took his eyes off the road to gaze at Mode as she spoke, trying
to pick up on anything distinctly human about her responses. The
organic parts of her face all moved naturally, but there was something
deeply unnerving about the way it would drop back into 'neutral'
expression after every sentence. Iggy wondered if she was truly
sentient or if she was just programmed sophisticatedly enough to
appear that way. Iggy had gotten used to being looked at with primal
desire and curiosity by Sil and underlying admiration from Clarissa.
But with Mode, she simply stared right through him.

"He didn't get a chance to tell me much about you," Iggy said while
pulling into a gentle curve on the road to the mountains. "I'm not
really sure what his plans were for you."

"He told me to live life, understand humanity and improve on it in
every way possible. I'm not sure how to complete that task, but I will
start by finishing my own construction," Mode said.

With the amount that she knows I shouldn't be surprised.

"Back at the lab?" Iggy asked.

"Preferably, but I could start anywhere with a workbench and key parts. Some are back at home, others need to be located," she said blankly.

"Sounds like a job, Tin Girl. He's still working for me so get in line," Clarissa interjected.

"Your assistance would be most welcome, Randall, though I have no money to pay you," Mode said with a more conversational variation of her cold tone.

"Okay, well just help keep us all alive while we get to our destination and then I'll think of something afterward," Iggy said with uncertainty.

"I will continue to guard you," she stated firmly.

A Werewolf, Vampire and an Android, you couldn't make this stuff up.

In Sil, he saw a wild passionate creature. A genius of the big waste, but curious and naive to the rest of society. Clarissa was a world-weary powerful specimen of deadly intellect and ruthless actions with a small but noticeable side of insecurity. Mode seemed to almost a hybrid of the two, as new to the world as a child but an archive's worth of data. He didn't think about it consciously, but Iggy wanted to get closer to her. He was once again intrigued.

As the Blockgain approached speeds of 180 MPH the jagged hills of Maim Creek became more visible. Small but vicious-looking mountains made of red and black rocks sat across the horizon in an intimidating fashion. The late morning sky was painted a dark orange and the air was bitter and rough like a discarded ashtray. The big waste was warning the weak away from here, but Iggy had come too far, he had no choice.

Holding a sleeve over his mouth to cough heavily as his throat adjusted to the new air, he began to hear the engine volume increase notably. As he leaned into his dashboard, he realized that it wasn't *his* engine making the added noise, but something else in the vicinity. Sil was asleep to the world but Clarissa and Mode picked up on it immediately, with the android lifting the assault rifle and turning to peer out of the window, being able to see perfectly in the light grey haze of the atmosphere.

"A poacher vehicle is pursuing us, Randall. How do you wish to approach combat?" Mode asked calmly.

No, no, no. I can't fight an Interceptor now! How long have they been following us?

Iggy's hand trembled as he spotted the large sand-colored battle vehicle closing in on him. It was more tank than car; six heavy-duty wheels and thick angled armor plating around the body and hood. Long serrated ramming spikes sticking out from the front of the grille and twin grenade launchers were affixed to either side of the hood.

Iggy's body went cold. His fearful mind brought him deadly premonitions of the mangled steel and burned chassis of his Blockgain Chaser. Turning to Mode and speaking into the voice box, he yelled in a hoarse and desperate tone. "I'm gonna try and outrun it, but I'm not sure if I can! Hold on to the safety bars and Sil, Clarissa. Mode, you ready to shoot if they get close?"

The android nodded calmly, aiming her weapon at the car window. "Good luck Randall," she said in her fixed tone.

The whooshing blast of the Blockgain's boosters screamed across the Hangman's Hills, reaching speeds of over 200 MPH. The interceptor was only slightly slower, not having a boost function but a mighty engine that let it keep Iggy's vehicle in front of it as they tore past a blur of wrecked infrastructure. The Poachers inside the interceptor didn't speak, even out of the view of the public they would stay in silent focus determined to see their 'poach' through to the end. Their training made them like machines, personality and conversation were taught as an obstacle to efficiency.

The rushing world around them was now one of populated society, with mostly-intact highways weaved around the hills. Medium-sized buildings housed gang hideouts and powder dens. Mutant run open markets littered the road-sides and nomad vehicles made up sparse traffic on the wide tarmac. A pre-skirmish billboard was heavily adorned in graffiti, with 'WELCOME TO MAIM CREEK BITCHES' scrawled in hot pink obnoxiously.

Iggy's heart was hammering through his chest, he was so close. But despite his highly skilled evasive driving, the interceptor was hot on his tail, trying to line up for a shot. Iggy was ignorant of most weapons but even he knew a citadel-crafted grenade launcher could turn his muscle car into a fireball.

"Just hit Maim Creek, Landlady! Now we just gotta shake this poacher!"

Clarissa once again gripped Sil and the safety bars inside the backseat as Iggy tightly drifted towards a dirt road that lead into a natural scrap yard. Seeing it as the only chance to outmaneuver their dangerous pursuers.

Huge remnants of pre-skirmish machinery lay half-buried in the landscape. The rusted remains of large aircraft made up most of the ancient debris, creating somewhat of a natural maze for the vehicles navigating the area. Iggy felt his own hot breath blazing over his knuckles, as he gripped the steering wheel in desperate survival. Mode looked over to him calmly and laid the assault rifle in her lap.

"The armor of the interceptor would repel all gunfire from this weapon with relative ease. On the contrary, the Blockgain Chaser will not survive a direct hit from the grenade launcher. What is your plan, Randall?" Mode asked.

"I'm still figuring that out, Mode. Just hang on!" Iggy barked through clenched teeth as he whipped the car around a partial jumbo jet wing.

Mode nodded, and placed her hand on a safety bar as her head moved left and right as if she was scanning everything around them.

It looked unnatural like some sort of wind up doll, but Iggy was grateful for any support he could get in this chase.

Approaching top speeds, Iggy steered through as many tight junctions of debris as he could. His expert driving narrowly keeping him from any nasty collisions with the large heaps of scrap that seemed to go on for miles.

A lot of planes were downed during the skirmishes here, or was it something else?

Despite the hasty but skilled maneuvers, the interceptor never seemed to be more than one corner behind the Blockgain. The interceptor was an S-Class vehicle with unparalleled acceleration and grip. The six tires were also fitted specifically for the terrain of the zone, unlike the 'all-purpose' tires that were currently on the Blockgain. Only Iggy's laser-sharp steering was keeping him out of the grenade launcher crosshairs.

Iggy cursed audibly as he saw the beige half-tank swerve around every corner in pursuit of him, not seeming to lose any speed. Iggy heavily considered using another boost but was not confident he could maintain the Blockgain's agility once pushing it past 200 MPH again. After cutting a hard 90-degree turn at a rusted jet engine, the voice box crackled on.

"I can hear how fuckin' close they are! Tell me you've got a plan, Crasher."

The plan is to not get my vehicle blown up. Man, they're fast!

"This scrap yard is a maze to drive through, they'll make a mista-"

The thundering blast of an explosion ripped through Iggy's sentence and the impact was so close it busted the window glass on the passenger side, a wave of fiery light and burning heat assaulted Iggy's senses before dissipating. Mode didn't move an inch.

"**SHIT!** Did they hit us?!" Iggy screamed as he refocused his eyes just in time to swerve around a fuel canister the size of a truck.

"Interceptor's weapon was an indirect hit. Damage moderate, mostly to the exterior." Mode said unflinchingly, overlapping with Clarissa's cursing from the voice box mixed with Sil's waking barks.

"Nishin! Move home faster! Home can't be **hurt!**" Sil demanded from the voice box.

The Blockgain fishtailed slightly, but Iggy was able to steady the vehicle immediately. The Derbies condition drivers to stay focused and keep the car's level right after impact, and that conditioning kept Iggy alive once again. His head throbbed as he tried to filter the voices of his companions to focus on his enemy. Glancing at the side mirror, he saw that the interceptor was fishtailing dramatically trying to regain control and trailing much further behind him.

That's it! I knew it!

Tapping lightly on the brakes, Iggy slowed himself down, bringing himself in line with the recently stabilized interceptor. Iggy clenched his teeth and bared a wild grin as he kept turning to the side mirror and checking the open paths in front of him.

"Crasher, are you fuckin' slowing down? Did they damage the engine?" Clarissa asked in a panic.

"Negative Clarissa, the engine is operational, Randall is decreasing speed **manually,**" Mode responded.

Iggy glanced at the unfazed android and winked at her, still holding his crazed smile. "Postpone your **fucking suicide,** Crasher, and hit that pedal before they get off another shot!"

Just as Clarissa shouted the 'Ka-thunk' sound of another explosive round being loaded was heard from the pursuing vehicle. Iggy held his breath and felt the tickling crawl of a sweat bead making its way down his cheek. He then pulled the steering wheel ever so slightly to veer his vehicle leftwards in the fairly wide lane the cars were on.

That's right, blow me up. I'm right here...

The boom of the grenade launcher was heard and the round exploded very close to the Blockgain once again. But this time Iggy reacted with automatic speed, yanking the handbrake and over-steering into a hard drift around a massive jet propeller on his left. Despite his ears ringing and his vision flashing, he maintained the perfect drift and weaved the Blockgain round the back of the rusted debris to emerge *behind* the interceptor. The powerful machine was spinning out of control, wildly propelled into the rotation from the recoil of its own weapon after firing from an angle.

"Yeah! **Fuck you, Poachers!** Everyone, brace yourselves!**"**

Just as the armored machine began to counter-steer out it's spiral, Iggy had already lined up and saw his opening. He smashed the boost button and the Blockgain Chaser launched into the Interceptor, charging it from the side during its backspin. The sound was thunderous. Between the blistering engines, screaming passengers and the high-speed collision of metal it could have been mistaken for a demolition project.

Crushed by the impact of the Blockgain's mighty charge, the half-crumpled Interceptor skidded over to a busted plane cockpit. The poacher's bodies inside were bloody wrecks, with only one twitching slightly. Iggy's world around him was spinning from the impact, but his chest rose and fell with the breath of pride. For he had just taken on a *Citadel Interceptor* and won. Tingling with elation, Iggy began to chuckle as he the gash on his head from the previous collision re-opened and blood trickled down his face.

"I don't think I'm gonna get used to this derby shit any time soon, Crasher... congrats on whatever nuts plan you had apparently working though," Clarissa spoke between heavy panting.

"Nishin, save house?!" Sil followed.

"I think they're dead, that interceptor looks like a beer can..." Iggy said while hitting the ignition trying to re-start the engine. "The Blockgain is pretty banged up too though."

Mode, who was completely unscathed and unnerved leaned forward curiously as her eyes began to glow green once again. "One of the poachers remains alive. Remo Ferguson age 35 born in-"

"Mode! Hurry up and kill him! He's still dangerous!" Iggy ordered while turning the ignition with more tenacity, still failing to start the engine.

"Affirmative Randall," Mode said as she rolled down the busted window, attempting to aim the large rifle with her single hand.

Mode pulled the trigger and high caliber rounds slammed into the front of the interceptor, blocked by the plating and missing the small window. The heavily injured poacher slumped in his seat to take cover behind the dashboard. Mode attempted another burst of fire, this time the recoil pushing the shots over the top of the vehicle, missing wildly. Iggy saw that despite her impressive physical feats, she wasn't strong enough to shoot straight at this distance with a two-handed gun using only one of her own. As soon as Mode's 2nd burst ended Iggy heard the 'Ka-thunk' of the interceptor's grenade launcher loading.

"No!! Fucking start!"

Twisting the ignition key with all of his might, Iggy cursed as the engine spluttered faintly, churning but not activating. Mode began firing at the Interceptor again, with no more accuracy than the first time. Iggy's derby instincts were screaming at him to bail out of the car, but knowing that Clarissa and by proxy, Sil couldn't leave the backseat. He held in his seat firm, gnashing his teeth as he punched the dashboard in rage while turning the key desperately.

"COME ON!!"

Clarissa and Sil both began to speak but the rupture of a deep explosion viciously canceled the commotion, a bright light blinded Iggy and the approaching heat was unbearable until he went numb.

Iggy's eyes blinked open carefully to see that it was the *Interceptor* that had just exploded, not the Blockgain. After patting himself down and confirming his own survival, he looked out of his window to see five heavily armed figures walking around the wreckage before acknowledging the Blockgain Chaser.

"Mode," Iggy whispered. "Are they Poachers?"

"Negative, they are Outlaws," Mode answered.

"Okay wheelie, step outta ya car. *Slow like sewage,*" said the Mutant holding a custom-built rocket launcher.

He stood out as the clear leader of the 5 figures, furthest out in front, making himself very visible and the only one out of the group to not be wearing some sort of face cover. His skin was dark blue, which had a slimy leathery quality to it. He had large black and red eyes that looked somewhat amphibious, that were contrasted with a set of front fangs that were so long and sharp they protruded past his bottom lip down to his tongue like a sabertooth. The rest of his body looked human enough apart from heavy plates of scales that covered his exposed forearms and neck. Adorned in high-level wasteland combat armor, Iggy found him intimidating enough to comply.

Turning to his android passenger who he believed hadn't been seen yet, he made a hand motion for her to hide herself and her weapons under the dashboard before leaving the vehicle, hands raised. The others in the outlaw group held their position as Iggy made himself seen and were all too far away for Iggy to identify beyond similar combat armor and various masks and helmets.

"A'ight, scav that Poacher wagon, they gonna have guns in there," the lead mutant shouted to his team. Resting his large weapon over his shoulder he walked a little closer to Iggy, looking him and his car up and down. "Must hav' a pretty fat bounty, to have Poacher-scum on yer ass. How much?"

Iggy gulped, knowing that he couldn't lie. His records were public.

"Hundred thousand and change. Bare minimum." Iggy said softly.

The blue mutant stared at Iggy for at least 20 seconds before finally making a scoffing sound.

"Yeah sounds bout' right. If it was more I woulda heard of ya. You prolly greased a merc out of zone or some shit, I couldn't give a Krok's arse."

Iggy did everything to mask his relief, exhaling slowly out of his nose.

"That still don't explain why a fuckin' Citi boi wheeler is out in Maim Creek, fancy gear can't hide tha way ya talk, soft-neck." the mutant said with a sinister grin, before reaching for a side pistol on his waist.

Iggy's hand threw themselves up once again in passive panic.

"Yotie, he's one of them derby wheelers, I's seen that whip on the vids, it's called the 'Blackchains' or something," the rough female voice came from a 2nd member of the outlaw group.

She was a pale green mutant woman with a shaved head and a forked tongue that darted in and out of her mouth as she spoke.

"No shit!?" the mutant called 'Yotie' responded. "Tha raises more questions than it answers tho."

"It's the Blockgain Chaser," Iggy said, correcting the woman. "And I'm just passing through," he lied.

"Krokshit, there ain't nothing past 'ere but the **Gaslands,** and ain't no Citi-Softneck driving through there willingly! Nah, matey, you got biznezz in the Creek." The woman started drawing her own pistol on Iggy.

"We just saved your life by junking that Poach-wagon. So, add all that to you toll for rollin' through here, and you owe me the rest of us here a... well a lot of fuckin' standards, Citi-boi."

Iggy stood pathetically with his hands up as the two outlaws threatened him while their 3 companions sorted through the wreckage of the interceptor. Calculating the odds in his mind, he went through a dozen scenarios of how he might try and fight them off, with all of them resulting in doomed estimates. His plotting was quickly cut off when the voice box inside the car crackled on and blasted full volume.

"**Koi, Yotie,** you fucking morons, it's me! We are going to see Baker!"

The blue mutant Yotie dropped his pistol arm suddenly white the bald mutant spun to point her gun at the source of the voice.

"Koi, tha' sounds like tha fuckin' Landlady," Yotie said with a slight quiver in his voice.

"K-Krokshit! Tha' aint' her voice...and why would she be riding with a Citi?!" Koi responded nervously.

"Koi, she called ya by ya fuckin' name. Ya know anyone else who'd recognize a four million bounty outlaw and call them morons?" Yotie asked pointedly

Four Million!?

Koi paused and considered her teammates point before aiming her gun back at a confused Iggy.

"If...if it is her, why she riding with a Citi-boy?"

"Who knows, might be fucking him."

Koi looked at Iggy up and down in mild disgust.

"Landlady fucks soft-necks?"

"It's been known ta happen," Yotie said while walking close to the Blockgain to speak directly to Clarissa.

"If you two are done speculating about my sex life, can you let Baker know I'm here? I know he's not in Creek for long but I got important business with him," Clarissa snarled.

"This Citi-Softneck with you Landlady? He delivering you?"

"Yeah, there's a Tin-Girl upfront with him, and I'm in the back with a mutant, avoiding a sun-tan," Clarissa snapped.

"Sil not mutant!" Sil barked gruffly before Clarissa hushed her.

"Right, this ain' proto-call, but I'll call ahead for ye," Yotie grumbled before pulling out a sleek communicator and punching a number in. "Your car is fucked, Wheelie. We are going to have to tow it to the shop," he said to Iggy with minor concern.

Iggy finally relaxed enough to take his eyes away from the Outlaw's pistols and assess the damage on the Blockgain. To his horror, the collision with the interceptor had pulverized his front bumper and warped the left fender along with the whole side of the hood that caused his front wheel to be bent inwards. The car was still technically intact, but it was no wonder why it had trouble starting. His stomach dropped as he came to the realization that in its current form it was undrivable. He was at the full mercy at these outlaws that Clarissa seemed to know.

*The infamous Landlady, even heavily wounded and trapped in my backseat behind sun-blockers still wields the authority to talk down to outlaws with **multi-million** standard bounties. Damn, Clarissa.*

Iggy wouldn't say it out loud, but he was a little turned on.

Chapter 22: Conference

The Blockgain Chaser and the remains of the Interceptor had been hitched to the back of Koi and Yotie's vehicles. They were being driven to an undisclosed location past the vast scrapyard. Both Mutants drove variants of a C-class pickup truck model called a 'Grip-Mule'. Certainly not fast or agile, but so durable and easy to handle that even rookies could put up a good fight in a derby if they could afford one. The outlaws had heavily customized their Mules with border spikes, black metal armor plating along with some crass graffiti in a language Iggy wasn't familiar with.

Along with Koi and Yotie who seemed to be leading the small group, the other three were introduced as Matchlock, Hayas, and Greem. They all kept their masks on, but Iggy noticed their skin colors and body shapes were not human. None of them spoke, they seemed to communicate with each other in grunts and nods.

Clarissa explained to Iggy that the Outlaws were not members of Cook's gang officially, but worked with Baker to split profits on their respective activities in Maim Creek. Which was mostly powder running and protection rackets on the markets. She went on to tell Iggy that Baker was the Cook-sibling most concerned with profits and had little interest in maintaining 'strict gang codes' (like not working with other crews) as long as he got paid. Baker was the one who fronted her the initial loan for her to lease and run the towers on their territory in Folsom and she had never met Cook or any of the others.

Having his car dragged by another vehicle made him feel physically sick. His pride in the Blockgain Chaser made the idea of it being 'assisted' in movement humiliating to his very core. The sound of its wheels being pulled across the dusty terrain was as painful as his own skin being dragged across it. He wasn't going to feel at ease until his vehicle was fully functional again. Peering out of the window he saw that they were getting further and further away from civilization and closer to the dark soil and moss-covered rocks of a dry swamp.

"So, after you see Baker you gonna head straight back to Folsom?" Iggy asked sheepishly.

"Uh...no probably not right away. Once I call Grady and confirm the handover, I'll have him come down this way and we will do some networking. New ventures and shit, you know?" Clarissa responded with a soft voice.

"Ah okay, so you won't be needing a ride back then, no problem..."

"No... but you did a good job, Crasher. I'm glad I hired you."

Iggy's voice barely disguised his uncertain feelings, but he did his best to hold his neutral tone.

"So, do you know where you are going to end up? I mean after Folsom; will you stay in the zone or move further out?" Iggy asked, trying not to sound too curious.

"I'll probably do a bit of drifting. Grady has a few contacts out of Zone, so I'll spend a while building a network while I figure out what I want to do," Clarissa said before pausing, realizing what Iggy was really asking. "But, heh...I'm the Landlady so you'll hear about me sooner or later, might even need you for a job down the line, who knows?" Clarissa was trying to sound positive, but she could feel the heavy feelings through the voice box.

"Yeah, who knows…" Iggy said dolefully.

He felt a weight on his stomach that wouldn't shift. These feelings were strange and uncomfortable to him; a freewheeling loner whose only family was his alcoholic grandpappy, who died by the same bottle he lived by. Thinking soberly about a life without Clarissa, or Sil or even Mode seemed inconceivable.

I can't be this attached, can I? I barely know these people. But then, I know them better than I know anyone else…

"I take it you're gonna stick with Mode and Sil for a while?" Clarissa asked, breaking Iggy's melancholy introspection.

"Uh, yeah. I want to find out about Sil's past, and what her connections were to my grandmother for sure. Not even thinking about trying to pay off my bounty now," Iggy said.

"Randall, as I continue to rebuild and upgrade, my access to personnel files will become greater. Including those of Sylvia and her background," Mode interjected.

Iggy smiled at Mode weakly, appreciating her offer of assistance. Still trying to understand how much free agency she really had in comparison to whatever programming she was given.

"I also made a promise to Mode to help her rebuild in exchange for keeping us alive… And I'm alive!" Iggy said with a little more spirit.

Clarissa chuckled along softly and turned to a half-asleep Sil, who was still incredibly weak, and only half-listening to the conversation with little reaction. Clarissa ran her newly four-fingered hand through the werewolf's hair before stroking her cheek gently.

"I'm gonna miss you too, Puppy," Clarissa whispered quietly.

The group inside the Blockgain felt bumps beneath the wheels which indicated to Clarissa were within the 'Badlands' territory. Which was where Baker's hideout was located.

"Oh, when we get there, Koi said you'll be led to an old gas station, they got some tools and parts there to fix your car, no charge," Clarissa said to Iggy reassuringly.

Iggy thanked her and sat back in his driver's seat, letting his eyes rest and clearing his mind of the soreness and stinging of his many injuries. While considering what locations he might travel after the end of his escort job, he drifted into a very shallow nap.

"Let's get moving wheelie!"

Iggy felt like he had only rested his eyes for a minute, but the harsh gruff of Yotie's deep voice indicated that he had probably been asleep for longer, as his body had a lot to recover from. As his eyes snapped open, he realized how dark it was outside of his car along with Clarissa and Sil climbing out of the backseat.

"Shit, is it night time already!? I couldn't have slept that long!" Iggy exclaimed.

"You haven't. We are in an underground area, you only slept briefly," Mode explained while calmly stepping out of the Blockgain, joining Sil and Clarissa in the dark facility.

Curious to his whereabouts, Iggy was quick to leave the damaged vehicle to examine his surroundings. Before his eyes could adjust to the dim lighting, his ears were assaulted with loud industrial punk music. It was being played from multiple sources, along with the commotion of dozens of loud obnoxious voices and the banging metal of tools on workshop tables.

"It's an abandoned train station, very popular forms of shelter during and after the skirmishes. You have to be pretty damn feared to secure one of these as a permanent hideout," Clarissa explained to an overwhelmed Iggy.

"Multiple mercenaries and outlaws populate this facility, bounties between two hundred thousand and thirty million," Mode mentioned while 'scanning' the area, eyes glowing green.

Before Iggy could react to those numbers, a tall figure in a long coat stepped out of the shadows and approached the group swiftly before speaking. "Thirty mil? I was at twenty-eight last week. What happened Koi?" the figure asked, his voice was masculine, commanding and full of confidence.

The female mutant, turned in slight shock as if the figure's stealthy approach caught her off guard before responding. "Uh, could have been that Lead-Slinger raid. Mashed up a few convoys in the crossfire," Koi said.

"You mean 3 days ago? How many died?" Yotie asked casually.

"Uh, 26 in the raid, another 12 during the getaway, mostly nomads, couple of merchants," Koi responded.

"I don't remember ordering that raid. When you reckless Mercs hit homesteaders, it raises my bounty by association, but whatever," the figure said before stepping closer to the towed vehicle and revealing himself in the headlamps.

He was a human with a long and chiseled face, complemented by a very strong jaw, that was peppered with dark stubble. His eyes were mismatched, the left one was a brownish-green like a hazardous pit of swamp mud, and his right was a bright mechanical blue of a cybernetic implant. His medium-length brown hair was tied into a loose topknot and his neck was adorned in tattoos. He stood even taller than Clarissa, Yotie, and Koi at around six foot four. His build was slim, but his form-fitting coat and shirt revealed very solid muscle underneath.

"Baker! Holy shit, you got older!" Clarissa said with a surprised but happy tone.

Placing a gloved hand on the shoulders of Koi and Yotie as he walked past them, the man revealed to be Baker briefly acknowledged Iggy and the others before putting an arm around Clarissa's waist. Iggy's eyes darted to this contact, not being able to look away.

"Older? Is the Immortal Vampire Landlady forgetting the aging process the rest of us have? I'm only Thirty-Five. But then again, it's been like eight years hasn't it?" Baker asked while leaning in slightly closer.

"Yeah well it ain't easy, getting all the way down here, this is why we started the monthly pay drops remember?"

"Hm, pay drops. More efficient, less contact. The nature of modern businesses."
Baker mused before turning to look at the Iggy, Sil, and Mode. "Quite a fetish party you got going here, Clar. You got a custom comfort-bot in a poacher jacket *and* a naked mutant girl? Kind of makes your driver look too ordinary!" Baker scoffed dismissively.

What a fucking prick, and why the hell did he call Mode a comfort bot?

"Sil...not...mutant" Sil stated once again, in a much drowsier tone.

Clarissa's eye darted between Iggy and Baker, deciding to speak up to break the tension.

"Ignition here is a hotshot derby driver, I had him escort me fast 'cause I knew you wouldn't be here tomorrow. Sil is a... w-wild woman who saved him from a waste lizard and Mode helped us escape those dickhead poachers. They are good people," she said respectfully.

Baker cast a lazy glance over the group again before turning back to Clarissa to pull her in closer to him. Iggy noticed there was no resistance from the proud vampire.

"Yeah poachers are a fucking pain, wish Yotie could have blown em up twice," Baker said firmly patting the mutant outlaw on the shoulder. "You came all the way here to talk business though, so I can make some time for that. Koi can take your friends up to the shop for repairs."

As Koi nodded and began to climb back inside her mule to tow the car topside, Iggy noticed Baker's hand slip closer to Clarissa's rear. The Landlady quickly glanced at Iggy before turning back to the towering gang leader, fully aware of what Iggy could see.

"Hey Baker, can I use the shower first? I don't even want to think of all the different crap I'm covered in," Clarissa said warily.

Baker pulled Clarissa closer to him as if she had no super-strength and inhaled a long whiff of her scent before locking her lips in a powerful open mouth kiss. Clarissa's head jolted slightly in surprise before slowly moving in rhythm with the make-out, moving her own hands to his rear and gripping hard. Iggy's eyes widened in anger, his chest became cold and his fists balled. Sil, Mode, and Yotie barely paid any notice.

"You smell like death and chaos, Clarissa, why the fuck would I want you to shower?!" Baker scoffed, before groping her chest fervidly as if no one else was around.

"You make a strong argument, Ritcher," Clarissa responded casually before pushing away from him gently to turn to Iggy. She found it difficult to meet his eyes with her own. "Well Crasher, I guess your job is complete.

"Guess so," Iggy grunted.

Clarissa kept her head down as she walked over the backseat of the Blockgain. With some fiddling, she opened a secret compartment under one of the seats that held a medium-sized strongbox and handed it to Iggy.

"There is your payment. Good work Ignition, and take care of yourself." Clarissa said before almost holding her hand out to shake, but deciding against it.

She nodded to Mode and waved to Sil before returning to Baker who was beckoning her over to his office. Iggy took the strongbox, turning away as quickly as possible, trying to put everything that just happened out of his mind. He couldn't return to the surface fast enough.

When he, Sil and Mode were back inside the busted Blockgain they were driven out of the underground facility up towards an abandoned gas station that was 'above' the train station on the ground level. There was no security door to the hideout, you could see the ramp leading to it from the waste outside. Iggy fully understood that with the kind of reputation the outlaws and gangs had inside, they didn't *need a security door.*

After a very short drive, Koi had parked her mule outside a badly bombed looking gas station that had a sign that said 'CRISPIN'S PIT-STOP' that was barely attached to the storefront. Right behind them was Yotie who was towing the remains of the Poacher's Interceptor to the gas stop too. After unhitching both the vehicles from their mules, Koi stayed at the station on guard duty while Yotie drove away.

"Tools an' parts are inside the shop, Wheeler. Fix ya' wagon quick so I can take an early break yah?" Koi ordered lazily before climbing the roof of the station and drawing a sniper rifle to keep watch with.

Well, I guess that's done then. Repair my Blockgain and get on with my life. Which means I need to find a life to get on with...

Sil emerged from the backseat of the towed truck and stretched with a deep yawn. She had finally gotten enough rest and decided to sit atop the hood of the car while Mode and Iggy tried to assess the state of the vehicle, seeing the damage on the Blockgain for the first time, turned to Iggy with concern.

"Home is hurt?" Sil asked with her familiar grunt,

"Sylvia considers the Blockgain Chaser, home?" Mode interjected.

"Since she met me," Iggy confirmed while examining an exposed coil spring above the damaged wheel. "Don't know why, and I haven't really asked." His voice was deflated and sullen.

"There is a high probability it is the scent; traces of the **sapphire vine** flower are in your car. Too faint for a human to detect, but a werewolf's sense of smell could easily identify it." Mode explained.

So, she's been calling my car home...because it smells like her home.

Iggy looked up at the naked werewolf who was now lazily stretched out on his hood, comfortably sunbathing in the harsh afternoon daylight of the clear sky. Iggy squinted at her bitterly with the new information, feeling like another ache was inside him right alongside the one for Clarissa.

*Wonder where or **who** she will run off to when the smell wears off.*

Iggy turned towards the android as she grabbed a large toolbox from the shelf of the station's front window. *At least Mode made it clear early, rebuild herself and then build a life, whatever that means for a... comfort bot?*

"Hey Mode, that name that Baker called you, is that what I think it is?" Iggy asked while vaguely recalling its usage back in the citadel.

"It's a high probability that you know of it in the context of humanoid sex devices seen in Citadels, which is indeed my base model," Mode confirmed.

"Wha? So Hughes made you to be a-"

"Incorrect. Father *salvaged* my base model from a Citadel scrapheap. But the work he has completed on me has been extensive. He built me for the purpose of living as the perfect human. My model's origins are incidental," Mode explained with a slight sharpness to her tone, interrupting Iggy for the first time.

Iggy was slightly taken aback as he watched her rummage through the toolbox with her single hand. Letting his eyes wander over her shapely legs and the gorgeous human parts of her face it started to make a lot of sense along with making her slightly more alluring to him.

"So, you...or your base model was being used as a comfort bot before being discarded in the scrapheap?" Iggy asked, realizing how crude it sounded.

Mode had retrieved a carjack and lug-nut wrench from the box and prepared to remove the bent wheel from the Blockgain Chaser before staring at Iggy with a silent pause as her eyes glowed a soft pink.

"My...memory banks in my base model's service chip are partially corrupted, but I have some recollection of the interactions with clients. Would you like me to detail them, Randall?" Mode asked.

"No! I mean...that's not necessary, but thank you for confirming," Iggy said in a flustered manner.

Despite that half of her face was an exposed metallic skull, she had a youthful innocent look about her. Iggy found it hard to believe that her body had likely been used in hundreds if not thousands of sexual encounters. Firstly, by the wealthy who could afford such an experience, and then the more common folk as her quality depreciated over time and became cheaper, before ultimately being discarded.

Iggy shuddered with the thought before beginning repairs on the Blockgain with Mode. Iggy was further away from his place of birth than he had ever been in his life, but fixing his car was so familiar, that his new environment was barely noticed.

Chapter 23: Blood Thinner

Clarissa's head was arched back, her mouth wide, and her face contracted. She wailed loud and long; each breath interrupted with another cry. Dripping with sweat and dizzy with head-rush, she slammed her slick, bouncy rear into Richter Baker's vigorous thrusting pelvis. Their flesh was clapping together so loud that the impact could be heard on the other side of the door of the sleeping quarters, where two armored gang members were standing guard. Baker was long and deep inside of her and she clenched down on him with all of her passion. He was so solid that she felt herself fitting around him, and it felt amazing.

Baker managed a few more minutes of thrusting before reaching his peak with an aching orgasm, shooting his fluid inside her for the 3rd time in a row. There was nothing extraordinary about his libido, he was just very attracted to her. She was skilled at foreplay and they had both sniffed a small amount of high-grade silver power.

"Fucckk, Landlady! All the powder in the world won't squeeze a 4th round of me." Baker said while flopping onto the mattress in a sweaty heap, palming around for his cigarillos. "Hope the loads were good enough for you. Did you get a nice warm blush?"

"Mmmm, nice and warm." Clarissa hushed as she fell into his chest, with her eyelid fluttering orgasmically. "I swear you get better every time"

Baker lit his cigarillo and pulled the vampire closer to him, enjoying the cushioned sensation of her large breasts. "It's been a lot of years of improvement, I was only, what, 17 the first time?"

"Heh, you mean **your** first time? Clarissa teased. "I can always tell."

"You got a thing for teenagers or was I just playing that well live?"

"I can't even remember the music Rict. I just always fuck the rhythm guitarist. It's like a personal tradition," she said while swinging her leg over his. "Glad I did though."

Richter took a long drag of his cigarillo before passing it to Clarissa and blew a cloud of smoke at the ceiling in thought. "It was so simple then; we were just about the music. No gang shit, just, like...*freedom* you know?"

Clarissa felt a pang of intense guilt before pulling away from Baker, sitting up to smoke and looking away to the door. She tried to keep her head clear, but only with partial success.

"So, Baker, I came here early for a reason. I brought a whole load of cash so I could pay of-"

"No, not here," Baker said firmly. "Not in the bedroom, we talk business in the office. Let this place be free of that necessary evil, if nowhere else." His voice was effortlessly commanding and Clarissa was in agreement.

"Okay Richter, we will talk in your office, but I know you're leaving soon so..."

"Yeah yeah, okay, I'm gettin' up. Half my guys have already left for HQ. I shouldn't even be here with so little in the way of protection. But procrastination you know?" Baker said as he peeled his sweat-drenched back off the high-quality sheets, and pulled on his studded jeans.

"The whole family's back at HQ?" Clarissa asked as she pulled her top over her generous bust.

"No, just me, Cook and Grille. Frye is running a huge chopshop outside of the Belgrave Citadel. And The Boil…" Baker paused as zipped up his boots. "Fuck the Boil, no protest from me when he misses meetings."

Clarissa chuckled softly as they finished dressing, mentally preparing herself for how to deliver her pitch.

It was a short walk from the sleeping quarters to the office. The train station had stalls, workbenches, and local maps at each of the former platforms, with a group of gang enforcers surrounding each one. The stench of sex was strong on Clarissa and Baker, which earned them both a few looks and nods of approval by the guards they walked past. They arrived at a door that had the faded letters ' TRAIN STAFF ONLY' where Yotie was standing outside with Clarissa's second lockbox of money that she gave to him along with a large set of keys that he used to open the multiple locks on the door.

"Hurry it up Yotie, how is it you know the names of every gang in the northeast zones but you can't remember four lock and key combos?" Baker said while tapping his foot in aggravation.

"It'd be easier if you didn't change them every week, Rick," Yotie grumbled as he fumbled with the final lock. "There we go. Here is your box Landlady. I didn't open it."

As the door creaked open, Clarissa was met with the smell of expensive cigar smoke and aged wine. The office was a former employee lounge, and it was furnished in the image of Baker's idea of luxury. Pool tables, a fully stocked mini-bar, a post-skirmish jukebox, and sound system along with pornographic holo-vids playing on the wall. In the middle of the room was a mismatched assortment of comfortable seating; A reading chair, liquid bag, a penthouse sofa, and a leather office chair.

Yotie slumped into the Liquid-bag while Richter sat in the office recliner, leaving Clarissa to perch in the incredibly soft sofa. She found humor in the fact that if someone didn't know who Richter was they would never know they were in the private office of one of the top 5 most dangerous people in the world, a title matched only by his siblings.

"Open the case, Yotie," Clarissa said while attempting to sit up straight in the quick-sand like cushions of the sofa. The mutant nodded and flicked open the unlocked case in a clear view of Baker's curious eye. He whistled in an impressed fashion and leaned forward.

"That's a lot of fuckin standards, Landlady. But I don't think we really need an expensive wedding. We just need to buy Yotie a few Root-waters and he'll act as a priest." Richter said with an easy smile.

Clarissa facepalmed before creasing up in laughter which was joined by a quick chuckle from Yotie himself.

"Goddamn it Richter, this is serious for once. I... wanted to bring this to you in person. It's the remainder of my leasing debt, and I won't be renewing it..." Clarissa said with a lack of her regular confidence.

Yotie looked back between the Vampire and the Richter who had paused silently and tented his fingers. After nodding very softly as a confirmation for her to continue, Clarissa nervously cleared her throat. Trying to form her sentences as clearly as possible.

"I... wanted to see you in person. I enjoyed the work I've done with you and Cook, but it's been 15 years. And I'm not getting any younger. I want to try and do something different now." Clarissa said sheepishly, finding it hard to meet Richter Baker's blank stare.

"You won't be working with us anymore?" Baker asked calmly.

"No, I'm sure I will! But as a freelance, ad-hoc set up like what you've got with Yotie and the outlaws," she said turning to Yotie for some sort of acknowledgment.

"Landlady, I'm just dumb muscle with a rocket launcher, I can't run a pair of apartment towers. I can barely keep my bunk bed clean." Yotie quipped with a smirk.

"He's right Clarissa, your abilities as a manager are pretty invaluable to me. You've been working with us for a long time, but your management skills are second to none. You really want to leave the towers behind?" Baker asked.

"Yes, Richter I do. You can keep all the weapons and contraband we confiscated from the residents. All that me and Grady will take are my standards worth in profits and the deposit on next year's security and zoning fees." Clarissa paused as her voice began to crack with nerves. "All the refurbishment and upgrades to the rooms stay in the tower of course. Those apartments are worth 3 times what they were before we took over.

Baker's stare was strong and direct. He swirled his chair to face away from Clarissa to retrieve a laminated sheet of paper from his desk and turned back to face her. The tension in the air was pulled as tight.

"Cook has some crazy idea about moving into more of a legitimate business with Citadel officials. You know we take a cut of the sex industry in Texcoco, but it's sloppy. We don't get paid on time and the Citi-Sec stays on our asses," Baker said.

"Killed 3 of my best pimps because they ate at the wrong restaurants. It's anti-mutant bullshit. The Soft-necks get a pass," Yotie added sourly.

"Basically, we need to start bribing higher up the food chain for this Citi-shit to work. Personally, I think the whole idea is cursed. I can't trust a Citizen as far as I can throw em down a tunnel. But Cook's pulling authority on this," Baker said as he leaned further forward and pointed to the case of standards. "We need **more money, Clarissa.** I got to prioritize business."

Clarissa stayed silent as her eyes flicked between Baker and Yotie.

"We need you to stay in Folsom and focus on expanding our territory. Not just the towers, but the brothels, bars, and garages. I know some of them are your friends, but we need to bring back the protection rackets." Baker handed the laminated paper to Yotie while pulling out a new folder. "Now this will mean going to war with other gangs in Folsom, so Yotie will take a small army to the Shell and you'll take over every corner of those streets. Obviously, it's a lot more risk and responsibility but you'll be compensated."

Clarissa's chest ached as her heart sank, looking at Baker and Yotie in mild disbelief.
"No, Baker. This isn't a request. I'm leaving the business and I'm leaving this contract. I'm not fighting a turf war in Folsom. I'm not shaking down good people like Blanch for gang tax and I'm not running those towers anymore. The debt is paid. I'm out." Clarissa asserted strongly.

Baker sighed deeply and looked at the floor. "There is gonna be a new debt and this doesn't cover it, Landlady. The contract will be renewed with Grady running operations if you refuse to take the lead on that. Either way, you're still in with us."

Clarissa shot up out of her seat, burning with rage and disgust. Her voice had snapped from a diplomatic inflection to a threatening snarl.

"Baker, I respect you. But if you even **think** about forcing Grady into your stupid war campaign, I'll feed you and every member of this gang their *fucking hearts*!" Clarissa was shaking with anger but also fear, pointing an assertive but shaking finger at Richter Baker as she spoke. "You can't strong-arm us into a new contract, we didn't sign up for this!"

Richter remained calm as he held is stare with Clarissa, showing no fear but only the slightest amount of empathy. "I didn't have to strong-arm Grady into the contract, it was his idea."

A cold lump rose into Clarissa's throat.

"W-what, n-no he would n-never…" she said as her body began to quiver violently along with her voice.

Heavy footsteps entered the office from a previously unseen side door.

"It's a good plan, L.," said the familiar voice.

The large mutant stepped into the seating area with a dark expression of concern across his amphibious face. *Grady* had revealed himself.

Clarissa's jaw dropped slowly, the air rushed out of her lungs like an emergency escape and her head throbbed with panic and sickness. All she could taste was cold metal and mucus. She felt like her eye was betraying her, she couldn't believe that Grady was here.

"You…you're in Folsom…looking after the towers…why, how?" Clarissa stuttered as Baker and Yotie looked back and forth between the duo.

"We have been in talks with Grady for a little while about stepping up. Again, it's just business, Clarissa." Baker said calmly.

"S-stepping up?" She said as she snapped her head to her mutant accomplice, who refused to meet her gaze out of what looked to be a mild shame. "You're supposed to be watching things back at home…what is going on?" she said with a shaking voice of total confusion and growing rage.

"I left right after you did. Cook's boys are holding the towers L, we won't get any trouble." Grady held the large folder from Baker's desk and sighed. "I signed the contract before you arrived, L. I'm gonna expand Cook's territory and take over Folsom. There is a future for me, for us in the organization. I know you were getting sick of ejecting powder-heads anyway right?"

Grady's voice was conversational, but with a solemn drop in his tone, he still couldn't make eye contact with his Vampire mentor as he spoke. Clarissa tried to respond but she was choked by shock.

"Grady has laid out how much more we can make once we start taxing the local businesses for protection money. I get that you have strong friendships with these people but we can't afford to look weak." Baker added.

"T-they'll never go for it! They won't kick up money to the gangs without me!" Clarissa shrieked.

Grady dropped his head and cleared his throat, finally meeting Clarissa's furious glare. "You're right, L. Out of loyalty to you Blanch was defiant...till the end. Hopefully, the rest will fall in line."

"Y-you...fuck...You...ungrateful shit!! **I raised you!** How could you!?" Clarissa shrieked.

Grady went silent, showing no remorse in his face and turned to Baker, who rose from his seat to continue the explanation.

"Grady and I both respect your wishes not to drink blood, but the streets are talking, rivals are getting bolder. They see it as a sign of weakness that you choose to not be a full power vampire. So, Grady is going to establish a more ruthless style from here on out. We will have jobs for you in terms of the handover and helping the troops take new turf in Folsom."

Clarissa could barely see anything, the tears of betrayal blurred everything in front of her. Balling her fists in indignation she bawled in emotional pain, drawing her pistol and aiming it at all 3 men in the room.

"It's empty Clarissa, I took out the clip in the bedroom," Baker stated flatly.

Clarissa pulled the trigger rapidly as she sobbed, struggling to breathe as she choked on her own tears. Feeling the reduced weight of the gun and hearing no gunshots, she dropped her pistol in despair. Before she could declare her hatred, her world was rocked by a devastatingly heavy impact, as Grady's punch rendered her completely unconscious.

Chapter 24: Deadline

Sil emerged from the abandoned gas station wearing a new makeshift poncho that she had crudely made from a rug found in the back room. She tore a wide hole open for her head and neck, and it fit just as comfortably as her previous one. The now-dark sky brought with it a cold breeze and Sil was comfortable wearing the only type of clothing she knew for the practical warmth. Iggy and Mode finished the last repairs on the Blockgain and were loading some of the tools in the trunk, knowing they might need them again soon.

"The Blockgain Chaser will require further maintenance to be back to optimum condition, but the vehicle is functional now. We can depart anytime," Mode said as she handed a monkey wrench to Iggy.

"Well now, I won't be paying off my bounty so I might as well spend a little of the job money on some upgrades," Iggy said as he wiped his forehead with an oil-stained sleeve. "Hopefully the next Shell isn't too far. we need gas."

"I will try to download a local map of the surrounding areas, though it may take some time. Also, you have multiple injuries that may need treatment," Mode said.

"Yeah, nothing that won't heal. It's only my shoulder in any sort of pain." Iggy said while clutching it. "What have you got there?"

Mode reached past Iggy and grabbed the shock-prod attachment that he had scavenged from the Nomad's Tin-Man. Her eyes glowed green as she turned it back and forth to fully examine it.

"A very primitive arm attachment, but could be useful with some modification." Mode mused, before placing it near the stump of her wrist.

"Yeah, it's all yours. I had no idea what we were going to use it for anyway. You need a proper lab to put that on though, right?" Iggy asked as he studied its size, noting the two large 'hook-prongs' which could be useful as a grappling prosthetic.

"I may be able to use these tools, but I'll need to download an assembly file for that procedure. This will take a few moments," Mode said.

Iggy rubbed his eyes and nodded in response to her comment and closed the trunk. "Alright, let me check the radiator. It's getting pretty cold out here."

After placing the shock-prod attachment on top of the trunk, Mode clasped her metal and flesh hand around Iggy's wrist, preventing him from returning to the car. In one swift motion, she stood in front of him, her eyes now glowing pink, with a noticeable expression of curiosity.

"Randall, let's engage in sexual activity," she said bluntly as she released his wrist to unzip her poacher's jacket exposing her mostly flesh naked torso.

"What? Really? Now?" Iggy asked in thrilled confusion. Feeling his body fully reacting to the sight of her.

"Yes, we have time while I download the area map, and you desire this. Also, I am curious about my first experience in this model. How would you like to begin?" Mode asked.

"Hang on how did you know that I-" Iggy sputtered.

"I was not certain at first, but your frequent glances were joined by heavy respirations, and increased body temperature, especially in your groin area. This was at its peak while we repaired your vehicle. I am assuming that despite my incomplete appearance, you still desire me," Mode said.

She wasn't wrong.

In the hours they spent repairing; Iggy had spent more time examining Mode than his own vehicle. Desperate to push all thoughts of Clarissa from his mind, he let his base urges take over and his eyes wander. In contrast to Sil's beastly lumber and Clarissa's roguish strut, Mode moved in an elegant stride that Iggy found difficult to look away from. Similar to Sil, Mode had little-to-no concept of human modesty and would regularly leave parts of her lithe body exposed as she was repairing the car.

Iggy glanced over to the rooftop of the gas station, seeing Koi still on watch duty, but facing eastward from their position at the car. He knew it was possible she might see or hear them, but he didn't care. Soon he would be far away from this hideout and maim creek as a whole and his attraction to Mode was undeniable.

Placing his hand on Mode's hip he pulled her closer towards him and locked his lips over hers. Her mouth shared the same blend of flesh and machine as the rest of her body. While her tongue was warm, wet and very human, the inside of her mouth was a cold metal alloy, creating a strange but exciting sensation for Iggy's tastes. Her kissing was soft but deliberate. Her 'experience' as a machine made for human pleasure was instantly apparent.

Iggy wanted to take the lead for once, but as soon as his hands could get to caressing her lithe frame, her nimble fingers had already breached his zipper and clasped around him, pulling and stroking in an automatic but effective rhythm, instantly bringing him to full mast. Feeling around her body was a fascinating journey, both soft and hard depending on where his palms found themselves. Eventually reaching down he felt her entrance, it was fully flesh, and slightly moist, indistinguishable from any other he had felt. Pulling away from the kiss, he worked his fingers in and around her with carnal intent, curious to what reaction he would get from a being such as her.

Iggy heard her make no sounds of pleasure and realized that she didn't breathe. Her reaction was the increased pink glow of her eyes, along with the hard, circular grind of her hips into his hand, it was different, but Iggy was still turned on. Sleeping with both a Werewolf and Vampire made him much more open-minded to non-standard forms of sexual interactions. However, he couldn't shake a curious uncertainty.

Is she actually enjoying this? Does she have the sentience to 'like' it? Or is it just a series of programming that makes her react like this automatically? But in the case of an artificially built person, is there really any difference?

Iggy's existential thoughts were interrupted by a very new sensation enveloping him. Mode had dropped to her knees and taken him into her mouth in one fluid motion. Iggy couldn't believe how fast she was. Her heated tongue was sliding around and pushing his shaft around the walls of her frigid mouth giving him a frightfully exhilarating experience that he didn't want to end. His eyes fluttered open to see the uniquely gorgeous android looking up at him with her pink beams of light. Iggy accepted he couldn't really understand if androids could receive pleasure, but he felt an intuitive certainty that she was enjoying herself.

Iggy's body was in such extreme levels of arousal, he didn't hear the quiet footsteps of a curious werewolf, who was brought over by the powerful musk of Iggy's thrill. As always, Sil stopped to observe the activity with natural intrigue before speaking.

"Metal-Girl...eat Nishin?"

Iggy's eyes shot open and snapped his head left to find the wild female only a few feet away from him staring intently at Mode's growing speed and intensity.

"Sil! Crap, it's uh...I ahhh, she's...Hnngg-"

The arrival of Sil had zero effect on Mode's rhythm and her tongue actions only became faster, overwhelming Iggy and impairing his ability to talk. Sil walked closer to the pair softly growling with mild concern.

"Nishin, being eaten...need Sil to save?"

Iggy's eyes widened at Sil's muscles tensing and her claws slowly starting to reveal themselves. Realizing her misunderstanding he forced himself to speak out before the situation turned ugly.

"**No!** It's not eating...ugh...it's like when we push? Just different..." Iggy stuttered as mode gripped his rear, pulling her mouth off to swirl her tongue around his tip.

"Push...in mouth? But not eating?" Sil said with genuine puzzlement, her growling settled.

"This is fellatio, Sylvia. Also known as a blowjob. A popular form of human foreplay to stimulate the penis orally. I am bringing Randall to full arousal before intercourse," Mode explained while her mouth was full, highlighting that her voice didn't actually come from her throat.

Iggy had no idea if Sil understood even some of what Mode said, but her tilted head and increased air sniffing around them made him doubt it. She glanced at Iggy one more time and dropped to all fours, smelling Iggy's groin area as Mode continued before licking around his crotch gently.

"**Sil!?**" Iggy gasped with surprise.

"Nishin likes Metal-Girl mouth-push...Nishin like Sil mouth push?" she purred gently as her lapping became more deliberate.

"Randall enjoys it, Sylvia. His heart rate is increasing. We will stimulate him together," Mode lectured before gently placing Iggy's balls in her mouth.

Sil's licking made its way to the underside of his mast, trying to emulate Mode's actions as best as she could. Iggy's mind entered pure euphoria as they used their mouths in tandem, both taking turns to lick, suck and kiss with growing speed. While mode was direct and methodical, Sil was chaotic and eager.

Looking down at the android and werewolf at their knees, cleavages on display with neither of their single items of clothing covering their legs or rears, all restraint rushed out of him like a vacuum. Gripping the Blockgain's side mirror as he leaned against it, Iggy ejaculated forcefully into Sil's mouth, catching her off guard as she was taking her 'turn' to handle the main organ.

After roaring long and loud with one of the most intense orgasms he had ever experienced. Iggy's entire body went limp. With no strength or balance to keep him standing, he slumped backward before falling into a seated position, with only his vehicle keeping his back upright. Avoiding the intense gaze of his two companions he lazily put himself away and pulled up his zipper.

*Me, Mode and Sil. I could get used to this, **really** used to this.*

 A half grin found its way on Iggy's face as she finally swallowed everything he released in her mouth, and crawled over to him, sniffing the air between them once again. Mode leaned in once again and kissed Iggy softly placing her hand on his thigh suggestively.

"Me and Sylvia would like to continue to full intercourse, are you ready?" Mode asked plainly.

"Ugh let me rest Mode, I need a while."

Mode's eyes lost their pink glow instantly and Iggy couldn't help but feel a little guilty. Sil, on the other hand, was still very eager to continue, attempting to pull down the pants he had just zipped up.

"Sil, I'm spent! Give me a second!"

Lazing on the roof of the auto-shop and scanning the area for threats that she was certain would never come; Koi rolled her eyes after listening to the noisy activity of the three outsiders. Impatiently wondering when they would finally leave. Her quiet boredom was broken by the buzz of her communicator which she picked up, knowing it would be Yotie.

"Yeah, they are still here, should be going soon...Uh-huh, yeah...really?!" Koi said before walking to the other side of the roof and lowering her voice. "Fuck off, she couldn't?"

Sil's advances suddenly stopped as she rose to her feet. Her head darting in multiple directions as her ears began to twitch. Iggy finally sat up, trying to follow her head movements but couldn't hear or say anything outside of the night's sky and the gentle wind.

"Rissa? They say, Rissa?!" Sil suddenly barked, loud enough to startle Iggy but not quite loud enough for Koi to hear from the roof. Mode turned to Sil with a blank expression, and her eyes began to glow green once more.

"What are you talking about? Who said, Clarissa?" Iggy asked with concern.

"Mutant up there, saying Rissa, talking to box, saying **capture** Rissa." She explained as best as she could while pointing at the roof. Mode turned towards Koi who was still on the communicator and began to focus intensely.

How could she even hear that? Are her ears that powerful? Why would they want to kidnap Clarissa?

Sil dropped to her fours and began to growl. Her face was that of a guard dog who had found an intruder. Iggy was surprised at her concern for Clarissa. He didn't think Sil had empathy for anything but the Blockgain and it brought him feelings of resentment.

Maybe they do want to snatch her. This ain't my business anymore. I did the job, she paid me and then she went off with that Baker guy. I don't understand the Gangster life, and I don't want to. Sil needs to forget her.

"Sil, it's fine, we are gonna leave soon, let's get into the house. We got a long journey ahead of us," Iggy said, trying his very best to sound detached. Sil turned to him with a tilted head and furrowed brow.

"Nishin...not save Rissa?" Sil asked.

"No, we won't. This is gang business, not our business," Iggy said.

Sil looked between Mode and Iggy with lost eyes before rising back to her two feet and plodded to the passenger side of the Blockgain waiting for Iggy to open the doors. Dusting himself off Iggy placed a hand on Sil's shoulder and kissed her softly, trying to keep only the future in his mind.

"Sylvia is correct; they are indeed discussing the kidnapping of Clarissa. Richter Baker, Yotie Caskey, and Grady Sullivan can be heard over the communicator belonging to Koi Kari," Mode said.

Iggy felt a cold shock in his neck and stepped closer to Mode. "**Grady?** As in, Grady that works with Clarissa in Folsom?"

"Grady Sullivan's file places him as Tower Security in Folsom, yes. The voice matches the file," Mode said.

Iggy looked at the roof of the shop and the back at Mode and Sil with disbelief. "And you're sure that's his voice and they are talking about taking away Clarissa? You can hear that from here? I can barely hear her mumbling."

"Yes, I'm certain. And the subject is Clarissa's fate," Mode said while turning towards the shop and walking slowly closer towards it. "They also mentioned an alternative – the 'Thorn Institute'. This area is not on my records."

Iggy's face went pale. "They are going to send her to the **Thorn?**" Iggy asked with shaking hands and a thousand-yard glare. **"**That Baker fuck and **Grady** are talking about selling Clarissa to that...place?!"

Iggy's face morphed into a scowl of disgust and rage. After glancing up at Koi on the rooftop again, he marched to the trunk of his car and immediately grabbed his 2-2 rifle. Sil and Mode watched as a scowling Iggy rested the gun barrel over the roof of the car and crouched with the butt of the rifle stock tucked neatly against his shoulder.

"Nishin…" Sil said as Iggy began to take aim at the roof. Watching Koi closely.

Hurry up and put the phone down, I got another call for you.

Iggy saw Koi pacing up and down with the communicator in her hand while chattering with a look of surprise and excitement on her face. This only made Iggy's nerves harder and his focus sharper as his finger hovered over the trigger guard.

Koi finally ended the call, dropping her arm to pocket the communicator and Iggy fired his rifle, shattering the peaceful silence of the night. The bullet punched through her skull, painting the large part of the roof with her blood and brain fragments, leaving her head a partially formed crater. She never saw it coming.

Sil dropped low into a wary stance looking around for more enemies, expecting there to be another large fight, but Iggy simply dropped the rifle back into the trunk and marched towards the shop with fists both tightly balled.

"Do you still plan to leave for the next Shell, Randall? I have the local area map downloaded now," Mode said calmly, not detecting any enemies.

"No, I need to get back into the hideout and get Clarissa out," Iggy said, turning to face his two companions. His scowl dropped into a frown of worry. "But I can't save her without your help."

Sil stood up straight and walked over to Nishin with a look of determination on her face. "Sil will save Rissa with Nishin…" She placed a clawed hand on his shoulder. "Not *Fenrir.*"

Iggy paused before taking Sil's hand and holding it firmly before nodding firmly and bringing her face towards him for a long kiss. Mode approached them both and nodded once, brandishing the shock-prod arm attachment with the slightest look of intrigue on her perfectly angled face.

"I will continue to preserve the life of you and your companions, Randall," Mode said.

"How fast do you think you can equip that attachment, Mode?" Iggy asked.

"With the tools here, I can affix in approximately fifteen minutes."

Iggy looked between Mode and Sil and gave a small but encouraging grin. "Alright, I might have a plan. We just got to figure out how to get them to open up the hideout. Any ideas, girls?" Iggy asked with a breathy tone.

Mode glanced at the roof, then Sil, then Iggy. Her green eyes were now a full emerald glare, "Sylvia, please retrieve Koi's communicator from the roof. We can attempt to have the hideout opened so we can proceed with Randall's plan."

Iggy raised an eyebrow as he watched Sil follow the request without question, dashing at the storefront and ascending to the roof with a single leap. "They aren't going to open up the hideout just because I ask them to, Mode," Iggy said.

"You are most likely correct, so **Koi** will be the one asking," Mode said.

Iggy glanced up to the dead body with confusion and the slightest of smiles appeared on the human part of Mode's lips.

Baker's office was filled with heated debate, a recently floored Clarissa was laid out on the luxury carpeting next to the pool table, while Grady, Yotie and Richter Baker paced while exchanging words candidly. The sound of heavy footsteps and muffled disagreement put the guards outside the room on edge.

"I told you, she was never going to go for it. This is why we **had** to do this here, Richter. She would have had me strung up from the towers if I had told her this back in Folsom!" Grady ranted, throwing his thick arms up in frustration.

"You had to do this here? You had to punch her out and make a permanent enemy out of her? We could have smoothed it over and had her transferred! Now we are probably going to have to kill her." Baker replied in a calmer but equally blunt tone.

"Fucking kill her then, just make sure you do it properly, this bitch has taken shots to the head before. It put her down but didn't finish her," Yotie spat while pointing at the knocked-out Landlady. Grady dropped his head again and took a deep breath before lifting her limp body on the pool table.

"Aright....just make it quick. Knife to the heart, drive it deep. Clean and painless."

Richter nodded at Yotie and the lead henchmen began to punch in Koi's number into his communicator. Richter walked over to Clarissa and ran the back of his hand down the Vampire's cheek before Grady slapped it away with a look of deadly rage.

"Don't touch her, Ricky. Don't even say her name. Just get it done."

Baker looked deep into the black pools of Grady's fish eyes before scoffing and turning towards Yotie and motioning him closer to them, away from the door. The mutant stepped between them and looked between Grady and Baker curiously.

"I just told Koi we were gonna crease her, but you look like you got an idea, Baker," Yotie said with a smirk.

"Yeah, I do. Why kill her when we can make some money? I just remembered that the Thorn institute was looking for new attendees," Baker mused before stroking his chin. "How much do you think they'd pay for a Vampire with a body like hers?"

Grady's eyes widened and his lips parted with mild shock. Yotie glanced at the sleeping vampire in thought before licking his lips with a fat yellow tongue.

"Them horny Thornys would pay at least two mil for her. She's a security risk though, don't know if a high-end house would be able to keep her under control," Yotie said in a hushed voice as he glanced between Baker and the front door.

"It ain't no 'House' you squid faced fuck, it's a torture fetish prison for rich Citi-Sicks. Do you **know** what they'll do to her there!?" Grady said in an unfamiliar thunderous growl as he stepped towards the smaller Yotie in a threatening manner.

"She'll be tortured, raped in half and fed to the highest bidders," Baker said calmly. "But that 2 million will go a long way, especially with your upcoming takeover, Grady. So, we are going to go with the paying option." Baker gently pushed aside the slightly quivering Yotie and pushed his chiselled face right up to Grady's, showing no fear or remorse. "Or you can kill her, *and be 2 million in the hole* with Cook's gang. Make a decision."

Yotie gazed at Baker's unflinching stance with awe as the lithe human underboss stared down the gigantic red mutant, who took a step back before wiping his hand across his scaled forehead.

"Do what you're gonna do," Grady said in surrender.

Baker nodded at Yotie and grabbed his long-coat from a nearby coat rack before opening the door and waving two of his guards in. Both of the helmeted mutants were momentarily stunned to see Clarissa out cold on a pool table but quickly refocused when Baker ordered them to bind her and prepare her for transport.

"Okay, get the cars. I've kept Cook waiting long enough. You and Koi are in charge of her delivery and price negotiation. Grady, it's been a long fucking day. Just go back to Folsom and take tomorrow off. I'll call you when I'm back from HQ," Baker said as he left the office in a swift manner.

Grady took a deep breath and looked at his former mentor with hollow eyes as the guards fastened black cords around her hands and feet and carried her away.

Yotie redialled for Koi but there was no answer. He stared at the phone intently, desperate not to make eye contact with Grady until the large mutant finally left the room. After a few more tries the communicator finally crackled on and Yotie heard his long-time partner's voice.

"It's Koi, can you please open the front gate? Randall and his companions have repaired their car and departed."

"Randall!? Ya mean the Citi-Crasher?" Yotie asked, slightly surprised. "Ya be talkin' like a damn Citi professor, don't be pickin' that talk up from em, it don't suit ya."

"You...Ya right, jus...open the door, fuckin, door." the voice said.

"Yeah...yeah, fine. We gotta leave right away for a drop off anyway so make it quick." Yotie responded before ending the call and walking over to the door controls outside.
"I gotta get whatever powder be giving her that Citi-speak, holy shit," Yotie mumbled to himself.

Slowly, as the front gate craned open, Yotie patted himself down for a cigarillo and headed for the toilet room, his bladder ready to burst after Grady was in his face. The mercenaries in the hideout began to pack up their gear and leave for HQ on Baker's orders, so they didn't pay much mind to the open front gate, or the intruder that entered.

Chapter 25: Ladykillers

The hideout was in full motion. The two dozen or so armed gang enforcers along with a handful of outlaw associates were packing their guns, powder, food, and valuables into crates, ready to be loaded onto their vehicles. The doors and gates were being locked down at every 'station' and shutters were being pulled down over stalls and workshops. Without the gang members and their loot, it would be hard for the average Wastelander to know the train station was an underboss hideout, which was undoubtedly the point. The creaking, slamming and hissing of hydraulic metal doors combined with coarse gang chatter and the thumping industrial hip hop would create the perfect cover for a noisier intruder. But for the almost silent entrance of Mode, it was just another distraction.

The lithe android avoided the well-lit platforms of the hideout, instead using the high verticality to traverse undetected. With perfect balance and precision, Mode leaped from across a network of pipes and steel beams that hung like tree branches across the ceiling. Even with her single hand, every step, jump, swing, and landing was perfect. She effortlessly balanced on narrow pipes that were half the width of her feet as she crouched to scan the space beneath her. Mode was able to pick up Clarissa's location quickly; surrounded by 5 heavily armed guards she was tied to a gurney which was being prepared for loading inside a large D-class pickup truck known as a **workhorse**.

Her green scanning eyes slowly began to shift to red as she jumped to a new platform, putting her above a large network of wires which converged at a humming generator. The large machine was guarded by a single mutant outlaw who was nodding his head to the current song blaring through the hideout; *'Case of Rickets' by The Boil.*

Mode reached into her poacher jacket's main pocket to retrieve a shard of broken glass, no bigger than her palm. Both her pockets were filled with them, collected from the smashed window of the gas station. With a simple flick of her wrist, she hurled the glimmering shard downwards with deadly precision, sinking it deep into the un-armored neck of the outlaw mutant. Despite seeing his own blood spew out over his chest like a garden hose, the loudest sound he could muster was a hiss and a gargle before he collapsed to the floor, pawing at his throat before expiring.

After confirming the kill was unseen, Mode fell down to the fuse box platform silently. She pulled out Koi's communicator from her inside pocket and dialled the extension for the Blockgain's channel.

"Randall, I'm in position," Mode whispered.

"Good work! How long will the fuse box take?" Iggy asked over the communicator with a hushed voice.

"It will take three seconds."

Mode lifted her newly-attached shock-prod tool that pulsed with live sparks. It had its two-prongs altered to resemble a long double hook for practical use as per Iggy's suggestion.

"Alright, try to remain hidden okay?" Iggy said over the sound of the Blockgain's engine rev in the background. "Remember, Clarissa is our top priority."

"Affirmative Randall, I will retrieve her," Mode said.

Mode ended the call and punched her shock-prod arm inside of the fuse box, instantly piercing the panel protecting the switchboard and activated the tool to full power. It pumped crackling electricity across the fuse matrix and violently shorted out all power in the hideout. Everything went black, and all the sound of machinery went dead. The silence was replaced by the confused murmurs and half-panicked shouts of the gang inside, who were scrambling through their recently packed cargo for flashlights.

"Which one of ya stupid pricks took a whizzle on the third rail?" Yotie shouted with amusement as he emerged from the bathroom.

"I left Matchlock posted near the fuse box. Probably fucked around trying to charge his portable-vid," said the outlaw Greem.

"Just find some lights and let's get out of here. We can call maintenance when we come back. I don't care if the door is open. There is nothing to steal here," shouted Baker as he dragged a sack full of silver powder out of his bedroom.

"FIND THE LIGHTS!" Greem shouted to a group of shadowed gang members who were rummaging blindly through their cargo. "Hey Yotie, why the fuck **is** the front door still open? I didn't see Koi come in?"

Yotie glanced at the wide-open door in suspicion before attempting an explanation to his fellow outlaw. But before he could speak, he witnessed two small red lights behind Greem, illuminating the space in front of them in a mild crimson.

"Ah, I see someone found a fuckin' ligh-"

Greem's voice morphed into a desperate wretch as blood ejected from his neck in chaotic fashion. Yotie couldn't muster a gasp before his comrade dropped to the floor as a twitching corpse, and the two red lights vanished from view. Instinctively grabbing his pistol from his hip, the panicked outlaw fired two shots into the air yelling at the top of his lungs.

"We got a break in! Get the lights on!"

The entire hideout was now on high alert. Narrow beams of light illuminated sections of the tunnel, most of which were flashlight gun attachments. Bursts of fire rattled through the air aimlessly as the panicked gang fired in the dark with little idea of what they were shooting at. Keeping his head down, Yotie ran towards the parked vehicles at the end of the train tunnel listening to chaotic cries of confusion as he went.

"Where the fuck are they?"

"How many of them?!"

"Shit they got Claine in the neck!"

"Fuck! Someone get those lights on!!"

Grady, who was still in the office when the lights went out was startled by the screaming and gunfire. He cautiously emerged from the door to find both office guards dead with bloody throats and eyes as wide as waste-geckos.

"I'd never hire *you two* for tower security," Grady scoffed before relieving the corpses of their submachine guns.

Crouching behind a railing panel with both guns held near his neck, he took a deep breath and tuned all the noise from his mind, letting his black eyes fully adapt to the darkness. Between the room flashing bright with gunfire every couple of seconds, Grady's advanced eyesight locked him on to the red glare of Mode's eyes and the crackling light of her new arm.

"Damn girl, you move fast..."

Grady carefully took aim and waited for Mode to leap to a set of beams that were right within his sights.

"Gotcha!"

With both guns, Grady squeezed off a hell-storm of fire at the android with bullets wildly slamming into the infrastructure all over the ceiling of the station. Mode was struck with a couple of rounds to the leg which caused her to miss her mark. She fell into the destination board directly above the 2nd platform, barely managing to hang on to the corner of it with her opposable hand.

"There she is ya dumbasses! The destination board! Watch out for the red eyes!" Grady yelled to the gang before making a sprint to the parking area, tossing both of his submachine guns aside.

The destination board was lit up with inaccurate but heavy gunfire and Mode was forced to let go and fall to the rails beneath her. Not being able to land correctly with a damaged leg, the android smashed against the tracks, causing her shin to break. Scrambling into a hopping motion, she began a slow retreat as the gang located the area where she fell and closed in.

Just as the crowd of henchmen began to gather around the platform, a new source of light flooded the hideout, along with the mighty rumble of a muscle car engine.

Just like pins in a bowling alley.

The Blockgain Chaser tore through the darkness, blazing its harsh headlights in the path of its speeding charge. Just over a dozen were grouped together in the same spot, and only had time to gasp before the derby vehicle plowed into them. The impact was wickedly violent; decapitating the bodies on direct impact while crushing and slicing through the rest. Iggy slammed the brakes and careened into a 180-degree turn before catapulting along the rest of the platform, smashing into everything he could see, living or not.

"Mode! Are you okay? Did you find Clarissa?!" Iggy shouted into his car's built-in communicator as the car finally skidded to a stop.

"R-**Ran**dall, the fuuuse box aff-fected my s-scanners, plus I have been d-**dam**aged further...S-she is **not** in my immedi-di-diate area." Mode said with a static, malfunctioning voice.

"Shit! I'll have to get out of the car, stay there!" Iggy said with heavy panic and dread in his voice.

"Aff-f-f-**firm**aaaat-ive."

A few stray bullets slammed into the Blockgain Chaser's new armor, reinforced by some of the platings from the wrecked interceptor. As the last few gang members jumped off the platform to avoid the roaming vehicle, Yotie stepped on to the far end of the platform, brandishing his rocket launcher.

"So it *was* you guys! We shoulda creased ya when we saw ya," Yotie shouted as he took careful aim. "This is for Koi, **Citi-slick**!"

As he went to pull the trigger for his heavy weapon Yotie was halted by a devastating stabbing pain in his shoulder, crying out and dropping to one knee. He turned around to the shadowy figure with burning white eyes who had buried a clawed hand right below his collarbone.

"You...**not...explode home!**" Sil barked deeply, leaning closer towards the shaking mutant.

"YYYYAARRRRRRRGGHH!!!"

With one savage motion, Sil tore Yotie's arm from his torso leaving his helpless body to flop around in agony as blood gushed from the gory stump.

"Sil!!! Find Clarissa! Get her ou-" Iggy shouted as he exited his car, interrupted by gunfire from some remaining gangsters alerted to his position.

The wild female sniffed the air obsessively, trying to pick up the vampire's scent. The stench of machinery and gunpowder obscured the trail, but Sil found a general direction and began to trot over to it, also watching for enemies in the dark with her nocturnal vision.

Iggy, armed with his Elephant Revolver crouched low as he slithered out of the line of fire, knowing that the cover of darkness was the only thing keeping him alive. Palming his way past the structures on the platform Iggy squinted his eyes, looking for any sign of his android companion, hoping the remaining gunmen wouldn't see the same indication.

A single pair of red lights flashed once which Iggy took as the most discreet signal that Mode would offer and scampered towards it as silently as possible. The red eyes flashed once again, revealing Mode to be on the train tracks in a crippled state.

"Shh, Mode, I'm gonna get you back to the car," Iggy whispered while scooping the android up, wincing at her mangled leg. "Sil will get Clarissa and we will get out of here; I'll fix you up...I'll fix you..."

Iggy lifted her extremely light wounded body back onto the platform before climbing on to join her on it. As he kneeled down to lift her back up, Mode's eyes flashed brighter than they have ever been.

"**R**andall! Evaaade!"

Mode's shouting voice was just enough to startle Iggy into a duck, which caused a bullet to tear past his scalp instead of inside it. The flash of the gunshot revealed the tall slim shooter, *Richter Baker*. Iggy instinctively drew his Revolver and fired back, once again unprepared for the recoil of the weapon and missing wildly, only causing Baker to flinch before closing in for another shot.

"I can see in the dark, Citizen. Stop fidgeting about and let me aim," Richter taunted before firing another shot that sunk directly into Iggy's thigh.

Iggy dropped to the floor with a yelp and raised attempted to raise the revolver to return fire, only to find his pain-stricken body unable to hold the gun straight, also barely being able to see his target in the shadows. As he grunted in frustration, the tall underboss came into point-blank range before smacking the revolver from his hand before centering his pistol on Iggy's forehead.

"You cost me a lot of fucking money."

"I... Will preserve your...Life **Randall**"

Mode's warped voice was followed by the buzzing jolt of her shock-prod as she jammed it into Baker's ribs from a downed position, completely catching him off guard. Mode could only muster a small shock but it was enough to jerk his firing hand to shoot wide and firing clear of Iggy's head. Seeing his chance, the wounded Driver charged Baker with a full-bodied tackle. It knocked them both to the floor with Iggy mounting him, throwing desperate punches with his brief advantage while cursing through his teeth.

"You...fuck! I heard **everything!**" Iggy grunted as rained his fists into Baker's chiseled face. "You were gonna take her to the **Thorn! You** sick-fuck!"

Once the shock wore off, Baker began to scramble off his back, tying up Iggy's arms and stifling his attack. Demonstrating his strength and durability, he laughed in the face of Iggy's assault.

"Hah! You simp! She isn't *that* good, Citi-boy, stick with your comfort bot's pussy." Baker taunted before snatching Iggy's wrist and pulling it backward following with an incredibly hard gut punch from the bottom.

Iggy scrambled to his feet with a choking cough and met Baker toe to toe, unable to put any weight on his now bleeding leg.

Why am I so useless outside of the car?

Sil had followed her nose to the other side of the hideout, ignoring the gunshots and cries from the platform, knowing that Clarissa was her priority. Navigating the network of the vehicles in the dark parking area, she stopped to sniff around, trying to confirm a location. Her acute hearing picked up the panicked shouts and random gunshots being fired off through the hideout and willed herself to not be distracted.

Sil persistently tracked the scent until she found herself at the backdoors of the workhorse van. After sliding a hand against the backdoors of the van, Sil pulled the door open, easily snapping its weak lock without noticing. After confirming the end of the scent, Sil reached into the back and laid her hand across a smooth cold surface of the large rectangular box. Pulling it out with one tug, she found it to be a coffin with the words 'To Thorn Institute' were engraved on the lid, though Sil couldn't read it.

After a final sniff of the casket, she punched a hole through the top and tore the entire lid off as if it was made of wet cardboard. Adorned in a black cocktail dress with a new matching eye patch Clarissa laid still inside.

"**Rissa! Rissa!**" Sil barked excitedly, licking the vampire's motionless face.

Clarissa's eye fluttered open slowly as she was met with the thick slobber of a werewolf's saliva. She instinctively wiped off her face only to find her own movements sluggish and drowsy.

"Fuckin' gettoff me, Sil...I'm awake!" Clarissa slurred as she draped her arms over Sil weakly. "Ah... think those cunts musta drugged me...or sumfing."

The Werewolf picked her out of the box and placed her upright, letting the Landlady find her feet in a new pair of heeled boots that she was now wearing. She only got a chance to glance at herself with puzzlement before Sil began to drag her by the wrist out of the parking area.

"Nishin and metal-girl are near home, Sil bring you back, we all move from here!" Sil exclaimed happily.

As they came out on the middle platform both the Vampire and Werewolf were hit with the intense stench of fresh mutant blood. Clarissa's groggy vision caught the blurry outline of a one-armed Yotie crawling to his feet, almost dead but with rocket launcher back on his remaining arm.

"What the...fuck?" Clarissa said, processing the new information slowly.

"Ey...dog-bitch..." Yotie sputtered with a bloody cough, nearly dead from blood loss. "Catch the frisbee!!"

With his last remaining strength of life, Yotie fired a rocket directly at the pair. In a split second, Sil turned to see Clarissa in sluggish motion and immediately embraced her, attempting to shield her from what she saw being launched her way.

Baker finished a powerful combo with a roundhouse kick, sending a bruised and battered Iggy skidding across the filthy platform floor. Baker retrieved his pistol and laughed as the overmatched derby driver struggled to find his footing. Before he could deliver the final blow, a thundering explosion shook the entire station as Yotie's rocket hit one of the vans in the parking space. Jets of orange fire pushed out in all directions and a wave of heat hit Baker's face, causing the first sign of panic to form on his face.

"What the hell!? They got bombs?" Baker said before firing his gun blindly in the direction of the explosion. "Yotie! Where the fuck are you? Where is my car? Shit."

Completely ignoring Iggy, Baker jumped down to the rails, desperate to see if his vehicle that was holding his money was still intact. Watching and listening carefully to the glow and crackle of the post-explosion fire, Baker still wasn't able to see Sil's hand swipe before it sent him flying backward, catching him square in the chest.

Moderately charred but very alive, Sil lumbered towards Baker with a heavy limp and her claws and fangs baring wide. Richter scrambled backward as the werewolf closed in him, with murderous intent in her white-hot eyes.

"You're no fucking mutant...y-you're a monster!" Baker said before firing his pistol and hitting Sil in the chest area.

Sil paused at the gunshot momentarily before snarling deeply and continuing her approach. Her face began to morph into something more savage, spikes of hair pushed out from her shoulder area, and her well-defined muscles began to bulge, Baker could only watch in terror as the bullet he fired into her pushed out of her chest and fell harmlessly to the ground.

"YOTIE, YOTIE!" Baker screamed as he fired more shots into Sil, each one having less effect than the last. "GET HER AWAY FROM ME!"

The audible crunching and popping of Sil's transforming ligaments were drowned out by the screech of tires and the roar of an engine. Sil was barely able to turn around before being struck by the front end of a Pickup Truck that sent her soaring through the air and landing through a communal bench on the platform.

The pickup truck stopped short of the Underboss, and its powerful horn blared loud enough to cause Baker to grimace and Iggy to jump back to his senses. A large, red-scaled arm waved the underboss over from the window, and Grady's nonchalant voice was heard again.

"Money is in the back, Ricky. You got one chance to get out of this alive," Grady said.

Baker scrambled to his feet and ran towards the passenger side only to find it occupied by Hyatt, the last living member of Yotie's outlaw crew. Similar to Grady he had a somewhat amphibious appearance but with blue slimy toad-like skin and fins around his face like a frilled lizard. He shook his large head at Baker and pointed a wet thumb behind him.

"Get in tha back Baker, you're a passenger," Hyatt said with a cruel chuckle that was joined by Grady.

"Motherfuck-" Baker grumbled before hoisting himself clumsily into the cargo bed and banging on the back window over the snickering of the mutants in the front. "Alright let's move! And where's the money?"

"Most of that is my money now, Ricky, seeing as I just saved your fuckin life, plus all your guys are dead," Grady said before gunning the engine and waving sarcastically to Iggy from his window before hitting the gas. "It's a long ride back to Folsom, Rick, just enough time to re-negotiate the money me **and** Hyatt are gonna get when we take over the Shell-"

Grady's demands were cut short by a trio of bullets smashing through the back of his truck, causing him to start driving immediately for the exit.

"**Baker, Grady!!**" screamed a dashing Clarissa as she fired Yotie's pistol at the Workhorse as it was speeding away. The bullets narrowly missed Baker who attempted to return fire, only to find his gun was empty. He gave Clarissa a nasty grin before the truck peeled out of the station, leaving Clarissa with no target.

"Clarissa!" Iggy shouted as he clutched his swollen, bleeding face while rummaging through the broken bench "Sil's still alive over here!"

"Good! Get her in the back with Mode, we can still catch those fucks!" Clarissa said as she snatched up the damaged android and loaded her into the backseat.

Iggy cautiously nodded as he did the same with a dazed and battered Sil who clearly had some broken bones. "You sure you want to go after them? We are all back together now and-"

"You can get your victory orgy after we splatter those two treacherous cunts, Crasher. Get in the **fucking car!**" Clarissa snarled.

Clarissa snapped with all of her fire and fury and none of the groggy effects of the drugs which had all but worn off. Iggy smirked with a throbbing face at her comment as he climbed in the Blockgain with Clarissa and brought the engine to life. "Your wish is my command, Landlady. I like your outfit too!"

The tires screamed intensely as the Blockgain launched from a swerving burnout and propelled out of the hideout and into the black night of the Big Waste. Iggy grit his teeth as he hit the boost function, trying to cover as much lost ground as possible as he desperately searched for the Workhorse. "I can't see them! Clarissa, which direction?!" Iggy yelled with a shifting neck, straining to see with a swollen eye.

"I can see them," The Vampire said with a newly solemn tone. "That Workhorse is slow. Just pull to the left a little and they'll come into view."

Iggy glanced at Clarissa to see her face drop into her palms before taking a deep breath and wiping her eye. "Clarissa..." he muttered empathetically.

"Eyes on the fucking road, Crasher! They are still dangerous. Grady was raised dangerous," Clarissa snapped before her voice dropped into a sob. "I raised him to be dangerous, smart, the best..."

Iggy saw the red and orange tail lights of the pickup truck on the horizon and lined up at its rear before pressing hard on the gas, accelerating rapidly. Iggy was impressed with how good a job he and Mode did on the clean sounding engine as they closed in on the Workhorse.

Baker was still in the back of the truck demanding that he swap seats with Hyatt but to no avail. Once he saw the menacing muscle car roar into view, he screamed at the mutants to hand him a gun. Bullets whipped by the Blockgain as Baker let off a few shots, with the panic and turbulence of the chase affecting his aim.

"Listen to me! I'm the Cook sibling in charge of accounts & treasury! I have no direct involvement in petty gang-beefs, turn away now and this doesn't have to be anything personal," Baker negotiated through a shouting, shaking voice.

Iggy turned toward Clarissa and saw the pain of betrayal on her face along with a single tear from her eye which Iggy was certain was because of Grady. His mind envisioned what he knew about the Thorn Institute. Terrified captured women and men subjected to the wills of rich sadistic patrons. Pin torture, electro torture, starving, partial drowning, blinding, forced cannibalism and other unspeakable acts that his vampire companion would have been subject to. They filled Iggy's mind and he was overcome with disgusted rage.

Iggy rolled down his driver's side window and shouted back at the underboss, "No, Richter Baker, you're wrong. It's *very personal!*"

Iggy flicked his harpoon mechanism to fire, once again launching the gas propelled hook from its cannon directly at Baker. The aim was perfect. The grapnel punched through Barker's chest, skewering his body in dramatic fashion.

"Clariss...**urk!!!**"

Baker's voice was canceled as both his lungs were popped by the bladed claw lodged inside him. With his dying strength, he desperately clung to the inside of the cargo bay. With his mangled body drenched in blood and eyes wide as saucers as he choked out his last few breaths of life.

A cold splash of horrified shock hit Iggy as he witnessed the gory mess in front of him before he was hit with a much stronger feeling of blood-lust rushing through him. Clarissa placed her hand on Iggy's thigh and he grinned as wide as his busted lip would allow before flicking the retract switch.

The grappling cannon's mighty withdrawal did not bring Baker's back with it, but tore him asunder from the middle, causing his flesh to explode in all directions from the back of the truck.

Richter Baker, the middle Cook sibling, was dead.

As a large splash of Baker's blood hit the Blockgain's windshield. Iggy turned again to Clarissa who exhaled with a small sigh of relief before nodding in approval. "One more, Crasher. One more."

The far superior Blockgain caught up to the Pickup Truck so quickly that Iggy had to brake slightly to line up the car for his famous PIT maneuver. Grady leaned out of the window and turned back towards the Blockgain. His calm and cheery expression slowly twisted into a cruel smirk as he waved a small device in their view.

"Hey L, it's a shame I had to break Blanch's neck, she was always so good with **insurance policies,** the range on this remote is pathetic, thank the Soft-neck for driving so close!" Grady yelled from the vehicle, hovering his thumb over the main button.

Clarissa's eye widened with dread as she heard the subtle beeping from the inside of the car, immediately gripping Iggy's arm and screaming. **"They put a *bomb on your car*! You have to get out now!!"**

Iggy snapped his head towards her with eyes of disbelief.

"What?! I just fixed it! I didn't see no bomb and neither did Mode, he's bluffing! I almost have him!" Iggy yelled while shrugging Clarissa off.

"No **there is a bomb!** I had Blanch put it on your car the night we met...but I decided to leave the remote with Grady, I... changed my mind about using it!" Clarissa said as she unlocked the doors in the Blockgain, shouting in the voice box for Mode and Sil to jump out.

Iggy's eyes began to well up with tears as he angrily shoved Clarissa off as he tried to line up for his attack.

"No!!! Mode didn't see a bomb! She has fucking **scanners!** You're wrong!"

"Raaaandal...explo-sisisive device was located, but was assumed to b-be part of your equipm-ment." Mode chattered through the voice box.

"Noooo!!!!! I'm NOT leaving!! Just let me drive!!" Iggy wailed as the beeping sound became loud enough for him to hear. "Just jump out! I'll finish this myself." Iggy unlocked the doors, motioning Clarissa to leave him.

"Mode, grab Sil and exit the car, it's an emergency escape," Clarissa ordered into the voice box.

"Afffirmative, I will preserrrrve **life,**" Mode confirmed as she hooked her arm around the dazed werewolf and yanked her out of the car with them.

Iggy screamed as he saw Mode and Sil violently tumble out of his beloved car at the speed they were at, but was cut off by Clarissa rocking his world with a swift punch and forcibly ejecting herself with him. The pair rolled through dirt at breakneck speed, compounding every bruise and cut they had received up until this point until finally slowing to skid.

Iggy lifted his head just in time to see his beloved magnum opus, the Blockgain Chaser erupt into a massive explosion.

"ARRRGGGGHHH!!!!"

Iggy cried loud and long repeatedly punching the ground with his swollen knuckles and before dropping his face into the earth, soaking it with his blood and tears. Clarissa slapped Iggy forcefully, the added sting causing his howls to drop into a whimper before dragging him to his feet, forcing him to limp with her.

"Shut the fuck up!! Sil and Mode are still back there! Or would you rather mourn your car for an hour longer?" she said with a stern tone, hiding a small hint of empathy in her speech.

Iggy's mind re-focused quickly and he called out for Mode and Sil while trying to ignore the new injuries he received from the ejection. After around five minutes of limped searching they found Sil crawling slowly with Mode clinging on to her neck, unable to stand with two fully broken legs.

"Ni...nishin..." Sil muttered before all four dropped to the ground together in exhaustion. "Where is home, Nishin...?"

Iggy threw his arms around Sil and sobbed softly into her chest, causing her to embrace him tightly.

I don't know where home is anymore.

The Battle-Mule pickup truck started to rock violently as it approached the off-road, causing Grady's sole passenger and only surviving outlaw Hyatt to complain.

"Ya gonna fuck up the tires, Grade! How the hell did you get to tha hideout so swift driving like that?" Hyatt asked as he was thrown around his seat by the road bumps.

"It's a shortcut. Dear, departed Baker told me about it months ago. Most cars won't take this route cause of the terrain but a tough old Junker like this can make it through," Grady said with a smirk before his face dropped. "And you can go ahead and call me boss now, Hyatt. Only choice you got now is Folsom and me."

Hyatt glared at Grady before his blue face went soft with a submissive nod. He peered at the side mirror to see the glowing flames of the Blockgain's burning carcass and blinked twice.

"Ya thank they are dead Boss-Grady?" Hyatt asked.

"They had time to eject but I don't know if they did, can you smell any burning bodies? I don't have a nose as you can see," Grady said.

"I don't have one either, these slits on my face are technically gills," Hyatt said flatly.

Grady facepalmed before he took one last look behind him as the wreckage faded into the distance. "Well worst-case scenario is they survived, but they are in the middle of the badlands at night," Grady said with a vicious smile. "Maim Creek is Cook territory so they gotta take their chances in the waste looking for an outpost or something on foot before the sun rises and cooks Clarissa alive. If they are lucky, a Radlion will munch em before that happens.

"Not tha classiest way ta go... probably betta than Yotie though, jeez," Hyatt responded with a shudder.

Grady scoffed before punching a number into his communicator as they finally drove through the rockiest part of the area. Grady signaled Hyatt to be silent as it rang.

"Who is this?" a female voice from the communicator asked.

"It's uh Grady Sullivan. Is this the Kitchen?"

"What do you want Sullivan? We are very busy."

"I need to talk to Cook."

"Everyone needs to talk to Cook. The questions is, why the fuck would Cook talk to some random affiliate?"

"Because it's about his brother. Richter Baker is dead," Grady stated firmly.

The communicator went silent for a few moments while Hyatt's eyes grew wide with suspense. "One moment, Sullivan, Cook wants to speak to you directly." the voice said in a much more civil tone.

Grady turned to Hyatt and reassured him with a very wide smile.

Chapter 26: Loose Ends

"Where? WHERE IS HOME?!" Sil barked at Iggy with moderate panic.

"It... it's gone. Sil." Iggy replied, drained of all energy and motivation.

Sil's head began to dart around, barking in different directions as she dropped to all fours. Iggy sat motionless, staring at the floor as his own tears dampened them in the dark. Clarissa cradled Mode as the mangled android's voice began to slur into a hushed stream of murmurs, and her eyes lost almost their entire glow.

"GONE!? Gone WHERE!? Find home Nishin!!" Sil snarled with a tone that was more rage than panic.

Iggy was barely able to lift his head and look Sil in eyes before pointing in the direction of the burning wreckage of the Blockgain in the distance. When Sil finally turned to face the fate of the vehicle she called home, she filled the sky with the longest, loudest and most painful howl she could muster.

Clarissa instinctively rushed over to Iggy and pulled him away from Sil as she saw the werewolf begin to thrash around as if locked in combat with a horde of invisible enemies. With each swing, her limbs were becoming longer, and her neck was growing thicker. Sharp white hairs pushing themselves out Sil's upper body seemed to glow in the all-enveloping darkness of the night. Clarissa, Mode, and Iggy both knew what was coming, but only the Vampire reacted.

"Crasher...your revolver, do you still have it?" Clarissa hushed urgently as Sil's bone structure began to morph in front of her.

Iggy sighed before patting the inside of his jacket, finally turning to Clarissa.
"Must have fallen out when we jumped, probably around here somewhere...maybe..." Iggy mumbled with a hollow tone.

Clarissa's eyes shifted between the sullen Iggy and the rapidly shifting Sil while palming around for her own weapon. Realizing that all of her possessions were probably back at the hideout along with her clothes, she sighed as she grabbed a fist-sized rock from the floor.

"*Daa*amage...Significant...**I**...**M**uST reB00T." Mode blurted out before her eyes lost all glow and her eyelids shut.

Mode's voice caused the heavily beast-like Sil to turn her focus back to the group, snarling deeply. Her face was almost completely wolf-like, with her new snout hosing a terrifying set of pointed fangs. The werewolf's shoulders began to expand into a broad powerful frame, rapidly filled out with primal muscle and growing bones to accommodate. The sounds of her insides changing were loud and disturbing, like an organic factory going into overdrive. Sil stepped towards Clarissa with her clawed hands at the ready, the vampire held her rock high, ready to engage.

"Who is in control? Is it Sil or Fenrir?" Iggy asked in a low monotone, walking up behind her with a limp.

The monstrous humanoid spun on her heels to face the driver. His eyes were vacant and cold, and there was no fear in his expression. Sil's stepped closer to him with a loud growl, her hot breath steaming on to his face like a dryer. But Iggy didn't blink, and he didn't move, he simply waited for an answer.

"FENREER HAS HOME, SIL DOES NOT." the werewolf gnashed with a barbarous grunt.

Before Iggy or Clarissa could react, the half-transformed creature rushed off into the waste, at a speed that would put the late Blockgain to shame. There was nothing left but a high mist of dirt that was kicked up on-departure. Clarissa's superhuman eyesight couldn't track the Werewolf's movement and Iggy didn't even try. Once again, Sil was gone.

After nearly 30 minutes of pained silence and inactivity, Clarissa finally rose to her feet lifting Mode with her. The night time allowed Clarissa's body to heal from it's very worst injuries quickly, though she was still in moderate agony. Iggy's body afforded him no such gifts, and he shivered with pain.

"Crasher...let's get moving. We...I have to get to some sort of shelter before I'm burned alive by the morning." she said, adjusting her fairly uncomfortable and mostly torn dress. "And I have no idea where we are. I can't see anything."

Iggy sat up, groaning as he clutched his wounded leg, and pulled Mode into a sitting position with him.

"You have a plan?" Iggy asked flatly.

"Yes, I'm going back to Folsom," she said clenching her fists. "I'm going to settle this with Grady."

"Wrong," Iggy said coldly. "**We** are going to settle this with Grady, and we are going to take your Towers Back."

A small smile crept across Clarissa's face, surprised and slightly aroused by Iggy's new demeanour.

"No, **you're** wrong, we are **all** going to settle with Grady. We'll find Sil, fix Mode, and take my Towers **and** the entire fucking Shell of Folsom!" Clarissa declared with a spirited tone.

Iggy's sullen face slowly twisted into a smirk before grabbing Clarissa by both shoulders in for a deep kiss. Clarissa's eyelid fluttered in surprise before clutching his face as she returned the gesture in full. Iggy pulled out of the kiss slowly and looked her deep in the eye with a determination she had never seen until now.

"And kill everyone associated with that fucking gang while we are there," he confirmed.

Clarissa smiled as she rose to her feet, lifting a limping Iggy with her left arm and a motionless Mode over her right shoulder. Though cumbersome, it was no burden for the Vampire's enhanced fortitude at night.

"Pick a direction Crasher," Clarissa said before turning her head around the wide-open space, seemingly on high alert. "I don't think we're alone out here."

To Be Continued...

C.W. ASHLEY

THANKS FOR READING

I hope you enjoyed the events of The Big Waste and can't wait to see what happens next! If you want to be kept in the loop on the sequels, upcoming and free sneak peaks, email me at c.w.ashley@outlook.com to join my mailing list.

If you are hungry for more of this universe and lore please check out

Which is 'Book 0' in the After-Skirmish series, serving as prequel anthology of the Big Waste.

C.W. Ashley

C.W. ASHLEY

Printed in Great Britain
by Amazon

23144032R00158